BRET EASTON ELLIS
AND THE OTHER DOGS

BRET EASTON ELLIS
AND
THE OTHER DOGS

Lina Wolff

Translated by Frank Perry

other stories

First published in English translation in 2016 by
And Other Stories
High Wycombe – Los Angeles
www.andotherstories.org

First published as *Bret Easton Ellis och de andra hundarna* in 2012
by Albert Bonniers Förlag
English language translation copyright © Frank Perry 2016

ISBN 9781908276643
eBook ISBN 9781908276650

Editor: Tara Tobler; Copy-editor and Proofreader: Sophie Lewis; Typesetter:
Tetragon, London; Typefaces: Linotype Swift Neue and Verlag; Cover Design:
Hannah Naughton.

A catalogue record for this book is available from the British Library.

This book has been selected to receive financial assistance from English PEN's
PEN Translates! programme. English PEN exists to promote literature and our
understanding of it, to uphold writers' freedoms around the world, to campaign
against the persecution and imprisonment of writers for stating their views,
and to promote the friendly co-operation of writers and the free exchange of
ideas. www.englishpen.org

We gratefully acknowledge that the cost of this translation was defrayed by a
subsidy from the Swedish Arts Council.

This book was also supported using public funding by Arts Council England.

CONTENTS

CONTENTS

meat is cut as roses are cut
men die as dogs die
love dies like dogs die,
he said.

CHARLES BUKOWSKI
'5 dollars'

NOT EVERYONE GETS TO CHOOSE
HOW THEY DIE, ALBA

'It was Friday two weeks ago,' Valentino told me on one of the days he drove me to school. 'Alba Cambó and I met up at ten that morning and went for a spin in the car. They were playing Vivaldi on the radio. I had pushed the top back and it was a lovely day, the kind of day when the air smells of figs, salt water and sweet exhaust fumes. Alba was sitting in the same place you are now, her head against the neck-rest, looking up at the roofs as we drove through the streets and avenues. I recognised the music they were playing on the radio and hummed along to it while driving. I could never make love to Vivaldi, Alba said at that point. Vivaldi's beautiful, don't you think, I said. That's why, she said. Imagine making love to the *Gloria*. Only saints can do that, and saints aren't supposed to make love. Saints should be saintly. I thought about what it would be like to make love to Vivaldi. Maybe she was right. Maybe it wasn't for people like us to make love to Vivaldi. It's the sort of thing some people are able to do while others can't. In any case it didn't matter in the slightest at that moment. I had no intention of asking her to make love to Vivaldi. I was planning to ask her something else entirely. I was wondering how I should put it. I wanted to say something really big, something really important, only no matter how I tried to word it, it sounded banal. Since the first time I saw you. On the beach in San Remo. It sounded banal. San Remo sounded banal. It is a banal town, but that was where we met. Ever since I met you, Alba, it's as though a bird has lodged itself in my heart and built a nest. It's the bird of love. It's you. That sounded banal as well, only then it struck me that the banal is sometimes what's most true. I was going to tell the truth and even if the truth sounded banal, I was going to say it anyway. That was the price I was prepared to pay for telling the truth. I went over the different ways of putting it again and again. I kept thinking I'm going to turn towards her and say it now. But when I had finally mustered the courage, I saw she had fallen asleep.

We parked near Pla del Born. She woke up and we walked around on the lookout for a good restaurant. We kept walking, and it felt as though Vivaldi's notes were dancing in my ears. Could you make love to this? I thought. Maybe if you were very old or very young. We sat at a bar and ordered drinks. We raised our glasses to each other and drank. The alcohol filled us up and made us happy. We started teasing each other. Then all of a sudden she put on a serious face and said: Valentino, do you want to marry me? And I couldn't take it in. I really couldn't take it in at all. This wasn't how I had imagined it. It was meant to be my question. In my world, it's the man who pops the question. In my world there are certain things the man has to ask and that's not because I'm old-fashioned but because everything turns out better that way. Who wants a feminist woman in his bed? Who wants a feminist man in her bed? We should always endeavour to be someone else when we make love. That's the only way out. She shouldn't have said it, I thought, and Vivaldi kept dancing in my ears; something about the situation would go wrong now. You see, Alba,

I said, I wasn't expecting that. I really wasn't expecting that. I'd imagined something different. I'd pictured something else entirely. I understand, she answered. You were the one who was supposed to say it. I got in before you. That's right, I said. You look so sad, she said and reached up to stroke my cheek. Where's the champagne? I thought.

We went walking round again, without a plan and without any pleasure either. We did not return to the question. We simply pretended it didn't exist. We walked along little streets and there was ivy hanging here and there. We came to a dusty little shop selling old clothes and things. Let's go in, said Alba. As we opened the door, the smell of mildew hit us. Pots, pedestals, busts, stuffed birds, a boar's head and fabrics in bold colours were scattered about indiscriminately. Behind the counter was an old lady with grey hair in a bun who looked at us suspiciously as we moseyed around. Alba opened a cupboard and a pile of clothes slid out onto the floor. She started lifting up one garment after the other. She picked up an antique shawl and a small jacket with gold embroidery. What's this? she asked the woman behind the counter. From the estate of someone who just died, she answered dryly. They only came in an hour ago and I haven't had time to put them on hangers yet. They belonged to an old aficionado and his wife. She added the last bit reluctantly as though she didn't consider us worthy of the information. She stepped behind a curtain and started fiddling with something and after a few seconds the sounds of *Nisi Dominus* issued from the loudspeakers. Alba looked up at me and smiled. Do you hear that? Yes, I said. So now we know what we're *not* going to do, she said, and continued rooting through the pile of clothes. I just stood there. She asked me to come over. Put this on, she said, holding up the goldwork

13

jacket. No, I said. I refuse to put on the clothes of someone who's just died. If you want to try them on, you can change behind the curtain, said the lady. I don't want to try them on, I replied. It felt as if drooping spiderwebs were entering my ears. There was itching all over my upper body. He died of a broken heart, the woman said. What a dull way to die, said Alba. Not everyone gets to choose how they die, the other woman replied. I just don't understand what you can do with all this, I said. Everything is old and dusty. It feels unhygienic. These are lovely garments, the woman said then, and her eyes seemed to glitter in the half-light. Aha! Alba laughed. There speaks the mighty Thor, who kills bulls with his bare hands but is scared of a few fleas. And the old girl behind the counter laughed as well, and I could see she didn't have any teeth. Her mouth was a black hole, a helter-skelter ride down to something that had no shape or form. That's right, I said, the mighty Thor has spoken, and tried to laugh along with them. Alba was rummaging around behind the curtain. Then she drew it to one side and stood there wreathed in lace and with a hat on her head. She wasn't wearing anything on top and you could see her breasts. Alba, I said. Put something on. Just give it a rest, she said. You really should cheer up. I could feel something touching my arm and jerked away before realising that it was the woman who had crept up beside me. The smell of old age seemed to waft from her and I moved a step further. So lovely, she said and her toothless mouth smiled broadly. That scarf was just lying there waiting for a woman like you. It was then I noticed that she was holding a silver tray in her hands with liqueur glasses containing something transparent. Do try it, she said and offered the tray to me. No thank you, I said. Go on, she said as her smile vanished. Just take it, Alba said, standing there in the black lace. Bloody old cow, I thought, draining the contents of the glass and then slamming it back down on the tray with a bang. Bloody old cow and her smelly dead-people-clothes. Come on Alba, let's go, I said. Not until you've tried on the matador jacket and stood beside me for a photo, she replied. She crossed her arms and looked defiant. The old woman held out the tray to her and she took a glass. On one condition, I said then. That we leave afterwards. Immediately. Of course, said Alba. We shouldn't spend too long in the air in here in any case. The other woman nodded and didn't seem the slightest bit offended.

I took off my shirt and struggled into the gold jacket. The old lady's hands wove across me like the fingers of a spider-woman, fastening buttons and adjusting loops. Then she and Alba stood in front of me and looked me over with a critical eye. There's something missing, the old woman said and went over to root through the pile. She returned with a cape that she swept across my shoulders. Then she removed a sword from an umbrella stand and put it under my arm. That's it, she said. Let's take the picture now. Alba handed her the camera and then came and stood next to me. Smile, she said. I tried out a tentative smile. The old woman took the picture. Alba got her camera back, and we looked at the image. I smiled when I saw us, despite the situation. And whenever I have looked at the picture since, I have noticed the assurance in my gaze, the indolent self-confidence in hers. Me as a matador and her as a prostitute. That was the way we were going to live. Full on, flat out and no teasing the brakes. Wholeheartedly. Otherwise why bother? We would live life even if it killed us. That was what we would do and that was the moment I realised it. Alba Cambó and I would live life, even if it killed us.

I struggled out of the coat and the jacket. Everything seemed to smell of elderly, mildewed man. Alba was still preening in front of the mirror. The old woman kept staring at her. Her mouth was half open, she had put down the tray and her arms hung loose along her sides. Come on, I said. Alba finally got changed while chatting with the other woman. The old lady was answering in hoarse monosyllables while peering intently at Alba. Thank you, this was fun, Alba said as we walked towards the door. Wait! the woman called. You must take the lace with you. You can have it, it belongs to you. Alba wound it around her throat and then shook hands with her. Then we stepped out onto the street and I could sense that the old woman was still standing there following us with her eyes, but I didn't want to turn round.

Something had changed when we got out into the fresh air. We felt happier. It might have been the liqueur, maybe the oxygen, but all the gloom suddenly seemed to have been lifted. We walked back and forth along the streets. We went into a bar and had several drinks. We talked about music you could make love to. The Verve, said Alba. I don't know who they are, I said. Nor do I, she said, only I've heard they're good for that purpose. We laughed. We walked on. We went into a restaurant and ordered grilled prawns. Everything was perfect. It wasn't too hot and it wasn't too cold, the cava slipped beautifully down our throats. Alba was sitting there with the black lace around her throat, saying apparently unconnected things like: "I can't understand why men are so fond of sex," and "Once I saw a skull in the water when I was swimming off Palmarola," and "When the main problem people have is that lack of lightness, it's all over for them." I just sat there nodding. Is that right, I would say. And I made no comment on her comments about sex. As for the skull, I told her I had seen a skull too, on Sardinia, only it wasn't floating around but in the cliffs. I had swum a bit away from the shoreline and turned around which is when I saw it in the rock face. The black holes of its eyes were staring at me. So I know what you're talking about, I said, you get this kind of tingling feeling in your toes when you've got a thousand cubic metres of water underneath you and you look towards land and see a skull. We continued in this vein, confused and drunk, and most of what we said was disconnected and meaningless but we were finally happy again and felt grateful for that.

The waiter was friendly and came over with our prawns. He put out bread, and all around us people were murmuring at the other tables but no one was loud or disturbing. I just can't believe what a great time we're having, I said and Alba nodded and stuffed a prawn into her mouth. So great we should feel guilty. You're so right, I said. We groped one another under the table. We talked about going to the cinema just to be able to neck for a bit undisturbed. A bad film, at the very back of the stalls. We ordered elderberry sorbet and daiquiris. Alba took a joint out of her bag and smoked it, and the waiter didn't seem to care. After a while I felt that the time was ripe to return to the question. So what about getting married? I said. We'll get married in May, she said dreamily while blowing out smoke. We'll marry in Albarracín in May. The poplar trees along the river will have just come into leaf. And the sun won't have scorched the earth. Everything will be warm and expectant. We'll be able to paddle down in the ravine and eat long dinners at open-air restaurants. We'll be able to make love in the Castilian four-poster beds at a parador.

Although I'd never been in Albarracín, I could see it in my mind's eye. A little village on a mountain. A ravine, poplars whose leaves twist in the wind and rustle softly. Black, heavy beds, black velvet, closed shutters, narrow strips of light that creep in during the hours of daylight. I could see it all before me and it was as though I had always been there, in Albarracín, as though I had always wandered the surrounding hills with the wind in my face, and the views. No lowlands. No tired cattle roving around. Just mighty birds hurling themselves into the air. Yes, we will, I said and my eyes filled with tears. Is it legal to be this happy? I laid my head on her shoulder. She stroked my cheek. They'll be tossing us into the dungeons soon, she said. When you're this happy, it can only ever be the last circle.

For a few hours I was convinced that I was, or at least could be, that happy. I looked out of the corner of my eyes at her walking by my side. I thought about the soft leather of her boots and the way it wrapped round her ankles, the tights that accompanied her body up to the navel. In my mind I traced every promontory and every valley along her. I could see before me how we would wake beside one another every morning from this moment on. As thrilled as it was envious, the world would look on. Time would stop as we passed by. I could see it all, and for a few hours I managed to forget completely the impossibility of the equation.

But at some point the day started to go downhill. I don't know exactly when, but it was after we had paid and were just about to get up and go. It was then that the day fell flat with as much grace as a wounded crow. The energy drained out of me and Alba was slumped listlessly across the table. I even think the sun went behind a cloud. That was the good bit, Alba said. Don't forget we're getting married in Albarracín, I said. Don't worry, I'm not going to forget that. But they mustn't play Vivaldi. I tried to laugh and felt the wine fumes back up into my mouth.

I got up and went to the toilet. It was filthy and someone had urinated beside the seat. I stood there and peed. I went back out to Alba again and she had got up and was standing there waiting, looking strained and reproachful, as though she was thinking where have you been all this time. We walked around. I looked at the clock and it was quarter to five. Which meant it was exactly four hours before the call from the hospital. How did we while away the hours? I don't remember. I think we felt cold even though it was hot. I remember that we moved out of the shadows and into the sunlight and I remember that we moved once again when the sun was blocked by a building that cast a shadow over us. I think maybe the conversation faltered and that talking began to be a bit of an effort, that we started to feel we had to last it out. I think I even wondered when the day would ever end, when we could go home go to bed and put out the light.

When the call finally came, evening had fallen. We had eaten again, at a different restaurant and this time just soup and some fruit and a bottle of still mineral water. Her mobile rang. She looked at the display, got up and went out. I remember thinking: who is this person she can't talk to in front of me? When we'll soon be sharing everything? I could see her back from the table by the window. She was in the foyer and the waiters were moving round her carrying their trays. She was standing absolutely still. I fiddled with the ashtray and the toothpick container. The salt cellar had swollen rice grains in it. They looked like maggots. She came back, pulled out the chair in front of me and said, That was the hospital calling. They've got the results of my tests and it looks as though it's malignant. What is? I said. The tumour, she answered. You never mentioned any tumour. Didn't I? I thought I'd told you. Well, you hadn't.

Really, that's odd. In any case it has spread and they think it's too late to operate. I laughed, thinking it was all a joke. They don't tell you things like that from the hospital. Not at night, not something like that over the phone. Not when two people are feeling so happy. Yes they do, said Alba. They didn't want to tell me at first but then I lied and said I was abroad and wouldn't be home for another four weeks. So then they told me. Her face looked as though it had been carved out of white stone. Her jaws moved slightly. Only, I said. Only. I didn't know what to say. We were going to, I mean. Albarracín. The poplars and the ravine. Time was going to stand still. Albarracín. In my mind's eye I could see a pair of cogs that had trapped a piece of flesh and were grinding it down. I tried to visualise something else. The future. The poplars. The leaves twisting in the light. The waiters walked past. One of them opened a window. The sounds from the square outside entered the restaurant. I could hear a man telling off a child, I could smell roasted chestnuts. A woman was laughing loudly. The church bells struck. I sat there thinking: the smell of chestnuts, a man telling off a child, the bells striking nine. This is how it is. It's nine o'clock and there's nothing to say I have to stop loving her.'

Not that Valentino's story was the first I had heard of Alba Cambó. Our initial impression of her would be based almost entirely on what we read in the magazine *Semejanzas*. The same day she moved in below us (we realised that someone had come to stay because the broken pots and abandoned crowbar that had lain down there for as long as we could remember were suddenly gone and in their place were two individuals having a conversation while the aroma of exotic food found its way up to us), Mum went to the market to find out what was going on. No one knew anything at the market that afternoon apart from the fact that there had been a moving van in the street the day before, and that things had been unloaded and that a woman who must have been Alba Cambó had stood there keeping a watchful eye on the moving men as they handled her boxes. This was not enough for Mum, however, and she went down to the market again the next morning. A few hours later she came home with the latest issue of *Semejanzas*, which she had walked all the way up to Fnac near Pla Catalunya to buy. We leafed through the glossy pages. First there was a feature about a man who devoted himself to the illegal fishing of mussels in the estuary outside Vigo, followed by an interview with a prominent writer from Madrid whose name I can no longer remember but whose photo etched itself deeply into my brain because of a minor detail in the background: the muzzle of a pistol peering out from a bookshelf. Then there it was, the piece written by our new neighbour. A picture was included of a woman smiling and looking at someone outside the image, and there couldn't be the slightest doubt it was her. Mum read her short story aloud. Nineteen pages long, it was about an extremely lonely man in the district of Poblenou. The man had no name in the short story but was referred to simply as 'the man'. He was described as rather short with thinning hair and large, slightly staring eyes that looked enormously unhappy. The man's problem was that he had been alone for so long that he had slowly but surely begun to develop a social phobia. Initially the phobia was nothing more than a vague reluctance to engage with other people, a reluctance that was manifested for the most part by his staying away from meetings with people he knew and regretfully declining invitations to family gatherings. But the problem rapidly developed into something else, something that could no longer be ignored and that imposed severe limitations on the way he lived his life. The clearest evidence that the man in the short story actually suffered from a phobia and not just from a common or garden aversion to the world around him was that he was no longer capable of eating without embarrassment in the company of other people. His hands shook so much that the food dropped off his fork and the fork would sometimes then fall out of his hands and onto the plate, landing with what sounded to him like a deafening clatter. His embarrassment was immediately evident in the colour of his face. Sometimes the man would even blush when there was not the slightest reason to do so, which meant that other people's eyes were drawn to him, making both the situation and his phobia worse. His nearest and dearest were most concerned. Finally his daughter arranged a surprise party for him. His sixtieth birthday was coming up and his daughter thought this would be a good occasion to gather friends and family together. Perhaps a large social gathering might also alleviate some of her father's phobia? She had heard that exposure to the objects that trigger phobias was always a positive thing. The daughter managed to get a group of about forty people together. They were all standing there in the dark in the hall of the man's flat in Poblenou one evening as he made his way home from work. The man opened the door in the same slow and effortful way he always did. The forty people could hear the key being turned in the lock, the man putting down his briefcase on the floor in the hall and closing the door behind him. For a second or two there was absolute silence. You could have heard a pin drop in the darkness, the daughter would say a few pages later in the short story. All the guests held their breath while they waited for a signal from the daughter to burst into a chorus of congratulations, to the accompaniment of the light from the ceiling lamp which had been wreathed in coloured paper along with streamers and confetti that would be thrown up into the air to rain down over him. But just before the daughter could give them the green light, the socially phobic man farted. He was easing the pressure in his stomach, a pressure that had been building up throughout the day at the featureless office the man worked at, a pressure that Cambó described as a kind of internal and repressed rebellion against the beige-coloured walls and the white, rather damp faces that are typical of many fat people, people who never spend time in the open air, and people who eat nothing but sausage, if such people exist, that is. The sound that came out of the man was lengthy and sustained. It echoed between the walls and was drawn out into a kind of lamentation; it was then transformed into the cry that issues from the gullet of a bird one evening on some isolated mountain lake, and was finally followed by a sigh of relief. The daughter stood there paralysed in the darkness. The whole thing fell apart. The signal for the festivities to begin was not given despite the fact that the noises of celebration might have drowned out bodily sounds. A smell of sewage slowly spread through the hall. After several more seconds (Cambó managed to make the duration of these seconds appear to be an eternity) the daughter gave the go-ahead, and the guests began their gaudy congratulations. But the congratulations were only half-hearted. Derailed, embarrassed congratulations, congratulations characterised by shame, embarrassment and sorrow. Some ill-concealed giggling could also be heard from the youngest female members of the family. The eyes of the guests kept shifting about and a murmuring started up although the voices doing the murmuring sounded uncertain. Bright red, the man stood on the threshold with his briefcase pressed against his chest like armour. He asked his daughter to gather together all the guests and get them to leave his flat immediately. He refused to see them and went into the toilet where he locked the door and sat absolutely motionless on the toilet seat until he heard the door close behind the last of the guests. The story ended one week later with the daughter finding her father hanging from a beam in the sitting room, rigid in death although wearing newly polished shoes, a ludicrous attention to detail that would be his last.

It was stated that Alba Cambó had won a prize for the short story and that the jury had referred to 'shame', 'loneliness' and 'the predicament of the modern man' in their verdict. The prize was worth €1,000, and she said in an interview in the same issue that she was going to use the money to construct a garden on her terrace, which she seemed to have put off for some time as during the coming months we saw no sign of a garden or of any increase in the number of pots down there.

A month or two after we had read the story of a lonely man, another short story written by Alba Cambó was published in the same periodical. Mum bought this one as well. It was about a little boy who had been kidnapped from Majadahonda, a residential district for the better-off on the outskirts of Madrid. The search for the boy went on for days and weeks, but he was never found. Finally a call came from the man who had stolen the boy. The family was asked to pay a ransom. A week or two later the kidnapper was found in a rubbish bag. He had been brutally murdered: his arms had been cut off and, according to the autopsy that had been carried out, they had been cut off while he was still alive. He had also been subjected to sexual abuse. The boy was never found. This was a peculiar short story with rather a lot of loose ends – why, for example, had the man made his presence known and why should the reader believe that it was the boy who had led the killing of the man when there could just as well have been another kidnapper involved? Nor was there anything to suggest that the boy remained alive as well. There was an interview with Alba Cambó alongside this short story too. In it she said that the entertainment value of a violated female body was infinite and inexhaustible and that in writing about violated male bodies her aim was to explore the kind of entertainment value they offered. Rather unwisely she pre-empted the journalist's questions by wondering rhetorically what was wrong with depicting violated male bodies when women's bodies were continually being used in literature for that purpose? Some writers wrote like lazily masturbating monkeys in overheated cages, she said. They wrote as though they had lost the taste for the real flavours of a dish and had to keep adding salt and pork fat in order to make it taste of anything. Raped and murdered women here, raped and murdered women there, that was the only way the readers' interest could be kept alive, said Alba Cambó.

The editor of the magazine had fixed on what she said about lazily masturbating monkeys. *Alba Cambó on Lazily Masturbating Monkeys* was written in bold above her image. This picture of her was not a particularly successful one. She was shown at an angle from the front with her lips slightly apart, an expression that actually made her look a bit retarded, even though Alba Cambó was not an ugly woman in reality. Mum said it was an unfortunate picture and an unfortunate piece of writing and that Alba Cambó might have gone a bit too far in what she said. In any case we both agreed that the first short story was better than the second. Mum put them both in a drawer in her bedroom where she kept magazine articles, obituaries and other things she felt somehow had to do with us.

Apart from the writing and the interviews there didn't seem to be anything special about Alba Cambó. She fit in to the everyday life that was typical of the neighbourhood without any difficulty. Her hair was bleached and in rather poor condition, she was not in the first flush of youth and often had too much black around her eyes. She had a hoarse voice: it might have been the alcohol or the tobacco smoke that had damaged it, Mum thought. She was not particularly friendly and never initiated a conversation. On some days you would see her with one man and on other days with someone else. One of the men was tall and dark and said hello in a friendly way if you met on the stairs, although he never started up a conversation either. All of which made it difficult for us to form an image of Alba Cambó in those first few months. But her ceiling was our floor, and there was only a set of beams a foot or so thick separating our lives. This was something I often heard Mum say during the period following the publication of Alba's first two stories. After all there's only twelve inches separating our lives, she might exclaim on the phone or over a glass of wine one evening. We could hear the water rushing through the pipes when Alba Cambó flushed the toilet, and when she had a drink we could hear the tiny thud as the glass was put down on the surface of the counter. I am sure Mum entertained various notions about Alba Cambó she didn't confide to me because even though I had read both the short stories I was far from being a sufficiently experienced conversational partner when it came to certain subjects. I think though that she must have spoken about Alba with some of her male acquaintances because on several occasions when one of them came to dinner, conversation would fall silent around the table when the sound of heels could be heard from the terrace below. The eyes of both Mum and her friend then turned towards the railing where they remained fixed as though they were both, each in their own way, visualising a version of Alba Cambó and what she was doing down there.

The building we lived in, and which I still write in, is located on Calle Joaquín Costa not far from the Universitat metro station.

It is two storeys tall, built sometime in the 1940s, and has never been renovated. On the street outside shades of grey shift across the trunks of plane trees that look as though they have been attacked by scabies. But their leafy tops are healthy and in the spring they are light green; they darken in the summer and are shot through with warmer colours in the autumn. During the winter they are bare for a few months, but winters in Barcelona are short and mild and after a while the trees turn light green again. The foliage moves back and forth in the wind that comes in off the sea in the mornings and smells of seaweed and salt. On some days there is a tinge of oil in the air, from the port presumably. Even in those days our terrace was an oasis. Mum spent all her free mornings and evenings there. On it she had a deck chair and a round table where she would put a glass of wine while she smoked. From our terrace you could see part of the terrace below because it was slightly larger than ours and stuck out a bit more.

Our apartment was better on the outside than in. In Mum's room you could see damp spots starting to form on the ceiling, and although my room was small it had a high ceiling, which made you feel as though you were sleeping in a can. The only window in the room overlooked a tiny inner courtyard. It was no more than a space for refuse really, and a means of letting light in, and had not been painted since the house was built. So my view consisted of a smooth dirty-grey surface the same colour as Blu-Tack or papier mâché. The whole building smelled in a way I believed at that time was the smell of an ordinary building but which I later realised was the smell of mould. And even though the refuse truck came every evening and the refuse space got disinfected, some vermin managed to survive. The cockroaches were red, several centimetres long, and had wings they could half-fly with. You would suddenly see them on the doorframe while you were brushing your teeth, and they would sit there calm and composed while washing their long reddish-brown antennae with their legs. The invasions were worse at the beginning of the summer and tailed off towards its end. Mum told me she had read a book by a Basque writer who suggested you should call cockroaches by name, which would make them impossible to kill. She experimented with calling one of them José María, and it really was impossible for her afterwards to crush him under her foot. This led to our having rather a lot of José Marías running over the floors on summer nights. Once I stepped on one as I was going to the toilet at night. Feeling its body scrabbling against my foot was revolting, and it was after that I decided to take things into my own hands. One night when Mum was at a friend's, I went on the attack with a spray I had bought at the Chinese shop on the corner. I turned on the light, shifted the sofa and got spraying. Afterwards I could see them dying with their legs in the air like the sails of little windmills. As I swept them up I felt a pang of guilt that Mum's José María probably lay among the cadavers. But new José Marías were bound to turn up, because there was an inexhaustible supply somewhere, and Mum would never have to miss her late friend.

There were maggots in the building as well although in their case Mum never suggested giving them names. It was almost impossible to get the better of these maggots, the caretaker said, because they seemed able to lay their eggs even in cement. They were everywhere and their shed skins turned up in flour bags and rice containers and on stale bits of bread. Eventually they turned into small moth-like creatures that were drawn to the light. You wouldn't see them for a very long while, and then suddenly, as you were having your supper on the terrace or in the sitting room, talking about something nice and Mum might be sharing a bottle of wine with someone, a winged insect would come fluttering through the air like a reminder that their nests were still going strong and that the refuse space would never be entirely clean.

If any of the men friends who came to see Mum brought up the state of the apartment (they might, for instance, say it was nice but that the need for renovation appeared pressing if not to say urgent), Mum used to reply that yes, the flat we lived in was like a sinking boat. Just as you plugged one hole, another one burst open.

'One fine day,' she would say, 'the water will flood in and it will sink to the bottom.'

She even joked about the need for renovation now and then and used to call the flat 'our castle, our grave and maybe our mausoleum'. The men laughed incredulously when they heard her say things like that. Presumably they thought she had some kind of plan up her sleeve after all, and that a gang of craftsmen would arrive one day and knock down the plaster, break up the old flooring and take down the damp-stained ceilings. And they probably thought this woman needs a man, and perhaps just for a second or two they imagined what life would be like for them living with us, how long it would take them to get to work, where they would put their computers and their bookshelves, how much of the mortgage remained to be paid off, that they might be able to write the book they had always dreamed of writing in exchange for lending a practical hand and a bit of masculine glamour – ideas that might flicker past for a moment before vanishing. But not one of them ever took any practical initiative and I think they were wise to keep their distance from us. We weren't a good match if it was financial freedom they were after. Mum's salary working for the local government was hardly enough for any kind of extravagance and we lived on soups made of carrots, potatoes and chickpeas. We did eat meat, although, like the working classes of old, only on Sundays. Mum would often leave the soup-pot simmering for hours just like it was supposed to in the ancient recipes she worked from and which were based on the principle that many cheap ingredients could be made into something special provided they were allowed to cook together for long enough. The smell of those endless simmers found its way into all the nooks and crannies of the flat and seeped into our clothes as well, which was worse. Sometimes when I was away from home I would suddenly become aware of that smell of overcooked food. What's that odour like mouldy old blankets, I might think, only to realise that the smell came from me. But there was a kind of pride in enduring, in bearing your cross and imagining that you were like a larva in its cocoon, trapped for now maybe but one day, one fine day, you would spread your wings and burst out and then everything would be utterly different. You couldn't exactly imagine what it would be like, but it would be totally different and that was all that mattered. Meanwhile our motto had to be that we made the best of what we had. And if you had nothing, then you made the best of that too.

We continued to be curious about Alba Cambó, who published several more short stories in *Semejanzas*. Some of them were really violent, and frequently the violence was perpetrated by women and children against men. According to one of Mum's

male friends, a psychologist who taught at the Complutense
University of Madrid, Alba Cambó's short stories were unnatural
and based on falsehoods about the human psyche in general
and the male psyche in particular. The stuff about the psyche
was not something we could judge. But we bought the magazines and kept them in the box for newspaper cuttings. I also
think that Alba Cambó won some more awards, which led to
some rather merry parties on her terrace, parties where people
smoked marijuana, sang and laughed while we sat up there
listening in the semi-darkness. She continued her excessive
lifestyle well into the night as well. She did not come home
until the early hours and always slept until late.

'A real woman with a real life,' Mum once said about Alba
Cambó, and there was no mistaking a note of envy in her voice.

It wasn't until a few days after she moved in that we realised
Alba Cambó had not moved in alone. A new nameplate on
the post box in the hall informed us that *Alba Cambó Altamira*
and *Blosom Gutiérrez Gafas* now lived in the flat below. We saw
Blosom that same evening, when we found her to be beautiful,
black-skinned, and seemingly reserved and rather large. Mum
said that she must be Alba's personal assistant because she had
to come from somewhere in Central America to judge by her
accent. We would soon discover that she was just as uncom-
municative as Alba Cambó herself, and never said hello if you
happened to meet her on the street. She would stride past instead
with an expression that declared 'I know you are there but I
have no intention of saying hello because we do not know one
another.' Her solemn and dignified manner (Mum referred to
it as carrying her tail in the air) made it impossible to take the

first step and start up a conversation of any kind. All the same she and Mum did begin talking one afternoon at the grocer's. I have no idea what they talked about in the shop but when Mum came home the focus of her attention had shifted from Alba to her home help. Mum screwed together the coffee maker in the kitchen and, while she was putting out the cup and the sugar bowl, she said that observing Alba wasn't particularly rewarding because she almost always sat still down there with paper and pen and a furrowed brow. The only action Cambó performed was focused on a cup she had beside her and which she drank from now and then, a movement not at all inspiring to a possible observer. Blosom, on the other hand, always had something going on. She hummed, laid the table, looked after the potted plants or laughed out loud at things she heard on the television or the radio in the living room. She shifted her body around in the heat in leisurely fashion, picking at Alba's pots, removing dried leaves and watering them with the hose once the sun had gone down, so as not – as the women of the neighbourhood used to say – to burn the plants with water during the heat of the day. Sometimes she would go round with a pair of clippers, taking a bit off this plant and then that, moving some of Alba's pots around and taking dirty wine glasses into the kitchen. From time to time she filled up the water in the little basin Alba had put up on one of the walls. Mum said that Blosom had acquired the habit of dipping her fingers very quickly into the little pool every so often when she passed it and then making the sign of the cross – it was a habitual movement, a reflex drummed in over years, decades maybe, and we wondered what Blosom's religion actually was. There was a kind of stiffness to her way of making the sign of the cross, the kind of stiffness that comes with learned behaviours that have never become entirely natural to the person who has learnt them.

In the daytime Mum would sometimes hear Blosom and Alba talking while Blosom hung out the washing. They chatted like two girlfriends or sisters and there didn't seem to be any differences between them then; when you shut your eyes and listened you couldn't tell who was the mistress and who the servant. If Mum went close to the railing she could see Blosom bend over the washing basket and pick up an item of clothing or a sheet, and then stand up and peg the fabric to the clothes line. When she bent down again her buttocks could be seen straining against the material of her dress, and they were large, soft and round with the fabric stretched across them, damp with her sweat. I've never ever seen buttocks like that, said Mum. Sometimes it looked to her as though the cloth might split and those buttocks would then bloom through the hole in her dress. That was what she imagined, Blosom's enormous buttocks suddenly bursting forth through a split in her skirt. And that wasn't some sort of indecent fantasy, Mum said as if to defend herself, it was the only thing you could think as someone observing the situation: all that fabulous physicality in all its magnificence.

Soon, though, it was at night that the real encounters between Mum and Blosom took place, if you could refer to real encounters at this point. Because once the door had shut behind Alba, Blosom would start clearing the dinner things. She went back and forth between the table on the terrace and the kitchen; you could hear her piling plates and dishes on top of one another. Then it was her turn to go out onto the terrace with a glass of wine. First she wiped her neck and arms with a wet cloth and her breathing was strained as though she had been for a very long walk or a run. Then she relaxed. Her powerful arms lay along her body, her stomach distended and her gaze lost in the windows of the building opposite. From the chair Mum sat in she could see Blosom's matted black hair sticking up just a few metres below. Mum used to sit there in absolute silence from fear that Blosom would think she was spying. Half an hour would pass in this way, an hour, sometimes even longer. Mum even wondered sometimes whether Blosom had fallen asleep down there. But then all of a sudden Blosom would get up, take the dirty wine glass with her into the flat and Mum would get up too and do the same.

At that time we used to buy our clothes at a market in Poblenou. I don't know why we went all the way to Poblenou to shop for clothes, there were cheaper places nearer us, but Mum insisted on driving there. We used to go early in the morning, before the start of work and school, and when we arrived we were confronted by mountains of clothes, together with house-wives and servants from the neighbourhood. We looked for bargains in the piles of underwear, skirts and quilted jackets of poor quality. If you found something you liked you pulled hard on the item of clothing, looking out of the corner of your eye at other people tugging at the same thing. Pitched battles could be waged in silence over beige knickers and nude bras at the market in Poblenou. When we drove home afterwards in Mum's car, we sometimes stopped to fill up at the neighbourhood petrol station. Mum never filled up more than the reserve tank. I think that said something about our lives, because how can you call the reserve tank a reserve when it's all you have?

Now and then we used to say how we longed to get away from this life and this building. How we were really nomads, not made to live between four walls, not suited to being locked in and having to live out our lives within ninety square metres. When we eventually shared these thoughts with Alba Cambó, she responded that it was true that you had to watch out for buildings because their main task was to maintain the decay going on inside their occupants. It does people good to wander, to be outside breathing clean air, she said. Letting yourself be confined inside walls just fuels the mould growing inside you. That's right, Mum said. One day maybe we will get out of here, go off somewhere. What are you waiting for? Alba Cambó asked. I don't know, Mum said. For Araceli's father to come back maybe. Cambó laughed. Crap! she shouted then. You're not waiting for any old dad, you're waiting for Godot like everyone else.

So no Dad, not that I've lacked for stand-ins. Only my fathers have all been mayfly dads, the kind that are here one day and gone after three days at most. Some left traces behind, a khaki-coloured toothbrush in the bathroom, an inhaler, a book on a bedside table, and sometimes those traces would give rise to hopes that they might come back, come in the door to the flat and suddenly be struck by the idea that this really was a bit like returning home, that everything was already here – a home, a wife and a child – all they had to do was enter and start living. I wrote about all of them in my diary, and because their names eventually started to blur (Valerio, Enrique, Álvaro, José María) I began calling them 'the Jogging Pants Man', 'the Chuckling Man' and 'the Tartare Man' instead, and then their images would immediately reappear before me.

'The Tartare Man' once made himself a steak tartare on our terrace. I had no idea what steak tartare actually was until he explained with a lofty expression on his face that this was what sophisticated bohemians in Paris ate. The sophisticated inhabitants of Paris were people whose taste buds had not yet been destroyed by charred meat and fried onions. He took the ingredients out of the bag and put the tartare together in front of us. The tartare consisted of cutting up a packet of raw mince and mixing it right there and then with egg yolk, salt and pepper. Have a taste – it's delicious, he said and offered the greasy plastic tray to Mum. She turned her head away and pretended not to look, but I did. His fingers closed hungrily around the mess and you could see the pleasure in his face as he pushed the morsel into his mouth. Uhhnn, he said. Then he swallowed and it was impossible not to think of a snake as his Adam's apple pushed the mouthful down his throat. Please don't let her let him move in, I thought, and she didn't.

For his part the 'Canary Man' made his mark with a rather distinctive present. Before he arrived Mum explained that this man was wasn't ugly, or attractive, but attractively ugly. He turned up one Friday evening, appearing in the gloom of our hall with a bottle he presented to Mum. Mum accepted the gift and put it on the linen cupboard.

'Thank you,' she said.

I knew what Mum did with the presents she was given by her male friends. She stuffed them in a box she kept under the bed, and when that was full, she shoved them in the wardrobe. Sometimes she would get bottles of wine and sometimes a bouquet of flowers. She also received chocolates, underwear and spirits and even though she always thanked them politely, it all ended up in the wardrobe in the bedroom. Once the man had gone, she would say that that wardrobe could serve as a storehouse in case of war or hard times. I used to think that a storehouse for hard times ought to contain completely different things like rice, beans and raincoats. Not Bowmore, corsets and Valrhona. But the Canary Man was to surprise us, because once he had handed over the wine bottle he said he had brought something else as well. He took a step backwards, and reached for something on the landing.

'Here,' he said. 'This is for you.'

He handed the cage proudly to Mum. An orange canary perched on a stick inside, its head aslant, looking at us with its black pinhead eyes. For a moment Mum just stood there staring at the bird as though she had been turned to stone. Then she laughed, said thank you and carried the cage, which had a little hook on the top, through the hall and put it on the cupboard beside the toilet door. I followed behind, looking at it. The bird looked back at me.

'Do you like it?' the man said when he had taken off his jacket and Mum had gone into the kitchen to get something to drink.

I shook my head.

'I don't like birds.'

'So what do you like?' the man asked.

'Ice cream,' I replied.

He laughed.

'Then I'll have to remember that for next time. Ice cream. I really won't forget. Ice cream.'

The canary stayed silent throughout the evening. It perched timidly on its stick, pressed against the bars at the far end of the cage and its eyes remained jet black. Finally it fell asleep and then it looked dead, although its claws still managed to clutch its stick.

'That's the way it sleeps,' said Mum's friend.

'What if it falls off?' I asked.

'They never fall off.'

And the canary didn't fall off its perch. The next morning it woke us with its chirping, which penetrated into every corner of the flat. It must have been no later than five o'clock when it started, and once the clock struck seven, Mum got up and put a cloth over the cage, but the bird continued to chirp. At nine

Mum and the Canary Man came out of the bedroom and went into the kitchen to make breakfast. They ate in silence and the Canary Man was now more ugly than attractive. I drew a canary on a notepad that lay on the table and that Mum used for writing down what she needed to buy at the shops. The bird was orange and flying towards a blue sky. Mum and the Canary Man both glanced furtively at the drawing although no one said anything. Finally Mum finished her coffee, put the cup on the draining board and went into the hall. She took the cage by the hook and moved into the bedroom. The Canary Man and I followed her. The Canary Man had a croissant in his hand and I could hear him chewing while Mum opened the window. When she lifted the cage to the window ledge and opened its door, a little clucking sound seemed to come from the man's throat. He stopped chewing at that point. The canary moved to the opening of the cage and then jumped onto the window. It stayed there for a good long while, as though considering something. It gave Mum, the Canary Man and me a sidelong look. Finally it launched itself into the air and flew out the window. It dropped rapidly, frantically fluttering its wings; it sank a bit more and then seemed to give up and tumbled through the air like a brightly coloured handkerchief. Finally it hit the ground and just lay there. I could feel the Canary Man's breath against my neck as we stood staring down at the street. It smelled of croissant, but he had completely stopped chewing.

'What a feeble birdie that was,' said Mum and closed the window.

'You killed it,' said the man.

'It fell,' said Mum.

Nothing more was said about the bird. In fact nothing more was said at all. Mum clattered the cups in the sink instead and then onto the drainer. By eleven the newly showered Canary Man was in the hall and saying his thanks. He said though he had to leave now, maybe they would be in touch again at some point in the future.

'Of course,' said Mum.

The Canary Man left and never came back.

After that Mum said:

'I'm ready for love, just not for lovers and husbands. I can't cope with them.'

As for me, I had nothing against men, whether they were husbands or lovers. I had also been in love, only once it's true, but as they say it's not the number of men who have filed past in your life that counts but the intensity of feelings you experience. Benicio Mercader was a nice man, not the kind who ate raw mince with his hands or turned up carrying a cage. Benicio Mercader was carefree, good-humoured, sharp as a razor blade and virile as a bull (those are not my words in that last bit but a paraphrase made afterwards by Muriel Ruiz). He came strolling along the promenade one day in Perpignan, this was a long time ago now, ten years, probably more. We were staying at the time with Mum's friend Geraldine who had her own parasol on the beach that summer. As she used to say, it was a 'prime-place parasol' that any foreign tourist would have to pay ten euros a day for, but which Geraldine as Geraldine had got for free. Mum had no trouble accepting Geraldine's diva-like airs, and just laughed and said that if Geraldine was given a parasol in the front row totally for free there could only be one reason – Geraldine's appearance. Any parasol-vendor with even an ounce of business sense was bound to realise that if you put someone like Geraldine in the front row, all the rows behind would fill up no matter how much you charged. And that was true. Because there are bodies and there are bodies, as Geraldine used to say. Some were like shamefaced shacks that buckled under other people's eyes as they moved along the shoreline. Those same people, in Geraldine's view, pretended to themselves that the physical was not important and that what counted was the soul. Then there were those who were born to be paradise on two legs. When they walked by it was as if everything stopped. Those who said it was the soul that mattered gazed in astonishment at these walking paradises, wondering how they could ever have been created, how their proportions could come together in such exquisite and therefore also such appalling harmony. The only answer the shacks could come up with was that if they were that beautiful, they would have to be incredibly defective in some other way.

'That's your basic algorithm of envy and pettiness,' Geraldine maintained. 'It sticks in their craws when they're forced to confront the fact that others have been favoured in so many ways at the same time.'

Once she had said this, she allowed herself to sink back into her deck chair and fall asleep with a contented smile on her lips.

A bit further along the beach was the ice-cream parlour owned by a Frenchman called Monsieur Leval. From afar his stand looked like an old shed equipped with faded orange awnings from the post-war period. The walls were made of planks painted brown, but time and salt water had worn away at them so that the whole shed looked pale and bleached by the sun. Although the windows were so clean you could see yourself reflected in them, and that made for a strange contrast. The queue of ice-cream buyers at Monsieur Leval's was always long, sometimes snaking all the way up the promenade to end in a little hook in front of Señor Javi's parlour, which was usually all but deserted. Everyone wanted to buy their ice cream at Leval's and when you saw people eating his ices you realised there had to be something really extraordinary about them. Some people emitted little groans of pleasure, others simply stared at one another as though spellbound and some people just shut their eyes and sat there with the sun in their faces, their entire being dissolving into the ice cream. Unfortunately Geraldine had a score to settle with Monsieur Leval. She always refused to discuss the details but it had something to do with the way Leval had once, a long time ago, placed his parlour in relation to the French windows of Geraldine's sitting room.

'He just dumped his shed on the beach like a lump of elephant shit and ruined the first fifty metres of my view,' she told Mum.

This meant that none of us could buy ice cream from Monsieur Leval. Although Mum reproached Geraldine for falling out with someone who made such delicious ice cream, she continued to insist in my presence that there were any number of ice-cream parlours along the promenade and that we really didn't need to rub salt into Geraldine's wounds by choosing the parlour owned by her long-standing enemy. This was why I was the only customer at Señor Javi's stand for several days that summer and whenever Javi handed me the ice creams, the people in Leval's queue looked at me as though I was an idiot, or a tourist, someone who had only just arrived and had no inside knowledge at all.

The more they talked about Leval and how forbidden it was to buy ice cream from him, the more irresistible my craving for his ice cream became. After a week on the beach in Perpignan the only thing I could think about was the ice cream at Monsieur Leval's. I woke up with a peculiar kind of hunger inside me and even though I ate breakfast on Geraldine's terrace it was like pouring water through a sieve because when I got to the beach I felt just as hungry as when I woke up. I hung around the shed and watched people eating Leval's ice cream. The children's faces got all sticky when their tongues splashed into the soft, pastel flavours. One time I went into the parlour. I could feel the chill from the ice cream boxes and the aroma of the freshly baked cones. There was a large bowl of whipped cream on the counter that Madame Leval used as topping. Monsieur Leval looked at me coldly and said that if I wasn't going to buy anything, I should leave.

The day Mercader turned up I saw myself reflected in the window of Leval's bar. First you could see the row of mums, dads and kids in the reflection, and standing behind them – as though in a different plane – was me. With my pale and slightly awkward body I was standing outside the image like an extra. I think that was the first time I ever looked at myself properly. Properly and as I really was, I mean. And, as if I had seen something I shouldn't have seen, or realised something too quickly and too soon, I backed away from the window and then turned round and ran towards Mum and Geraldine under the parasol.

'You've got to give me some money for ice cream now,' I said.

'Not if you are going to get it from Monsieur Leval,' said Geraldine.

I set off towards the ice-cream parlour again. Behind me I heard Geraldine shout that there was no point in my hanging around there if I wasn't actually going to buy anything. A girl in the queue stuck her tongue out at me. The girl's mother said that if I was going to buy an ice cream I had to go to the end of the queue.

'Though she hasn't got any money, has she,' said the girl.

It really is hard to imagine any of it turning out differently when you think about the circumstances at that moment. All Candyman had to do was push against an open door. Suddenly there he was, in the picture. In the mirror of the window I saw him walking towards the post-war awnings, the row of kids, and me. I thought there is no chance in the world he walks towards me. No chance in the world that someone like that man would be walking towards me. But it was an odd day, a day when anything could happen. Because he definitely was walking towards me and he had his hands in his pockets, strolling along like a lord with a bored expression on his face, which appeared somewhat amused when he looked at me.

When he was only a few metres behind me, he stopped.

'Hello,' he said. 'What's your name?'

Our eyes met in the window.

'What's yours?' I replied.

He looked at the sea and laughed.

'My name is Candyman,' he said then.

I turned around. He smiled, and he was unshaven. He toyed a bit with his linen shirt, which was buttoned up at the neck.

'Candyman isn't a real name,' I said.

'It's a name like any other name,' he replied. 'So what's yours then?'

He took off his glasses and put the top of one side of the frame in his mouth.

'My name is Candygirl,' I said.

Candyman laughed and took a step closer. He bent down towards me and whispered in my ear:

'That's lucky. Because when Candyman meets Candygirl she is allowed to ask for whatever she wants from him. And he has to give it to her.'

His words were like warm bits of cotton wool in my ear. Over his shoulder I could see the beach and all its inhabitants stretching out. Kilometre upon kilometre of heavenly bodies and shamefaced shacks. Closest to us lay two women with surgically enhanced breasts that stuck straight up.

'The ice cream in there,' I said. 'All the ice cream inside Monsieur Leval's ice cream parlour.'

Unlike ordinary men and their bullshit, Candyman didn't back out. Candyman was a real gentleman who understood what you said right from the start. He didn't say to Leval: Just give her a large ice cream and that'll keep her quiet, and he didn't wink at the other adults in a tacit conspiracy. Instead he took my hand, walked past the whole queue and into the ice-cream parlour. People muttered and someone called out in a muffled sort of way that the last place was at the very back. When we got to the front, he said to Monsieur Leval that he was going to buy all the ice cream in the entire parlour for the little lady at his side. If we could get it loaded onto a cart and driven over to the promenade, he'd be most obliged. At first Leval said it would be quite impossible. All the ice cream – all at one go and for a single customer? His wife came and stood beside him and asked: what would all the other people who were craving ice cream say – and what would she and her husband have to do for the rest of the day?

But objections of this kind posed not the slightest problem for Candyman. He said that surely this was a matter of money like everything else? People glared at us as we left. After a while Leval and his wife turned up on the promenade carrying the boxes. While I opened them Candyman sat on the wall and smoked. He smiled when he saw me eating with a spoon Leval had also provided. I tasted each and every one of the different flavours. Violet, liquorice, strawberry, condensed milk, chocolate. Passersby stared and laughed in disbelief; presumably they had never seen a child eating an ice-cream mountain with a cigar-smoking lord at her side. It was hot, although every now and then there was a breeze off the sea that brought a bit of coolness with it and the smell of salt.

'Damn, what a great time we could have,' said Candyman and puffed on his cigar. 'You and me, Candygirl.'

Before Mum and Geraldine could come running over, I had managed to point out Geraldine's flat to him, and also told him that I had been without a father for the last few years. Candyman asked what had made Dad pack his rucksack and leave home and I replied I had no idea. Parents are mysterious, he said then, you can't get a proper handle on them, they slip away from you like eels; they're not really interested in solving the problems. The problems? I said. Yes, he said. The problems. The really difficult ones. The ones even you can barely bring yourself to talk about. Childhood on the other hand was something we could talk about, he thought. Being a child was difficult, it has to be said, but childhood was far and away the worst thing he had ever experienced. That was why he had repressed it and now he felt like a prince. He really couldn't remember any of it, when he thought about it. Apart from the fact that his Dad, like mine, was gone. His Mum was as old as the hills and currently in an old people's home, where she guzzled porridge to the accompaniment of dance band music. Now and then she would shout something into the ears of the other living dead and that was how she passed her time: a kind of countdown towards what would be a far from solemn and tragic exit and more of a customs formality instead, a transit from one world to another. She did not recognise Candyman any more, and when he occasionally brought a present with him, some perfume or a scarf or a necklace, she used to flush it down the toilet as if by reflex.

'If you'd like, you could come with me to meet my mother some time,' he said. 'She likes children just like I do. She cheers up then, she sings and stamps her feet to the beat.'

I laughed at him as he talked, it sounded to me like he had a slight speech defect whenever he said f and s. I also asked what his name was when he wasn't called Candyman, and he replied that then he was called Benicio. When he asked me the same question, I said my name was Araceli. Benicio thought that Araceli was a lovely name. That it went very well with Benicio. Benicio and Araceli. Araceli and Benicio. I laughed and Candyman said I had a lovely laugh. Then he said that he had been looking for tenderness all his life and he believed that that was what everyone was doing, deep down.

'Me too?' I asked.

'Maybe not right now,' he said. 'But it's bound to come.'

After a while the ice cream started to melt and trickled across the paving stones and onto the sand below. A dog walked past and got ice cream on its paws, and afterwards you could see the tracks disappearing into the distance behind the dog.

Then we heard someone calling my name. When we looked up Mum and Geraldine were running across the sand, brandishing towels and hats in the air.

'That's my signal to go now,' said Candyman.

He got up off the wall and smoothed out the creases that had formed in his trousers.

'But if you want more ice cream another day we could meet here,' he said.

'What day and what time?' I asked.

'Don't worry – if you're here I'll find you, Candygirl.'

'Candyman,' I mumbled, and his name tasted of violets.

The next day a package arrived at Geraldine's flat, written on it was *For Araceli*. The package contained a pair of glossy red shoes. It's that bloody paedophile, said Geraldine when I opened the box. I'll take care of those, said Mum and snatched them from my hands. Only Mum has never been good at hiding-places. She hid them at the very top of the hall cupboard, and it was child's play to clamber up a stepladder inside Geraldine's cupboard and take the shoes out of the box and then put them back without disturbing anything. I ran down to the promenade in my trainers, but changed them as soon as I was out of sight of the house and then tottered down towards the shoreline.

I waited a long time for him. People stared, laughing and pointing. I would stand there like that for several mornings and was almost about to give up when I suddenly saw him come strolling along again. He was walking exactly the way he did the first time I saw him, and I felt a pang. There's the man I love, I thought. At his side was a woman in a white linen dress. They stopped when they saw me and the woman smiled warmly. I thought she must be his sister.

'We were going to see each other again some day,' I said.

The woman's phone rang and she continued on her way while talking into it.

'You look really lovely in your shoes,' said Benicio, 'but unfortunately I am too old for you.'

'Love has nothing to do with age,' I said.

'That is true,' he said. 'But only swine go to extremes.'

He pulled his hand through his hair.

'You know my name,' he said then. 'If you still remember me in ten, twenty years' time, you can look me up then. I promise I'll try and . . . '

He tried to find the right words.

' . . . be someone for you.'

He started walking towards the woman in white.

'But what about me?' I called.

'You'll be fine, never fear,' he replied.

I have often thought afterwards that I should try to find Benicio Mercader. After all he did say, Look me up, if you still remember me in ten years' time. Ten years have passed, and I still remember him. Whenever I meet a man, I always compare him with Benicio Mercader. I know this is idiotic because what do I actually know about Benicio Mercader?

But I think about him, and I dream about him, sometimes I can even see him before me when I come home and the flat is empty. He's in the kitchen, and he's still wearing the linen shirt and has sunglasses on. He pours some chilled white wine into a glass and takes my bag and puts it on a chair and he asks me about my day as he hands me the glass. He puts his cheek against mine and he still smells of salt water like that day by the sea. Then we sit down and he takes my shoes off and sits for a while with the soles of my feet in his hands. And then he says, Let's go out now. And we go out into the night, out into Benicio Mercader's night of adventure, and we keep holding hands the whole time and he is the person I want him to be, and I am the person he wants me to be. I am not worried about having to play a role because I know how. I have been playing a role all my life and whenever I have stopped, I have always started again. Benicio knows this and it doesn't bother him. Neither he nor I think there is anything odd about it; after all we are always playing roles. Then we walk around Barcelona and everything is warm and funny and enveloping.

And that is, of course, why I do not look him up. Because just imagine if I did look him up, rang the bell on his door, and then he opened it and was a sick old lover with a sick old linen-wearing wife, and maybe he would grasp my wrist and whisper: At last, Araceli, at last. I've longed for you so, I've needed you so. No thanks, I would be forced to say, backing away. That sort of intimacy isn't for me, goodbye.

In reality it all ended on the promenade in Perpignan. Benicio Mercader strolled away with the linen-wearing woman at his side. I remained standing there in the red shoes and would never see him again.

A month or two after she and Blosom moved into the flat below us Alba Cambó went to Italy. To Genoa for a change of air, she said to Mum when they met by the post boxes in the entrance. The home of pesto, she said as well. Incredibly beautiful rocks and sea, air you can actually breathe and language that is like a bubble bath of pearls. She was going to travel around, eat well and write whatever occurred to her, little short stories she would then try to sell to *Semejanzas*. Oh yes? we said. That sounds nice. We saw her leave home one morning; she crossed the street and stood there waiting for the bus to Pla Catalunya and the airport coach. She had a kerchief tied around her head and wore large sunglasses that covered almost her entire face. I thought she was looking at her own terrace with a certain superiority as though she was saying here I am and now I am off and who knows what I will get up to and who knows if I will even come back and, if I do come back, who knows with whom. The inherent mystery, the upper hand, of the traveller over those who remained behind and had to watch as she got on the bus, which went up the hill and turned round the corner.

For two weeks there was total silence from the flat below. There was no sign of Blosom either. And then one morning there they were again, Alba and Blosom on the terrace, only this time they were not alone. There was a third person present. I remember it was a Tuesday, because Mum and I had been at the market in Poblenou and bought clothes. We had our bargains packed in the yellow plastic bags we were carrying. Once we had parked the car and were walking towards the flat, we could see immediately that there was something different about Cambó's terrace. The old plants had been swapped for new ones. Now there were lemon and olive trees on it. An abundant bougainvillea was hanging over the wall to the neighbouring building. Alba was sitting at the table. Good Lord, Mum mumbled. 'What now? She must have gone completely mad over in Italy. Because a man was sitting next to Alba. A real bullfighter, a turkey, a rooster, Mum said under her breath as we approached them. Alba and the man came over to say hello. They stood there, all attentive politeness, on the other side of the fence; they each held a glass of wine and were both obviously drunk. Blosom stayed sitting at the table and raised her glass to us. Cambó and the man told us about the holiday when they had got to know one another, about the beach outside Genoa, and about San Remo and other places they had made trips to. They asked where we had been and Mum said that we had been at the market in Poblenou to buy clothes. Alba smiled the whole time and told us that we might be getting a new neighbour, Valentino Coraggioso, the very man standing beside her. They laughed together. How beautiful they are, I thought. Mum asked Valentino what his job was. I'm a *porn* star, Valentino replied. Oh yes? we said. Alba giggled. Did you really have to tell my neighbours that? she said. I'm just joking, Valentino said then. Mum and I didn't know what to say, we just stood there holding our bags, and then he laughed and Alba Cambó laughed even harder, and we had no idea what they were laughing at, whether it was at something they had said, or if it was just a way of making fun of something or if they were laughing at us. Nice to meet you in any case, said Mum. We'd better go in and hang up our clothes. Come on Araceli. Don't take it seriously, Mariela! Alba called. Valentino could never be a porn star, he's much too ugly. You should have seen the way the fish kept staring at him when he was snorkelling! Mum did not reply, just shook her head as we walked up the stairs. They were royally drunk, the pair of them, she said when we closed the door behind us. It's on occasions like this I feel deeply and profoundly grateful not to have a man of my own.

Then she said that she had always thought highly of Alba Cambó, and that she had always managed to be straightforward and unpretentious on the surface at least, 'so perfectly normal', and this new hilarity felt wrong to her, it didn't fit in, not in this neighbourhood.

How to describe Valentino Coraggioso? You could describe him the way Mum did the Canary Man: attractively ugly, though with a certain inclination to the lymphatic. A suitable husband for Alba? That was impossible to tell, because we didn't know him or Alba. We had no idea what lay in their past, or what the future held in store. We had only seen them standing there with the sun shining on them, surrounded by the flowers that had been newly watered.

It would not be long, however, before I had an opportunity to get to know Valentino. His place of work was not far from my school, so it seemed entirely natural for me to get a lift with him in his car every morning. He kept talking, which he would never do in Alba's company; his voice was different and he took liberties in asking questions he would never have asked if Alba or Blosom had been present. Have you got a boyfriend? he asked. In the beginning he would ask this every day: Have you got a boyfriend, someone you've just got to have, you're quite the grown-up lady after all? I didn't answer and just kept looking out the window. When I failed to reply, he would eventually give up and start talking about himself. He sounded anecdotal when he did this, as though he thought his life was a string of pearls, each one a successful episode about himself, a photo album you could leaf through in as much time as it took to drive between Joaquín Costa and Parque Güell. Valentino Coraggioso as a child with his mother in the park in Genoa. Valentino Coraggioso fishing with his father and how the two of them, Mum and Dad Coraggioso, stayed together all their lives, how they understood that it was all about staying together, that that was what everything was all about. He remembered them as the last happy couple. Something happened after them. Everyone started thinking of themselves. Tender egos were allowed to grow uncontrolled, to overflow every bank. The glue between the sexes split and most people became unhappy.

I laughed in an attempt to defuse the issue. You've got to have at least one bad memory from childhood. No one's got only good memories of growing up. And if someone does have only good ones that's because they are lying to themselves which means they are still in a state of denial, and that suggests real repressed traumas.

He thought about that.

'No,' he said then. 'There really are people who haven't got any traumas, even if it's hard for other people to believe that.'

He continued driving that gigolo car of his with a grim look on his face.

One time he asked me:

'Don't you want to find love?'

I replied that I did want to find love, but that I couldn't cope with husbands and lovers.

'Husbands and lovers?' Valentino shouted then. 'Husbands and lovers! What do you know about them, Araceli Villalobos?'

Come to think of it, what did I know about husbands and lovers, and what did Valentino Coraggioso know about Alba Cambó? You never really know anything about anything. At best you have an aching feeling in your stomach and a compass that sometimes points right, and other times spins crazily. And what did we know about Blosom? Blosom whom we thought had crossed the Atlantic to do Alba Cambó's washing-up. Mum and I had not the faintest idea of whatever plans Blosom might have, and to what extent we might be part of them. What we felt towards her was that pleasant and proper sympathy people who are safely removed from problems can permit themselves to feel. We would stand at the railing and look sympathetically down at Alba's terrace where Blosom was moving around. We had no way of knowing that while we were looking at Blosom, Blosom was looking at us out of the corner of her eye, the mother and daughter in the flat above: women who were not yet overcrowded, needy perhaps, and still hadn't let a man move in. I can see it all before me now, looking back, and it makes the whole thing slightly comical. I realise she must have had intentions of some kind even then – because there came a knock on the door one Saturday morning just a few months after Coraggioso's arrival. The three of them stood there in a row: Alba Cambó, Valentino Coraggioso and Blosom. Alba Cambó had lost a little weight and looked pale and sickly, her hair was all flat and dry. Coraggioso was smiling wryly with the whole of his face and his hair had been slicked down with water.

'Hello, Araceli,' said Alba. 'How are you?'

Without waiting for a reply, she went on:

'Please excuse us for turning up so early on a Saturday morning. Is Mariela home?'

I let them into the hall. Valentino held out a bag of croissants. I invited them to sit in the living room. The flat was silent and the air musty. What light there was came in through the blinds. Blosom went over to the terrace doors and opened them.

'Ah,' said Valentino as the smell of the sea and exhaust fumes filled the living room.

I went out into the kitchen to make coffee. I put the cups on a tray, together with the sugar bowl. When I returned, the rituals of greeting and the apologies appeared to have been completed and Alba had got to the point.

'It's about Blosom,' she said and took the coffee cup I passed to her in both hands.

Mum looked uncomprehending.

'Blosom?' she said. 'What do you mean?'

Alba bit into a croissant and chewed slowly.

'As you know I've met Valentino here. And he's going to move in permanently. We've been trying it out for several weeks now, and we've decided that we want to be together for good.'

Alba smiled at Mum while she took Valentino's hand. Valentino also smiled at Mum.

'I see,' said Mum and squirmed in her chair. 'That sounds nice. Congratulations.'

'Thank you,' Alba Cambó replied.

'And?' Mum said then.

'And,' said Alba, 'that's where you come in.'

'How's that?'

'You see, I can't keep Blosom on now that a man is moving in.'

Mum looked confused.

'And you want me to . . . ?'

'That's it,' said Alba nodding. 'That's it, Mariela. I would be eternally grateful.'

'Only I . . . ' Mum began, but Alba interrupted her.

'We've talked about it a great deal, Blosom and I. We've been over it back and forth. We've gone over a lot of old wounds and tried to come up with a good solution. And the only solution that we can see is you.'

For a short while there was absolute silence. Mum looked at Alba, and Alba looked at Mum with a stubborn smile. Blosom stared out through the terrace doors. Valentino Coraggioso sat perched on the edge of the chair Blosom had pulled out for him, his legs crossed and his eyes fixed on the floor. Outside on the street a lorry could be heard driving past, and then a rubbish container being slammed shut.

'Only, you see,' said Mum and cleared her throat, 'I don't need anyone here to help me.'

Blosom looked around the room with an expression of command.

'I don't think an extra pair of hands would do any harm, Mariela,' she said and her tone suggested she and Mum had known one another for ages. 'There's one or two things here that could definitely do with a bit of looking after. Including you.'

'What?' said Mum.

'You need someone to take care of you,' Blosom replied.

'What do you know about what I need?' Mum asked.

'Don't take it as an insult,' said Blosom calmly and started looking at her nails.

Mum shook her head.

'But why did you pick me in particular,' she said and spread her arms. 'There are lots of women who are in a better financial position and can afford that level of everyday luxury. But I . . . I've got neither the money nor the room. In any case there are men coming and going here as well. I've got a lot of male friends and I like having men around me.'

'So we've noticed,' said Alba, nodding with her eyebrows raised. 'But your men don't *live* here.'

'No,' Mum admitted. 'They don't.'

'Where is the girl's father?' asked Blosom.

'Gone,' said Mum. 'I've no idea where he is. One day he was just gone and . . . I've no idea.'

'I am so sorry,' Blosom said. 'I really am.'

Only, despite both expressions of sorrow, there was a note of expectation in her voice.

'And besides,' said Alba, 'Blosom says you already know each other pretty well.'

'I'm not really sure I know what you're talking about?' said Mum.

Blosom cleared her throat and looked straight at Mum with resolve.

'What about all those evenings, Mariela? All the evenings we spent out on the terrace, you and me, you on your terrace, me on mine. All the silences we've recently shared. We may even have shared each other's thoughts. Doesn't that count for something?'

Mum stared at Blosom and I could see a blush spread across her cheeks. Valentino Coraggioso nodded thoughtfully, as though he understood exactly what Blosom was getting at.

'May I speak to Mariela in private?' Blosom said.

'Of course,' said Alba. 'This is between the two of you now.'

Mum sat there in bewilderment as Valentino and Alba got up, put the chairs back at the table and then went into the hall. Then Blosom got up as well, as though it were the most natural thing in the world that she should now be the one to show the guests out. She shut the door behind them and settled down on her chair again.

'I wouldn't have come here unless it was absolutely necessary,' she began. 'I'm very fond of Alba, she has saved me from quite a few difficult situations and we share a past now, so to speak. But ever since she met Coraggioso it's as if she's become another person. And while I'm sure you don't need me to go into the details, let me just tell you what I witnessed yesterday afternoon when I got home from the market. I don't think they heard me come in, and after I'd unpacked all the shopping in the kitchen, I went into the living room to find out if they wanted a cup of coffee. And the sight that met my eyes then, Mariela, was an intimate moment that involved Alba lying across the sofa and Valentino lying on top of her. All of his attention was focused on an egg that lay across her buttocks. A little later they called out to me, and I went in. Yes? I said. We've had a bit of an accident, said Coraggioso. An egg got broken on the sofa. Could you clean it up? What was I supposed to do? I went and got the bucket and started cleaning up the egg and the bodily fluids that were mixed in with it. Alba and Coraggioso just sat there in the other armchair giggling all the while. They giggled like a couple of teenagers, and while I've got nothing against having a good time, I couldn't stand that giggling, Mariela. I need somewhere to go. I can't stay in their love nest. They can do whatever they like, it's no skin off my nose, but I just don't want to be involved in wiping up any more eggs. I've cleaned enough toilets in my day and there's something happens to you when you're on your knees dealing with other people's bodily fluids. There's this twig that snaps, you can hear it clear as a bell.'

'But I don't know you,' Mum protested. 'I don't know anything about you, you just knock on my door and want to move in and I . . . '

'Have you got a moment to spare?' said Blosom. 'You don't know me, for the simple reason that we've never had any kind of serious conversation.'

Blosom did not wait for Mum's answer but turned to me.

'Araceli, could you get us another pot of coffee, and some hot milk.'

While I went into the kitchen, I could hear her sighing deeply. Then she began her story.

'I left Livingston because that town was a godforsaken hole stuck between the swamps and hell. I lived in a tiny shed on the beach, and it always smelled of greasy fried chicken and swampy air where I lived. The gringos used to drive around in boats staring at the beach and at us poor blacks. People did their business just about anywhere. Sometimes turds would float by on the water, and sometimes there would be other things, worse things, like red liquids and empty bottles with poison symbols on them. At our backs we had the jungle and in front lay the sea and to our right, if we faced the sea, was the Río Dulce. Salt water from the ocean forced its way up the river and with it came sharks and other sea creatures. There were crocodiles and snakes in the fresh water of the river. But even if the big animals always seem to be the ones that terrify you most, the real horror was the dirt. And that was the delta I grew up in: a kind of no man's land where two worlds came together, a saltwater world and a freshwater one, in a deep and impenetrable filth. The air used to throb with insects after the rainy season. The mangrove swamp skirting the sea gurgled softly. You could see pelicans watching and waiting on floating logs, and the tourists from North America took pictures of those birds, they thought they were exotic, only I could never help thinking that if I fell into the water one day and died it would be those beaks skewering me. Carrion-eaters and scavengers, birds and rats are just the same, and poverty was forcing us closer and closer to them, inch by inch, day by day. So when the chance came to get out, I didn't hesitate for a second. I am going with you, I said, I'm coming too, and so I went home and packed a bag and then I stepped aboard the boat that would take us up the river to the Banana Palms hotel, where the laundry van was waiting to drive us to Guatemala City.

At Banana Palms we caught glimpses of the bodies lying in the sun, the staff with trays of fruit and a very overweight man who was carried away by helicopter from the hotel's private landing pad. I have never seen luxury like I saw at Banana Palms. Then again that luxury was nothing compared with what you could see on the Camino Real and that was nothing in turn against the kind of luxury that exists in places I will never get to see. We were flown to Mexico from Guatemala City, to a town on the US border. From there we would have to make our own way.

There was a factory in the border town where thousands of women and men worked. I stood at a conveyor belt sealing tins. I went back to my home every night. I lived in a shed that was pretty much like the one I had lived in in Livingston, only this one was better. I had running water, for instance, and some other stuff that made it feel like there were options here at least, and that things could change, that you weren't stuck for good in a brackish nightmare along with anacondas and turds. You were close to a border and one day, just like that, you might cross it; a feature of a borderland is that it only takes a few manoeuvres to get from one side to the other. And that gave you a sense that anything could happen. Perhaps that was why I met the man I did, because I trusted in the feeling that everything would turn out all right. Let's call him the Mexican worker. He used to read to me before I fell asleep. That is what I remember most about him: his voice while he was reading to me before I fell asleep. He always read the same book but I can't remember what it was called. He said that book was a curse, everything was a curse, the whole of Mexico was a curse, but he liked the curse the way you imagine a bacteria likes the wound it lives in. Those were his very words:

"I love this curse called Mexico the same way a sick microbe loves the infected wound it can grow and thrive in."

I said I thought that sounded grotesque. He said that life was like that, that was exactly what it was like; grotesque was the right word, a very good word, a very useful word. And then he continued reading the book, slow and drawling as though he was falling asleep while he read, although he never did. He always read to the end. You would have to call that real consideration, ensuring you had fallen asleep first, wouldn't you? And not to stop reading before he could hear your breathing change and knew you were somewhere else, and then he would reach over and turn out the light, and then he would fall asleep too, and the bed would become a boat that embraced two people who really loved one another. You mustn't think that love is something that doesn't exist, Mariela, because it does. You live alone, and you may have lost faith and I have too sometimes, but then I think about the Mexican worker and I believe again with the whole of my being. I wish I had managed to save the book he used to read. I don't even remember what it was about any more.

We were happy in that cabin on the border. Every day we got up, washed ourselves in running water, drank a cup of hot black coffee the Mexican worker brewed on the stove. Then we walked to the factory. We worked all day. And all day as we stood at our stations and sweated and the factory kept pounding away like a truck engine all around us, we were thinking about each other's bodies. In any case the first thing we did when got home to our flat (we called it a flat even thought it was a hut; that was a means of surviving, I think, calling things by different names than were rightly theirs), the first thing we did was to take all our clothes off and go straight to bed. I don't think I have ever been with anyone else in that way in my entire life, not like I was with the Mexican worker in the hut we shared on the border. Lorries with raw materials for the factories drove past on the road outside. We barely heard them. The heat was oppressive and we sweated like the damned, but when you are together with someone the way we were together in that place, everything becomes meaningful and you no longer have to keep looking or thinking.

So we were happy almost all the time, apart from the odd night when I woke up thinking it felt as if we were lying in a grave or on the bottom of the sea. Those unimaginable nights. Everything was quiet, the trucks had stopped running and the Mexican worker's breathing had become so slow it sometimes felt as if several minutes went by between each breath. I lay there listening and kept waiting for the next breath to come. I was thinking about what I would do if he died, because there were a lot of deaths in places like that, people died all the time and not just women but men as well. They died like flies, and even if they weren't raped or maimed, they got crushed in a press or sawn apart by an automated machine and they were rarely talked about because many of them had no relatives; it was as if they had sprung fully formed from the soil, born to be ghosts, because that soil was so dry nothing could grow out of it. If the Mexican worker died, I would never love anyone again. Like a hunger-striker protesting against God, I would deny pleasure any access to my body. I would be content with keeping my surroundings clean and that was all, I wouldn't have sex and I wouldn't eat good food. I had time to think all of that as I was lying there in the darkness just waiting for his next breath to come. In the end it did and then I began waiting for the next one.

Looking back I realise that those nights were a kind of practising for being dead, a sort of dress rehearsal if you like. I lay there twisting in the sheets until they were soaked through and wrinkled, giving off a sensation of bodies and dirt. I would leave the shed then and go and stand outside, and on some nights the whole sky was covered in stars and you could hear the cicadas playing even though it was so cold. I could be standing there, looking upwards, and still have the feeling inside me that I was at the bottom of the sea. I used to stand there smoking my fag with a sore groin and the Mexican worker's bodily fluids running together with my own down the inside of my thigh. Then I would back go in and lie beside him again. Sometimes I lay awake until dawn, and then all I could do was get up, drink coffee and walk to the factory.

And that was how our lives carried on until I became pregnant.

The child was born, and everything seemed to be fine. We formed a little family. We formed a little family on the border, three people on the borderland. But as we were both working in the daytime, we had no idea what to do with the child. There were women who tied their children to the table at home. Who left food out and came back ten hours later. That wasn't something we would ever have done. There was a nursery we left him at every morning even though it cost us a pretty large part of the miserable wages we earned. We knew he would meet other children there and that he was safe. Whatever precautions you take though, danger always comes at you from the direction you aren't looking in, that's just the way things are and it doesn't make any difference that you have understood that and started taking different precautions, because the danger will always come at you from your blind spot no matter what you do. And after a few years that terrible morning dawned. I was getting ready and was about to leave, I just had to put my lipstick on in front of the mirror in 'the hall'. It wasn't something I normally did, because no one would care at the factory, only that morning I just felt I wanted to be cheerful, and have brightly coloured lips. I thought: Maybe this will be a better day if I put on a bit of colour. I carefully sketched out the outlines with the lip pencil, highlighted my cupid's bow a bit more firmly and then filled it all in with the lip brush I had dipped in the glossy lipstick. And it was just as I was putting the cap on the lipstick and inspecting my now-painted lips in the mirror in front of me that I heard the brakes screech. I looked out the window and saw something flying through the air. I couldn't work out if it was a bucket or a spade or a shoe but while I was looking at the object fly through the air it was as if everything came to a stop inside me, as though all my organs ceased to function and just let go and dropped through my body. The child made no sound. You couldn't even hear the thud over the sound of engines. I rushed out and the truck driver was standing there by the road in his three-day stubble, completely bewildered. The engine of the truck was running behind him, like a great beast from one of those films set in the deserts of the American Southwest. I've got no idea what happened, he shouted through the din. The kid just suddenly ran out. We started searching but he was nowhere to be found. Don't call the police, the man who had run over our child shouted. You'll just screw things up for me if you call the police. I'll lose everything if you do. I've got three kids and a wife. If I lose my job, I'll lose the whole lot. I didn't mean to hurt your kid. Maybe he is here somewhere. Playing in the grass, maybe he got scared of this monstrosity. He laughed desperately and touched my shoulder. I called my son's name again. I wandered through the grass scared out of my wits. The truck driver got out his wallet and gave me three hundred dollars. You'd better not say anything, he said. I've got to get going. I can't risk getting the sack. You'd better not say anything or I'll come back and kill you. I hope you find your little boy. Goodbye.

He scrambled up into the cabin and put the truck into gear. I stood there by the side of the road listening to the sound fade away. There was complete silence after that. I walked back over to the ditch. My son's lifeless body was lying thirty metres away. Blood was coming out of his mouth and his eyes were open, looking straight up at the sky, which was covered in cloud that day. I stood there and stared at him. Somewhere inside me I was falling like a gigantic glass ball, at ten thousand kilometres a second, to land on an asphalt road. The bits of glass whirled up around me; I was standing in a kind of rain. Blossom! I heard the Mexican worker call from our place. I turned round. Freshly shaved, he was standing there on the other side of the road with his jacket in his hand and a smile on his face. Where's that little pixie? he said. We've got to go now. I couldn't say anything. Blosom? he said and came closer. Where's that little dumpling? he said again, and this time there was something in his voice, something scared or maybe already terrified. He came closer, and I knew that it was all over.

We could never find our way back to what we had had. We died there, in that village by the border. We died slowly and we held on to one another like two people in a wreck at sea. Like two dead plants clinging to each other's stalks or trunks, we tried to feel that there was something remaining inside us, some fluid or a sap that could still flow and pulse and give us life. But there wasn't anything like that any more. One time the Mexican worker took me by the head; he grabbed my hair and pulled. I screamed. And then he whispered in my ear, asking if I remembered that our son had been run over while I was putting on my make-up in front of the mirror. Do you remember that, he hissed in my ear, that our son died because you were painting your lips? I forgave him immediately. It wasn't him speaking; it was the corpses inside us speaking. The corpses, the bones and the stones.

Now that I was dead, I packed together the things I owned, took the three hundred dollars I got from the truck driver and made my way to Europe to find a new life.

I ended up in Madrid with a family made up of a man and a woman. They called themselves a family even though they didn't have children, and I had nothing against them doing that, only you are not a family unless there are children. I had sex with this man as well, but it was as joyless on his part as it was on mine. That's how it is if you insist on sexual intercourse when you are dead. Compulsive and mechanical, your standard master and slave relationship, just to confirm who is who and who wears the trousers and has the power. I often used to think that it wasn't actually us who wanted to do it, not me and not really him either. But his wife's suspicions were so obvious, they sort of isolated us. She made us feel we had already done what she was picturing in her mind and that kick-started our imaginations, and there is always something tempting about what you imagine and so we might just as well anyway. I can't explain it in any other way than that it was a result of the mechanical nature of things, ideas and actions. Not that you realise it, but that mechanicalness is at work and you do the kind of inconceivable things that just drag you further and further down, as though what you were really thinking was let's get it over with because it's all going to rot and ruin anyway.

The husband had a cat he adored. Her name was Marilyn and, as he himself said, she was the only person he really loved. He didn't love me and he didn't love Jessica, his wife. He didn't love his mother and he didn't love nature, even though he very much wanted to be the kind of person who loves nature, who can find peace, who can nurture hope for themselves, who can just sit outside and be present. The kind of person who doesn't need things and doesn't spend the weekend at shopping malls. He had come to realise that there was something he couldn't buy, because money couldn't buy that peace of mind. His cat was the only thing he loved; it was as simple as that. And even though I had nothing against that cat, it would be me who killed it. It sounds strange when you say it: even though I had nothing against that cat, it would be me who killed it. But I didn't know this when I started working there. Then I thought the cat and I had an understanding, that there was something honest about animals and that the real animals were people.

I got pregnant by this man as well. I didn't feel able to tell him. I just couldn't bring myself to say: I'm carrying your child, look after me. And he was just as blind as any other man. He didn't notice how pale I was, my swollen breasts, that I was getting bigger and smelled differently. But his wife did, of course she did, women don't suffer from that kind of blindness. Her own childless state made her hate me, carrying her husband's child in my womb as I was. She could have killed me with all her piles of ironing and the skirting boards she had me clean. *Blosom, don't forgot the skirting board behind the sofa.* She liked me to fetch her drinks while she was in the bath and she had me massage her shoulders.

"Blosom! The martini!"

And one of those days, one of the last with the two of them, it was hot and the air was throbbing with spores and humidity. I was in the second month and the nausea used to hit me in waves. I got the ice out of the tray, put a cube on my tongue and it slowly dissolved as I went upstairs with the martini for Jessica. I went up to the bathroom. I sat on the edge of the bath and massaged her shoulders.

"Did you forget the bath salts?" she asked.

I got up and got the bath salts from the bathroom cabinet.
I poured them into the water, swirling it with my hand.

"This city is bursting with people," she said. "We ought to
move somewhere else. To the country. Living like this is madness. What do you think, Blossom?"

"Yes," I said, thinking what nice problems they had.

She changed the subject.

"Have you noticed how sweet he is with that little cat of his?"

"He looks after her," I said. "The way you're supposed to
look after pets."

"He's like a father to her," Jessica said. "He's developed paternal feelings for her. I think that's lovely. That's so sensual, isn't
it? I mean when a man like him develops paternal feelings?"

"You should have given him a child, Señora Jessica," I replied.
"So he wouldn't have to go and develop paternal feelings for
a cat."

The nausea surged inside me like a wave as I said that, and
for a moment I thought I would vomit into the cool, perfumed
water.

"You pretentious little ignorant cow," Jessica cried. "Is that
what got drilled into you while you were growing up, that there's
nothing more important than giving a man a child? Hah. Along
with all those Venezuelan soaps you watch. That's soft porn for
old ladies, all of them thinking the best thing you can do for a
man is to give him a child and then the women are left with
chains around the ankles and a ring through the nose, stuck
with life in a cage. Fortunately, Vicente doesn't belong to the
old school. He *doesn't actually want to have children.*"

Our eyes met in the mirror on the other side of the bathtub.
I hate you, I thought. I hate you so much it's killing me.

"You've got something in your hair," she said.

"What?"

"It looks like sperm."

"Well it's not that."

"Would you mind washing it off, please."

I got up, went over to the sink and washed away what was in my hair. Then I went back to the tub and massaged a knot in her shoulder she pointed out to me. Again I thought, how much I hate you, Jessica. And she must have been able to sense that from my fingers in some way because suddenly she said, slowly and without opening her eyes.

"You hate me, Blosom, don't you?"

I stopped short and my hands dropped onto the edge of the tub. What was I supposed to say? My son was run over by a truck. Or: I used to love the Mexican worker. Or: I am going to have a new child. But I didn't say any of it. Instead I said: "Yes."

Jessica smiled, still without opening her eyes.

"I can feel it in your hands. They're stiff as a board when they touch me."

I squeezed a dab of cream out of a tube lying on the edge of the bath. I oiled my hands and could see her watching me in the mirror.

"You ought to work on forgiveness, Blosom. Not so much for our sakes, but for yours. Carrying around that much bitterness is a terrible burden. Being bitter makes you ugly. You get wrinkles, stomach ache, high blood pressure and everything that goes along with it."

"I'm not sure what I'm supposed to forgive in that case," I said.

"You could begin by forgiving me because I am who I am."

I laughed.

"That sounds absurd."

"No more absurd than the fact that you actually hate me for being who I am."

We sat in silence for a while and she drained her glass and handed it to me, her eyes closed once more.

"You're carrying his child, aren't you?" she asked.

"Yes," I said.

"That isn't going to change anything," she said.

"I'm not so sure," I said. "Perhaps something really will change."

"He's no one without me," Jessica said and opened her eyes. "And he'd rather be someone than just a father. Besides he would never love your child. All he loves is Marilyn, and you know that just as well as I do."

It was a hot day. We closed all the shutters in the house but the heat got in anyway. This is only spring, I thought. What is it going to be like in summer? A nightmare. Hell on earth. Jessica got out of the bath and lay down in her room with the air conditioning on. Marilyn was lying sprawled across his stomach in the living room. When it cooled down, she was let out to go hunting in the garden. I let her out, and even then I had no idea I would kill her only a day or so later. Here kitty, kitty, I said opening the door. Out you go and hunt some rats. I made a gazpacho in the kitchen. Every now and then I would look into the garden and once I thought I could see Marilyn lying in the shade. I felt sorry for her in the heat. I thought it was cruel to keep a cat in this climate. When the gazpacho was ready, I sat on a chair in the kitchen for a while. The house was filled with a great sense of peace. Everything was quiet, and my nausea had disappeared for a bit. The heat was oppressive and it must have felt like something was about to happen, only I had no idea at that moment anything would. I thought everything had just come to a stop because of the heat and that was all.

A few hours later and I could hear Jessica laughing in the kitchen. I was plumping up the cushions on the sofa, and Vicente was sitting in his armchair watching the sport.

"Come over here," she called to her husband. "Come and have a look at what your little kitty is getting up to. Ha-ha. Come and have a look."

He got up, went out into the kitchen and at first he refused to laugh out loud; there was something shocked about the hesitant sounds he was making, as if he didn't dare laugh at what he was seeing, as if he couldn't quite let himself do that. Jessica's laughter on the other hand was all-pervading like a machine gun. "Ra-ta-ta-ta! Your little Marilyn. So your little Marilyn's not that innocent after all. Ra-ta-ta-ta!"

I went into the kitchen as though in a trance. I saw them there looking out the window, which had been locked shut with the insurance company's device. A desperate mother blackbird was hovering outside the window. She stopped in mid-air and shrieked. Flapped her wings and shrieked. What's going on? I said.

"Marilyn is eating," answered the man whose child was in my belly, and there was a lopsided grin on his face.

"Marilyn is eating the blackbird's chicks," Jessica shouted. "Ra-ta-ta."

And I could see her in one of the cypresses; she was gobbling down the contents of the bird's nest. I can still hear those tiny cries. I can still hear their mother's desperation ringing in my ears.

"For God's sake," I cried. "Get that bastard cat away from them!"

I threw myself at the window but it was secured with the insurance company's special locks and couldn't be opened. I pounded and screamed and shouted Marilyn's name. Jessica just kept on laughing.

"That's not going to work, Blosom," she cried between her fits of laughter. "It's quite impossible."

I turned to face her and all I really wanted to do was slap her in the face, but when my hand landed on her and I could feel that cool, cream-softened skin beneath it I couldn't restrain myself and my fingers crooked by themselves and drove my nails into her skin and pulled. A huge scratch opened across her jaw and she shrieked the way a middle-class housewife screams when you ruin her cherished skin. Blood welled out over the hand she had placed over the wound. I kept listening to that scream. I liked the sound of it, only there was another sound that was drowning it out and at first I didn't understand what it was, but then I realised it was my own laughter. It was loud, frantic and quite mad.

"Just calm down, Blosom!" Vicente shouted. "You're totally hysterical."

Jessica kept screaming and suddenly I felt a sharp pain in one of my arms. Vicente had twisted it up behind my back and was pressing me into the floor. The man whose child I was expecting twisted my arm behind my back and spat into my ear.

"That was quite a scene you staged," he hissed. "My cat has the right to eat. It's nature's way. Eat or be eaten. Eat or be eaten, Blosom, do you understand?"

"Yes," I whispered.

His hold loosened. Jessica shouted from the kitchen.

"You can stop that howling now, Blosom. All the chicks are in Marilyn's belly. They're sound asleep in there, the way children in bellies are supposed to be. *Duérmete niño, duérmete ya . . .* ra-ta-ta-ta."

The pipes were blocked the next day. The house couldn't deal with anything more either. It finally came to a complete stop and nothing moved – in or out. The plumber arrived and left again. I was sitting on a chair in the kitchen. The house smelled of drains and I was thinking: Forgive him for what he did. He doesn't know about the child, I haven't told him about the child, I should have let him know, maybe things really could have changed. He wouldn't have done what he did if he had known. I sat there for a long time trying to forgive him.

That evening Jessica and Vicente went to bed early. I went into the kitchen and saw her lying bloated in a corner. Here kitty, kitty, I said. Come here, little kitty. I opened a tin of foie gras that the man whose child lay in my belly was no doubt planning to eat at midnight, when it cooled down, along with a glass of chilled white wine. Here kitty, kitty. And the cat came to me, all languid and sated, with her swollen belly. The water was boiling on the stove. I picked her up and put her in. The animal screamed. I put the lid on and turned up the gas. I could hear scratching on the inside of the pan and I had to hold on to the handle for a bit to make sure it didn't tip over. It was quiet after that and I turned off the gas, and all you could hear was the fridge ticking over. I picked up the bag I had packed and that was waiting for me in the hall and walked to the bus stop.

There was a different coolness to the air. A scent of clean water had blown into the neighbourhood and I thought I could hear a bird singing somewhere.'

I knew what was going on in Mum's head when Blosom had finished her story. First she thought, this woman's off her rocker. Then she thought, while that was true, it was the man who had been a beast and sometimes you have to turn into an animal yourself to deal with one.

She sat there just as slumped as Blosom, holding tight to the cup she had drained. She was thinking, if I help her, I'll be putting something of my own at risk. And, if I do, what'll happen to what I have now. To my friend from La Complutense? And what'll happen if I meet a canary man who might not be the man I am waiting for, but a man I could spend the night with in any case, as a distraction? If you help someone you've got to do it seriously. There aren't any half-measures when it comes to helping.

'I'm as poor as a church mouse,' she said finally. 'I can't afford a luxury like that. And where would you sleep in any case?'

'I could take Araceli's room,' Blosom said without any hesitation. 'Araceli will soon be of an age when you won't see her for dust. You should also think about how nice it can be to have a bit of company. We'd be able to sit on the terrace and drink cognac. And talk about our lives, and the future.'

Mum looked at me. I shook my head. I wasn't prepared to sleep on some sofa. I didn't want Blosom living with us. I had no illusions about what good people we were. Anyway, seeing as the boat we were in was the sort where the moment you plugged up one hole, another would burst open, how could it support Blosom as well?

'No,' Mum said. 'We don't need anyone else living here with us. We're fine just as we are.'

Mum was right about what she said. We were doing fine just as we were and besides we didn't have any room, no money to pay her with, and I wasn't prepared to sleep on the sofa in the living room. All the same, three months later, Blosom had moved in with us. And it had started to become more and more obvious that Blosom's moving in with us was part of a carefully thought-out plan being staged by Alba and Blosom. After Blosom had been to see us and told us her story, Mum would encounter Alba more and more often on the stairs. It was hard not to feel that Alba was standing behind her door listening for the sound of Mum's footsteps because they just happened to meet far more often during the next few weeks than they had since Alba had moved in. When they started talking, the conversation turned immediately to Blosom, and Alba would tell her about the exquisite dishes Blosom prepared, how beautifully ironed her blouses were because Blosom had ironed them and how lovely and clean and gorgeous everything was down in her flat, all thanks to Blosom. Blosom simply exuded that natural love of cleanliness and tidiness only a person who is acquainted with the deepest filth is capable of. Blosom could make you feel that anything to do with sadness and depression could be banished as long as you could have a hot bath and slip between clean sheets. Thanks to her scars she could make you appreciate life and feel a sense of joy in the small things, which was beyond price, Alba Cambó said. She also said that Valentino, who had had a lot of people to help around the home, didn't want Blosom to move at all, because he had never felt so well taken care of, so looked after, as on the weekends he spent at Alba's, and that had nothing to do with Alba as she didn't have a practical bone in her body, a fact that Valentino had predicted might create a number of stumbling blocks to their future life together (Alba told Mum this as if it were merely an anecdote and seemed not to attach any significance to Valentino's fears).

Alba started inviting Mum down to her flat. They would sit at the table under the bougainvillea, and the little fountain of holy water hanging on the wall would murmur away. From where I was sitting in our flat on Mum's deckchair I could hear their laughter and their voices until well into the early hours. Blosom's laughter cut through the other sounds, it was loud, resounding and unconstrained, and sometimes I used to think there was an undertone of despair in that laugh, despair or something inconsolable that would then quickly fade away among the other voices. I could hear a chair being pulled out and then dragged back in as though someone was constantly getting up from the table and then sitting at it again. I imagined it was Blosom coming and going with carafes whose contents were ice-cold and had orange slices floating around and I could see her serving Mum in lovely glasses with tall stems that Alba Cambó had bought in some exclusive shop on Paseo de Gracia. Whenever Mum came back upstairs after one of those evenings she would be in a good mood. She smelled of smoke and her voice sounded different. She would hum when she wiped off her makeup in the loo and when she went to bed she had the radio on and you could hear the sound of one of the channels that played jazz. And as Blosom would say to me much later on it was not the force of the drip but its persistent nature that made holes in the stone that spring. Slowly but surely, glass of wine upon glass of wine, cigarette upon cigarette and conversation upon conversation, Blosom and Alba succeeded in persuading Mum that it really was a brilliant idea for Blosom to move upstairs. And one morning at breakfast she told me Blosom would be moving up to live with us in a week's time.

'Where am I going to sleep?' I asked.

'On the sofa in the living room,' Mum said.

'Can't Blosom sleep there?'

Mum shook her head.

'Blosom needs her privacy. Just think of all she's been through.'

There was no point discussing it as everything had already been decided. Alba Cambó would continue to pay Blosom a monthly salary and in return Blosom would clean her and the Italian's flat once or twice a week. The rest of the time she would look after Mum (my name was never mentioned). I would move into in the living room. My desk would be placed in one corner along with a lamp and a reading chair. My bed would then be fitted in as well along with a little screen which would 'make the whole thing a bit more private'.

I said nothing. All that was left was to pack my things and put a good face on it when Blosom arrived.

Freshly combed and perfumed Blosom arrived at our door, carrying a little case in her hand. There was a ceremonial quality to the day. We had cleaned the entire flat and bought flowers that we put in vases. The windows were open and a cross-draught stirred the curtains gently.

'Is that all?' Mum said when she opened the door.

'That's all,' Blosom replied.

The case turned out to contain two dresses and a toilet bag, some underwear, an exercise book and a little box in which she kept her spare cash. She went into her room and unpacked while we stood in the doorway looking at her. Do you want some coffee? Mum asked, and Blosom shook her head. Water then? Lemon water? Or juice? Blosom gently shut the door on us. It was a whole day after that before she came out again, only then she took possession of the entire flat with a self-assurance worthy of a queen. She strode into the kitchen, poured water into a wineglass and then went out onto the terrace and looked down at Alba's. Alba was drinking coffee with Valentino Coraggioso and they both waved at Blosom, who lifted her hand to them in turn like a royal personage passing a crowd in a procession. Mum asked if everything was all right, and Blosom replied that everything was under control. She then went into the toilet where she started moving our things around and also dusting off a shelf where she placed her crocodile-skin toilet bag. When she came out there was a soft fruity smell about the flat. I opened a window. Mum was filing her nails on the sofa. Blosom rearranged the bathroom, stowing away bottles and boxes and then moved swiftly on to pour out all the old perfumes into the bathtub and soon the whole flat was reeking with an unbearable scent of stale Poison. Mum told Blosom off for pouring out the contents of those bottles: they may have been old but the scents had sentimental value. As soon as she dipped her nose into one of those scents she could see the past as clearly as if she was watching a film.

'If you keep looking in the rear-view mirror, you'll end up driving off the road,' was Blosom's only response, and the empty bottles ended up in a large bag that was put in the hallway.

When she had finished with the bathroom, she moved on to the kitchen. She went to the Chinese shop on the corner and bought little boxes she put the herbs and spices in. Then she wrote their names on the containers in straggly letters. Blosom's handwriting was the kind of handwriting people have who never write, uncertain and wobbly with awkward letters that often sloped backwards. Now and then I would see her do the oddest things. She once took a handful of coarse salt, opened the kitchen window and threw the salt over her shoulder out the window. When she saw that I had caught her in the act, she gave a start. Why do you do that? I asked. To ward off the evil eye, she said without any hesitation.

I continued driving to school with Valentino every morning. Valentino became even more chatty and talked about relationships and politics. One time he told me that he hated Zapatero for what he had done to the country, because Zapatero had slammed Spain's face into the mud like the owner who shoves his dog's face into its own shit whenever it shits indoors. I couldn't understand the comparison. Valentino said no matter how many nice friends he had on the left, he could never vote for those 'sad bastards'. The only good thing about this country during rule by the left was that the food was still just about okay. Compared with Germany in any case, he said. I didn't understand what Germany had to do with it. They eat dog food in Germany, Valentino said. And when you eat dog food every day, you end up becoming a dog.

What are you supposed to reply to something like that? You say nothing. You just keep looking out the window. And then he said, to provoke me further:

'So that school of yours is, I take it, a sort of refuge for girls who are too ugly to be models and too stupid to be engineers.'

Another time, one rainy day at the end of autumn, he stopped the car in a parking spot behind a shopping centre and told me about the time he and Alba went wandering around Barcelona, believing they were going to be happy and get married on a hill outside Albarracín.

THE PROUD WOMAN
OF POITIERS

So okay, there was a grain of truth to what Valentino had said that time in the car about our school being a refuge for girls who turned out too ugly to be models or too stupid to become engineers. Put it this way: none of the pupils could have been models and none of them could have been engineers either. Maybe one or two of us, after Sisyphean efforts and several years spent abroad, could have become the kind of mediocre interpreter who works at trade union conferences where the main aim is to keep the delegates from southern Europe happy, a feat best accomplished by a friendly and accessible interpreter, accessible in more ways than one, and vast quantities of food and alcohol. Becoming a translator was out of the question as far as any of us were concerned. You have to have a fiendish degree of self-discipline to be a translator, and we couldn't care less about anything. Most of us were probably going to lead fairly mediocre lives emotionally speaking and stumble through long marriages while earning only pocket money in temporary jobs. Some of us, like me and Muriel Ruiz, would soon find ourselves drifting onto a very different path. But at that point we were just a gang of happy and carefree girls. We loved watching soap operas, and our biggest goal was to find a man who would allow us to lead a life that was gilt-edged; gilt-edged in the sense that it didn't have to be sullied by shabbiness, reduced circumstances and or other barriers to a full and genuinely glamorous existence. When I look back, I can see that, despite our good intentions, we were really a group of pot-smoking, left-voting philistines. Though we did learn something during those years all the same. The most important lesson may not have been in what was said to us during the classes, but the helping of real life we got served into the bargain.

The best thing about the School for Translators and Interpreters was Muriel Ruiz, and I had the good fortune not only to be in her class but to sit on the same bench and spend all my breaks and free time with her. Muriel Ruiz and I were very unalike both on the inside and the outside but particularly on the outside. For instance, while I tend to keep my eyes peeled like a herbivore that has to keep watch in every direction, Muriel Ruiz' gaze was always fixed dead ahead, like a bird of prey that knew exactly what or who she was after. And that wasn't the only birdlike thing about Muriel Ruiz. She was small and slender; her physique remained that of a young girl, in fact, she never really stopped looking like a twelve-year-old, which was an advantage, she said, when it came to men because what men were always after was youth.

'Men are men,' she might say precociously and just a bit categorically, 'and no man is ever any different from another. Men hunger for youth, because their lives are ruled by the notion that youth is something that belongs to them, the birthright they have been illicitly deprived of later in life. The same men can, of course, get terribly bored when they have to spend too many hours in the company of young girls. Once the physical activities are over, they've no idea what to talk about. The disappointment is enormous when we, as the young women we are, fail to be impressed when they go on at length and in great detail about old writers, nostalgic fishing trips or exaggeratedly important football matches. That's when they're likely to long for someone who has learnt that essential survival instinct of appearing to be listening while thinking about something else. And that's also when it may occur to them that what they really need is not a delicate, fragile rose but a proper potted plant.'

The school was housed in an old and rather grand building not that far from Parque Güell. You went in through an imposing and spacious entrance, and then there was a wide staircase that led up to all the various floors of the building; our school was situated on the second floor. The main door to the school was made of solid oak and once past it you entered a long narrow corridor with the classrooms on the left and the administrative offices on the right. There was no cafeteria in the school; we had to make do with a coffee machine in the hall. The woman who worked in the office had had her lips operated on and when she smiled they tightened to the point you were worried they would split open (Muriel imagined that what would pour out, if those lips really did split, would be slippery and granular like the pulp of a pomegranate). The headmaster was a nobody and only appeared at the beginning and end of term. Then there was the so-called school caretaker whose name was Camillo Pochintesta and who always wore the same grey shirt, with loads of pockets, that was reminiscent of overalls. A set of keys he kept in one of those pockets would jangle as he walked, and he used to speed along the corridor with short steps and his head raised so you got the feeling he was uncomfortable about something. Or maybe he felt he was being watched.

Domingo was in our class and he was the only guy at the school, apart from Camillo and the headmaster. He had a vibrant mane of red hair that used to glow like a burning bush on those afternoons when the sun shone through the window into the classroom. He was tall and thin, with freckles and small hands, and his nails looked as though they had been filed with an emery board. When we started at the school, he used to go out in the breaks and meet up with other people he knew, to hang around a bar or sit on the tracks behind the station and smoke a joint, or drink the coffee they bought inside the station and then took with them. But Domingo gradually came to feel more comfortable in himself and when the second year began he no longer left in the breaks but stayed inside with us by the coffee machine or stuck bits of gum we had finished chewing on the walls when Camillo's back was turned. Camillo said that Domingo was absorbing all our bad habits like a sponge. When Domingo was absent, Camillo used to say that only queers studied to be translators and, if you weren't a queer to start with, you would be after three years at this school where you gained a profound and pitiless insight into the nature of woman.

We didn't just study; we did a lot of other stuff as well. We read poetry and smoked dope. We promised one another faithfully we would never read Rimbaud unless we were high, just as we would never read Baudelaire's pornographic vampire poems unless we were having sex at the same time (once again it was Muriel who said this and then she added that the best thing of all would be to have those poems read to you *while* you were having sex, alternatively you could skip the poems and just stick to the sex (she laughed at this point and you just couldn't help laughing along with her)). On other days she would say we should stop thinking about sex entirely, and the Arabs were the only ones to understand what the whole thing was about, and giving women their freedom was like shoving a knife in the hands of a murderer.

We also shoved, in addition to the soap operas, a lot of good literature inside ourselves. Latin American in preference to Spanish – Borges, Rulfo, Nicanor Parra (Muriel thought that Cortázar was antiquated and Neruda positively nauseating). At times we just stopped reading trash entirely and focused on what was, according to Muriel 'worth the effort'. It all went round in circles, as she put it, and the closer to the centre you got, the closer you got to the *real* truth.

'As literary anorexics we have to make sure we get some Borges inside us,' Muriel said. 'A few words a day, a few words that are like the extremely nutritious parts of the tuna. Those are the bits that will feed us, and those are the bits from which we will be born.'

Later on, one of Muriel's lovers, his name was Paco Parra and he came from Tarragona, would say that he loved Borges and that to him Borges was literary perfection incarnate. Muriel insisted at that point that he come up with a line from Borges, and when he couldn't quote a single word, Muriel said he had to come up with the title of just one of his works – it didn't matter if it was a short story or a poem – and when Paco Parra couldn't do that either, Muriel said it was impossible that Paco Parra had read Borges because, if he had, the swamps in his brain would have dried out long ago and there could be something growing inside. Someone who reads only Borges can never die of literary starvation, Muriel said as well, and now I think about it I don't think she has either.

We had two teachers for French, one we called Dauphine and one we called Madame Moreau. Dauphine lectured on French literature, and Madame Moreau taught translation. Domingo said he was attracted to Dauphine; he liked her approach to literature and her body. I couldn't understand how he could feel attracted to Dauphine. I said to Muriel, I just don't get how Domingo can feel attracted to Dauphine. Muriel responded: Are you jealous? Domingo's hardly my type of man, I replied. No, said Muriel, I suppose you prefer people like Benicio Mercader? Yes, I replied. That's the kind of man I'm going to have. You may have to make do with what's available, Muriel said, and then she went to Domingo and told him I found him attractive. I tried to avoid catching Domingo's eye but on one of the breaks he came up to me and asked if it was true that I was attracted to him? I replied that no, that wasn't the case. I was just surprised that he could be attracted to Dauphine. What's wrong with Dauphine? Domingo asked. For starters she is over twenty years older than you, I said, and then there's just something about her I don't like. What's that? Tell me what you don't like about Dauphine. First of all, I said, she's not just twice as old as you are but she is almost twice as tall as well. What's wrong with tall women? Domingo asked. There's nothing wrong with tall women. Only you would have looked like a lapdog next to her. What else disturbs you? Domingo asked. I can't stop thinking she looks like a monster, I said. Domingo laughed out loud.

She looks like a monster, does she? You'll have to explain that one, Araceli. He looked at me scornfully, and I tried to explain that it had something to do with her way of being happy. So you think women shouldn't be happy? Domingo asked. I didn't say she shouldn't be happy. It's just there's something about her *way* of being happy. There's something monstrous about her happiness. When she smiles, it's as if she's smiling because she could have killed you if she wanted. Do you get it? That's why. You can see the predator in her. She isn't smiling at something you've said or about something nice that happened. She always smiles the same smile and it's a mad smile, a smile that would like to kill you. That's true, Domingo said and stopped laughing. You're right. Only don't you see that that's what's so wonderful about her? One day I'm going to mount her like you climb a mountain and when I've got to her peak I'm going to pound my flagpole into her flesh. I am going to stand on those long bones and that soft flesh, and I will look out and survey all that is mine and be as proud as the first man to land on the moon. You're sick, I said and started to leave. We're all sick in our own way, he called after me.

I avoided him from then on.

Domingo also dangled a number of hooks in front of the other French teacher, Madame Moreau, but he was a lot more cautious in her case, and I never heard him say anything compromising about her, or ever even mention her body. He probably didn't dare. Madame Moreau was not someone you could joke with as a student, not even Domingo joked with her. She was close to fifty and came from Poitiers. She told us on the very first day when she came into the classroom:

Je m'appelle Elaine Moreau et je viens de Poitiers. It seemed to be important to her emphasise the bit about Poitiers: she came from Poitiers and it was at Poitiers in the eighth or ninth century that the French had driven back the Arabs who were pushing up from Castile. It was thanks to Poitiers that Europe was still Europe. You could just see it – a horde of Arabs thrusting up from the Iberian Peninsula and Madame Moreau's town mounting the resistance. You could even imagine Madame Moreau standing on a hill with the French flag fluttering behind her shoulders while she decapitated Moors as they advanced on horseback. Madame Moreau de Poitiers, the proud and resolute warrior. And it was that hard shell of hers that meant you couldn't stop thinking about her, she was there at the back of your mind the whole time, you imagined what it would be like to get underneath that shell, and be appreciated by her or even have her be kind to you. To win Madame Moreau's appreciation, to feel her kindness, would be an enormous privilege, like discovering a valley or a landscape that no one had ever seen before and that was exotic and extremely desirable. I could only have a sense of that pull, but as a man Domingo must have felt it all the more strongly. In any case he seemed determined to find a way in, even though he must have realised it would be a huge challenge. To mount Dauphine and capture Madame Moreau really could be likened to being the first man on the moon, planting his flag on a peak like that. The obvious question, though, was whether there was anything erotic about Madame Moreau at all. Or whether, as Camillo put it, Moreau really was completely frigid, one of those rare human beings who never think about sex and can live an entire lifetime without feeling a twinge of desire.

'The height of eroticism in the daily life of the translator ought to be the undressing of the word,' she said once. 'Anything to do with desire simply saps your energy and sows confusion.'

Was she frigid as Camillo said or had she got her fingers burnt? You couldn't work that out just by looking at her. But Domingo wanted to understand, to force his way in and get to the bottom of it. He was attracted by something outside what he previously considered normal, and when that happens to a person, the attraction can feel much stronger than when you are drawn to something this side of normality. When you allow yourself to be attracted by the repulsive, or rather when you manage to grasp the delight in something superficially repulsive, you are more vulnerable. You can't share the experience with anyone else. You have been taken over, sort of, by the irrational, and you can't bring it out into the light of day; you can't say, 'I'm attracted to something on the other side and I'm no longer one of you, I'm someone else now,' but that was what happened to Domingo when he found himself obliged to sit on a school bench facing Moreau on a daily basis, having to look at her body and write down what she said. It wasn't of course possible to feel desire for the woman who was standing before him, but if you allowed yourself to do it anyway, if you could imagine the repulsive as an option . . . He fell headlong because there are no manuals for that kind of attraction.

Muriel Ruiz never understood what motivated Domingo. As far as she was concerned although you could certainly give yourself to someone repulsive (she would, after all, do that with Parra, for instance) there had to be a reason behind that, a rationale for lowering your standards. She dismissed Madame

Moreau as the biggest joke ever perpetrated by womankind. A freak, an irrelevance, a punctured soufflé, something you put back in the fridge and forgot about. You had only yourself to blame if you made as little effort as Moreau. Muriel's scornful attitude to Moreau was made worse by the already powerful, not to say desperate, female rivalry that had existed between the two of them right from the start. Muriel must have forced Madame Moreau to re-evaluate one of her most cherished and vital credos, that vanity and talent could only coexist to a certain limit within the same individual and that anything else was a violation of that equation of fairness so fundamental to life. Vanity was the antagonist of talent, two elements that could never share the same individual; they cancelled each other out like the pH of alkalis and acids. According to Madame Moreau's algorithm, experiencing too powerful an attraction towards your own reflection meant you were a blockhead ('As far as I know Narcissus' only claim to fame was as a narcissist,' she once said.). Muriel refused to be fitted into this scheme, because Muriel was the most self-absorbed person ever to have walked the corridors of the school for translators and interpreters, and yet she could read and speak French far better than the rest of us. So there had to be something fishy going on and Moreau kept sniffing around it like a dog that has caught the scent but can't find the trail.

As I write this, I realise how easy it is to despise someone like Moreau for her narrow and categorical views. It's just that, looking back, I have no real idea where I stand. In a way I think you ought to be sceptical about people like Muriel Ruiz. If I remember right, she once said about someone else, 'She reminds me too much of myself. I wouldn't trust her.' Muriel came out with things like that, and it was confusing, you couldn't be sure whether there was a great honesty behind her words, a vast openness that most people are unable to allow themselves because of their fears, or if she was having us all on. But every door was always open to her. People like me, and Moreau for that matter, because you could lump us together in some respects, find it harder to take shortcuts than people like Muriel. Shortcuts do not invite us to take them. No Paco Parras remain with their gaping wallets to act you might say like walking slot-machines. Instead the terrain we find ourselves in is on the periphery (although even there we manage to get by, obviously).

'So, to the undressing of the word,' Madame Moreau said, and the light used to fall on her sitting at her desk in front of the class so that half her face was left in shadow, and all you could see was her mouth moving while her eyes were in twilight.

'If you succeed at the verbal undressing, if, that is, you succeed in freeing yourself from the surface of the text, and manage to *undress the words* and *get at their core*, you can spend long hours doing nothing more than savouring that core. Everything you have missed out on – everything you wanted to do, all the wings you wanted to try out – all of that becomes irrelevant. Only when you succeed in laying bare the words, getting rid of all the frippery, all the false connotations and all the senseless monopolies that people, companies and other interested parties have placed on them, can you enjoy them and that is when one of those rare states occurs that Joyce used to refer to as . . . '

She tried to find the word.

'Rare what?' said Muriel.

'Just wait, it'll come back to me any moment,' Moreau said at that point, though it didn't before the bell had rung.

'That's all for today, thank you,' she said then, and that brought the lesson to an end.

Camillo, who was Italian in origin, was the only person to openly challenge Moreau. He used to call her *zitella*, which means 'maiden'. *Mo' viene la zitella*, he used to say with scorn in his voice as she came through the door in the morning. And it was as if everything came to a stop when Madame Moreau entered the school. The way Camillo put it, it was as though 'the cars stopped honking in the street outside, the flowers withered in their pots and the putty dropped off the walls' when she came in. While that may have been an exaggeration, which it most definitely was, if we were standing by the coffee machine, which was just by the main door, and she opened that door it felt like a little spasm passed through the group: everyone straightened up, we fell silent in the middle of a sentence and stopped laughing with our mouths open. We sipped at our plastic cups, looking down at the floor until she had gone past.

Moreau walked slowly and in a controlled manner through the corridor, and there was a sort of transparent armour over her eyes. Her entire posture cried out that she didn't really want to be here, that she came here because someone or something, fate maybe, was holding a pistol to her head and forcing her to take each step. One step, two steps, three, a few thousand steps perhaps until she arrived at the grand entrance and the marble staircase that led straight up to the hell that was us. She strode along the corridor without saying hello to anyone and closed the door to the classroom behind her, refusing to let us enter before she had taken off her red coat and hung it on a rack of hangers in one corner. Then she put out all the books, papers and pens she was going to use on the table in front of her. The pencils were always sharpened and their points were turned outwards, towards where we would soon be sitting on the benches. Then she opened the door and stood silently by her desk, watching us as we went to our seats. Once everyone had sat down, she said: *Bonjour*, though that word usually sounded so dogged and so seething we couldn't be bothered to feel we were actually being addressed, so we just mumbled an indistinct response.

She called us by our surnames. '*Mademoiselle Ruiz! Si je vous vois encore une fois mâcher du chewing-gum, je baisserai vos notes dans toutes les matières, ceci n'est pas une école qui abrite les clochards!*' Or: '*Mademoiselle Villalobos, votre traduction est très insuffisante!*'

'She's been dumped or I'm a Dutchman,' Camillo used to say.

He tended to pass on to us by the coffee machine the rumours he said were going around. The gist was always that Madame Moreau had been abandoned and couldn't get over it; she was desperate to fill the empty space the absence of a man over so many years had created inside her, and that was why she had devoted herself to the accumulation of theoretical skills. She could read herself into being high, that one, Camillo told us, saying that he had seen her sitting for hours on end on one of the sofas in the staff room with the same book open in her lap. Only she didn't read like other people, who have to lie down after a while, or have a nap for a minute or two or put something in their mouths or get a cup of coffee. The *zitella* would sit there as straight as a rake, reading as though she were reading the Bible on a Sunday in church. There was something inhumanly rigid and mechanical about her way of reading, because there was no element of joy to it (however little Camillo might know about that kind of joy). Madame

Moreau has read everything there is to read in French and Spanish in that rigid and exaggeratedly attentive way of hers and at some point, Camillo said, all that reading has warped something in the *zitella's* head. Her loneliness, her reading and her disdainfulness are totally warped, he insisted.

Madame Moreau must have suspected what Camillo was saying about her, or perhaps her antipathy towards him was spontaneous and completely independent of his dislike, because she made attacks on him as well and they were often more cunning, or at least more calculated, than his attacks on her. She never stopped addressing him with the formal *vous*, for instance, which was a wall she erected to keep him out. He attempted more than once to use a less formal form of address between the two of them, using *tu* to her, and you got the sense there was something beseeching about that word, as if he was asking for a chance for intimacy, to get up close and personal maybe, if only she called him *tu* like she did all the other teachers at the school. But Madame Moreau obstinately denied him any opportunity like that and continued to talk to him using a glacial *vous*. She also chose to address him in such a way that that *vous* was repeated several times in the same sentence; thus failing to apply the technique she had taught us of using impersonal constructions so you weren't obliged to define the exact distance required to the person you were addressing. She would frequently go even further and end her sentences with *Monsieur Pochintesta* – a phrase that always made the distance between them seem more like a yawning gulf.

On several occasions she also forced him to carry out humiliating tasks in front of the rest of us in the classroom. *Monsieur Pochintesta!* she might call out. *Come and help me put this microphone together; Mademoiselle Ruiz is going to interpret a radio programme for the rest of us.* And Camillo would come in then and have to stand before us with his leads and cables, unable to get it to work, while Madame Moreau stood beside him with a smile of satisfaction on her lips as she told us that the caretaker who had worked at the school before Camillo could connect up the microphone in less than thirty seconds. Once Domingo stepped up to help Camillo and soon found out there was a bit missing. I see, said Madame Moreau, dry as dust: Well then, we had better manage without a mike this time. Camillo had to pack the whole lot up and leave the room. During the break Domingo opened one of Madame Moreau's drawers. And, as expected, there the little piece was.

One day Camillo was summoned to the classroom to help adjust the volume of the loudspeakers prior to our interpreting a congress about feminism we were supposed to translate from Spanish into French. When Camillo realised what the conference was about he said, Right, what a load of drivel. What exactly do you mean, 'load of drivel'? Madame Moreau asked him, which made you feel that Camillo had been trapped in Moreau's fingers the way a scientist captures a beetle with a pair of tweezers to study it from all angles. Only Camillo was oblivious to the danger. What I mean, he said, is that all that feminist stuff is drivel. Drivel, drivel and more drivel. We could all see, though Camillo couldn't, how Madame Moreau's eyes dropped to the floor and stayed there.

'Given the curriculum of the male gender over the last two thousand years,' Moreau began, 'as the arrangers of gladiatorial games, as witch burners, inquisitors and the perpetrators of abuse against women as a whole, there is of course much to reflect on, and to re-evaluate' (here she used the French phrase *remettre en cause)* 'if men as men are to rediscover themselves as beings that can be allowed in civilised company.'

'I am reflecting,' Camillo replied from one of the loudspeaker sets. 'I'm reflecting, I'm reflecting so hard smoke is coming out of my ears, can't you see that?'

Moreau laughed out loud.

'I hardly think that the great male re-evaluation is going to start with Camillo Pochintesta.'

She walked slowly across the classroom over to the window where she remained standing with her back turned to us all.

'You might as well stop reflecting, Monsieur Pochintesta,' she said absently, her fingers on her lips. 'The human race is not very likely to go under because a man like you stops considering the matter.'

Had Moreau turned round at this point and seen the defeated look on Camillo's face, she might have tried to soften what she said. For a moment Camillo actually looked completely crushed. His damp lower lip drooped sadly as though he had quite forgotten that sucking it in suited him better. His eyes were wide and staring.

Moreau nodded to herself. An ambulance rushed down the street outside and for a few seconds the classroom was filled with the noise of sirens.

'Have you finished?' she said and turned round. 'How could it take so long to fix a couple of loudspeakers? I'll do it myself next time. Au revoir.'

She shut the door behind him.

When I told them about the incident at home, Blosom said that the kind of warfare being waged between Pochintesta and

Moreau was almost bound to be something both of them found rather stimulating and if they really were forced to choose neither of them would want to do without it. I couldn't say. But even if what Blosom said was true and the conflict had a stimulating effect on all of us, including Camillo and Moreau, Moreau didn't have the strength to resist the decay that was slowly but surely forming around her person. That sort of decay may have something to do with there being no one who really likes you, and your not playing an essential role in anyone else's life, and that nothing would come to a stop for even the briefest of instants if you suddenly disappeared one day. There is something unsettling about people who suffer from that kind of decline, perhaps because they have to keep inventing and sticking to a raison d'être for every second of their lives, a raison d'être that in Moreau's case was nothing more than a few feet of shelving for old books, which are, when all is said and done, just the ashes of other people's lives and not even proper ashes as most of what is said in books isn't even true, and the more you think about it truth has no meaning and the only thing you can know for sure is that to really be alive you need far more courage than reading requires, and writing too for that matter. Then again maybe decay isn't the right word. It was more a matter of neglectfulness, a fatigue she fought against every day, and in her defence you would have to say that the fact that she actually turned up at the school was a sign she could manage the daily battles against tedium. So she was fighting it, but she fought like someone who is being deprived of her weapons one after the other. First the shield, then the sword, then the knife, then the shoes. Muriel said rather pompously that the battle Moreau waged against tedium was like the struggle every human being wages against life itself, you have to make all the deals on your own for the simple reason that you are the only person with any interest in doing so. And at the same time your weapons are taken from you one after the other; you are never really any more powerful than you were when you were born and had an entire regiment of parents and grandparents to protect you, and in the end you are left naked on the battlefield with only your bare hands for weapons while the machinery of war rumbles on around you. That's when, Muriel said, it's time to turn your back on it all and leap off the cliff. Though that isn't really the worst thing, she went on, the worst thing is that just a little bit away, on the other side of the hill or in the neighbouring village, there is an alter ego made of very different stuff who is living that other life you could have lived if you had done everything differently. If you'd chosen to settle somewhere else and learnt to do other things, taken a different job and made completely different friends. And that double will stand there strong and beautiful and happy when faced with the tanks. And if the double has to die, they know how to do so with dignity. The double never dies like a dog.

Whatever. In any case Moreau's eyes became increasingly armoured the longer term went on, which you could only consider to be proof of a profound inner weariness. Her red coat began to look increasingly drab, as though she couldn't be bothered to take it to the dry cleaner's. Her thin, short hair grew out and its split ends hung around her shoulders. She put on weight and her trousers started to pinch across her stomach, now and then you could see a bit of soft white flesh peeping out. She didn't seem to care. Camillo kept on saying repulsive things about her; he continued telling us all the rumours that were going around and that she had been dumped and how the womb in women who had not given birth could tear away from its moorings and start wandering around the body; that was the origin of hysteria according to the ancient Greeks, and even if you couldn't see the hysteria in Moreau, it was there under the surface. Camillo said he had a nose for that kind of thing, he could pick up the spoor of repressed female hysteria from miles away. Here in the school it was so thick it made the walls bulge; as a man, it hit you the moment you started up the stairs and you had to steel yourself, to the point of recklessness even, to enter the corridors. The function that armoured gaze of Moreau's served was to keep all that hysteria at bay, according to him, like a thin lid over a dark well, only there was nothing to say that that lid wouldn't crack one day from the pressure and then Madame Moreau's true self would be revealed as scorned, dumped, childless and totally insane.

It was thanks to Domingo that our class finally got to see another side of Madame Moreau. It was also, perhaps, because of Domingo's kindness to Madame Moreau that everything that followed actually took place, I have thought about that, and while I've never mapped out the connections exactly because that would be impossible, I really have given it some thought, and something definitely changed in the whole situation at that point, a kind of descent began. One day Domingo turned up with a tray of *petits choux* he had bought in the bakery below the school. He also had a bottle of cava and a pack of plastic wine glasses with him.

'No pastry in the world could sweeten that sour cunt,' said Camillo when he realised what Domingo was about.

'You can just keep your trap shut,' Domingo said then. 'Just for once you're going to keep a lid on it, Camillo Pochintesta.'

Camillo was glowering in the corridor while Domingo laid everything out in the classroom. The rest of us sat silently in our seats. Don't you get it? Domingo said. This is what we should have done a long time ago. Yes, we said. Madame Moreau opened the main door as usual a few minutes before the lesson was supposed to begin, entered the corridor and said a barely audible hello to Camillo who was leaning against the wall grinning at her. When she came into the classroom, she just stood there as though turned to stone while her gaze ranged across what Domingo had laid out. The tray with the pastries, the glasses, the three bottles of cava. And then the rows of seats, the sharpened pencils on the teacher's desk, us, the windows and the station building on the other side. Then she turned on her heels, said 'just a moment', and went into the toilet where she remained for almost four minutes.

When she came out, it was obvious she had put on a dark red lipstick that made her mouth look different. Her hands must have been shaking when she applied it, because from the second row where I was sitting you could clearly see that one side of her cupid's bow was higher than the other. But what was really astonishing was that she was smiling as she came back into the classroom. It was a strained, stiff smile, but a smile nonetheless. For the very first time I could see Madame Moreau's teeth, and they were even and pearly grey, like they end up in very old people or in people who have drunk a lot of tea.

'So what's all this?' she asked, her arms crossed over her chest.

'It's just that it struck us how rarely we show our appreciation,' Domingo said.

'Appreciation?' Madame Moreau said.

The last word came out like a gasp. We all nodded at that. Domino opened the cava with a confident hand and the festive sound of the cork being pushed out of the bottle got us onto our feet and made us walk over to the trays of *petits choux* and take a glass each. Madame Moreau accepted the glass Domingo offered her and carried it to her lips. She moved over to the window and stood with her back to us looking down at the street. She raised the glass to her lips again. There was a long, drawn-out silence. We were all struggling to come up with something to say because it felt as if the reason Madame Moreau was standing silently with her back to us was that she had no idea how to deal with the situation; she simply had no experience accepting appreciation, and we would have to save her from the embarrassment we were actually responsible for. Then she suddenly said, aloud and without a tremor in her voice:

'If I'd been more brilliant, I would have become something different.'

We looked at one another uncertainly.

'Different to what?' Domingo asked.

'Something different to what I am today. A teacher. A lonely, mediocre teacher.'

'Mediocre?' Domingo said.

'Mediocre,' Moreau said, her back still turned to us. 'It really wasn't that likely. There was nothing to say I would end up as mediocre as this. I speak two languages perfectly. I have contacts in several fields. I could have done those interpreting jobs, sat in a booth and earned seven hundred euros a day. Here I am instead. Trying to make people out of a bunch of losers.'

She drank from her glass again. We looked at Domingo, unsettled by the sudden confidence and that insult you couldn't just ignore.

'Anyway,' Moreau said and turned to face us. 'I can see you've tried to be kind to me. I appreciate that, and I will pay you back. It has been ages since anyone was kind to me. I can't actually remember the last time someone was. So I am going to pay you back,' she repeated.

'Haven't you got any friends?' Domingo asked.

We looked at him. How could he have been so bold? Madame Moreau stared at him as well and for a moment I thought she would send him out of the room, but she didn't.

'No,' she said sadly instead. 'I haven't got any friends.'

She laughed, looked out the window and went on:

'I'm actually terrified of other people. People are really terribly dangerous.'

'Maybe not all of them?' Domingo said and smiled at her.

'No, maybe not all of them,' Moreau conceded, 'but the vast majority are judgmental, narrow-minded, cowardly and, what's worse, they appear to be in it together.'

'Ha,' said Domingo. 'It sounds like you suffer from paranoia, Madame Moreau.'

He's in for it now, I thought. Domingo is going to get slapped down so hard he'll never get up again. But he wasn't. Instead Moreau laughed again and her laughter sounded almost happy this time.

'Maybe you could put it like that, but then I suppose even a paranoid person can be persecuted, what's your view on that, Monsieur del Rio?'

'Sure,' said Domingo.

'Do you know what I read on the train coming here?' Moreau asked while Domingo topped up her glass. 'They've done a study of which marriages survive the best. And get this, the marriages that survive the best are the ones where the partners are able to ignore what the other one says. I mean, doesn't that tell you something?'

'It does,' Domingo said.

'That's really creepy, isn't it?' Moreau cried and she was standing in front of him.

'Yes,' said Domingo and his voice sounded thick.

'So no, my friends,' Moreau said, and turned to the rest of us. 'Take my word for it. It's best to let your wounds bleed when you're by yourself.'

Her eyes seemed to be hooded from intoxication. Her lipstick had smudged a bit.

'I'd just like to say one thing,' Domingo said and took a step nearer her. He was standing so close that she had to be able to feel the warm air of his words against the nape of her neck.

'Not a single hair on your head is mediocre. You are the most knowledgeable and able teacher I have ever had. And besides, Elaine, you're . . . beautiful.'

Madame Moreau looked straight ahead. At first we couldn't make out the expression on her face because the light streaming in behind her was so strong, but then the sun suddenly went behind a cloud and we could make out the exact expression in her eyes. It switched from a kind of total and almost rapt openness into something that actually looked like an attempt at a new smile. Only then a shadow fell across it all and the usual glazed veil was back in place.

'Since when,' she said coldly, while turning towards Domingo, 'since when have Monsieur del Rio and I been on first-name terms?'

The spell had been broken. Domingo gave a little gasp and took a step back. Madame Moreau walked over to her desk and dropped her plastic glass into the waste bin.

'Make sure you get rid of the dregs. You're just standing there looking like dogs waiting to be fed. This is over now.'

We helped Domingo pack together what was left.

That was the only time Madame Moreau opened up to our class. The lessons continued as usual after that. She addressed us by our surnames, humiliated Camillo who humiliated her in turn although always in her absence. She failed us on almost all the papers we wrote and sneered openly at us when we were interpreting, either on account of our accents or because we couldn't memorise the entire contents of what was being read, or because we were dressed too conspicuously, given that a good interpreter should be wearing more or less the same pattern on his or her jacket as the wallpaper on the room where the interpreting is to take place. Not to put too fine a point on it, you could even say she destroyed our self-confidence when it came to expressing ourselves in French. That might sound sad, said Muriel, but the more you think about it the more you realise that self-confidence in expressing yourself in French is completely irrelevant. What does it matter? The heavens are not going to fall because I no longer have any confidence expressing myself in French. I can express myself in other languages. I can use body language or simply stay silent. I don't give really give a damn, I've never liked French, I'm glad I speak it so badly.

Which was a lie after all, because Muriel spoke French like a native.

As for me, what I was going to learn from Madame Moreau would be learnt a few months later and in the company of Alba Cambó and Valentino Coraggioso. And that knowledge would have little to do with vocabulary lists and conjugations, but more with something of wider human relevance that might be summed up as the fact that beneath the thick skin of even the most armour-plated person there is always a crack that runs straight to the centre and you should think it over very carefully before raising a hand to signal your willingness to fall inside.

'THE STORY OF LUCI'

ALBA CAMBÓ

Semejanzas 2008:11

The first thing a visitor to Caudal de la Ribera sees of the village is the cemetery. It sprawls around the outskirts almost insolently and then marches unchecked up a hill, and that is why there seems no end to it from the road. Then 'the club' comes into view, which is pink. The restaurant comes next and is ochre-coloured, like Leonor Albornoz' house and all the earth around Caudal for that matter. You can't see Maderas Del Pozo from the village – you have to go all the way through it and then out the other side – and there by the dried-up riverbed is the timber yard, not painted any colour at all. This yard is the destination for all the heavy lorries that pass through the centre of the village every day; it is at the timber yard the lorries stop and load up. Then they set off again, driving the same way they came except that on the way back they stop at neither the brothel nor the restaurant.

If extenuating circumstances exist for what happened in the village that year when the new priest arrived, they are to be found in the geography. A landscape shapes the people who inhabit it, and it has been said of Caudal – not totally in jest – that it is the last outpost of civilisation before you get to hell. The knife-edged dividing line between pitiless light and dense shadow has become etched into the villagers over the centuries. Their eyes are as steady and as penetrating as tacks; their capacity to arrive at swift judgements and to decide what is right and wrong would alarm anyone from hazier, darker and therefore also more hesitant regions. What they say about an opponent in Caudal is that all they have to do is sit on their steps and wait and soon enough they will see their enemy's coffin pass by. And there they are, sitting on their steps. The sun starts to climb in the east. It treks across the vaulted sky to linger at the zenith and then sinks with an endless slowness. Every now and then the church bells ring. Often for a funeral, more rarely for a marriage, never for a baptism. No one can remember when a baptism was last held in Caudal. And that makes it easier to understand why, on the night when Leonor rang for her, Daniela Hernandez was feeling such a vast, warm joy the moment she went out of the door of her house. She was looking forward to the childish babble that would soon be filling the church, to hearing it bounce off the walls and purl like a spring in all those old ears. The desiccated and ancient mumbling that normally filled the interior would turn into something very different the day Leonor's son was christened: something joyous and hopeful.

And so there Daniela Hernandez was, pedalling along, the night Leonor's child was to be born. The gravel crackled under the tyres; the veil of cloud had broken up and the stars were shining brightly in the firmament above her. She parked in front of the large ochre-coloured house in which Leonor had been living on her own for almost six months and lingered in the courtyard for a moment listening to the night. How silent it all was, she thought. Not a puff of wind, not a single cricket, no cars in the distance. Just peace, as though the entire landscape was holding its breath, waiting for something. It is waiting for the child, she thought. The dry earth is waiting for a little child it can feed. The dry soil is tired of swallowing old bodies. It is sated and bloated, and now it wants to give back something of itself. She picked up her bag and went into the house. As soon as she entered the bedroom, she discovered that the waters had broken long ago and that Leonor was already dilated by ten centimetres. What this made her think was that Leonor had been intending to go through the delivery on her own but had changed her mind at the last minute and rung for help. Daniela Hernandez would have liked to give her a piece of her mind. There was something deeply irresponsible about a plan like that. The entire village was waiting for Leonor's son; they were waiting like the desert waits for rain. But Leonor had now suffered through almost twenty hours of torment in the dilation phase, and the pain, the fear and rage were plain to see on her face. Daniela Hernandez chose therefore not to say anything at all, but to set to work and get the child out.

Several hours later, however, as she was disappointedly holding a little girl swaddled in towels, she asked Leonor what her daughter's name was to be. Leonor replied that the child would be called Lucifer.

'But it's . . . a girl?' Daniela said, perplexed.

'I made my mind up long ago that the child would be called Lucifer, whether it was a boy or a girl,' Leonor replied. 'I never asked for this child. All I wanted was peace and quiet. Now that Arcadio is dead, all I want is peace and quiet. But we all have to sup from the cup of sorrow with our own spoon, and what I got in my spoon was this child. That's why she will be called Lucifer and that is my last word on the matter.'

'Arcadio will be turning in his grave to hear you say that,' Daniela cried. 'He was a good Christian and would never have let you christen the child Lucifer.'

'What Arcadio gets up to in his grave is no longer my concern,' Leonor replied. 'He'll be bloating when it rains, I expect, and drying out when the sun shines, just like any other corpse.'

'Have you got any idea how much everyone in the village has been yearning for a child to be born?' Daniela persisted. 'Do you realise how happy everyone is that there's going to be a baptism in the church at last?'

'A baptism!' Leonor cried. 'Are you all out of your minds? There'll be no baptism for little Lucifer, over my dead body.'

'The girl could help change your life,' Daniela appealed, unable to let go of the image of all those aged, happy faces listening to the childish babble. 'You'll no longer be lonely in this huge house. This child could represent something new, she could help you find . . . '

'Help me find what?'

'The kind of thing that makes . . . things . . . meaningful,' Daniela said, already regretting her clumsy choice of words.

'When the blind lead the blind, they both end up in the ditch,' Leonor observed. 'Could you please clear off, now the child's finally out.'

Her cheeks flaming with annoyance, Daniela Hernandez cleaned up around Leonor. Then she rode off on her bike, shaken and relieved all at once. There was a feeling of sickness in Leonor's house, a kind of madness lying in wait in the walls.

The first few years Daniela Hernandez saw no sign of the girl. The insults she had been forced to endure were so fresh in her mind she could not bring herself to go over and see how they were doing. There were long stretches of time in which Daniela entirely forgot about little Lucifer, but then she would happen to think of her. Suddenly and unexpectedly, like when you wake in the middle of the night and remember something you had forgotten or a mistake you'd made that had become muffled in the cotton wool of your everyday preoccupations during the hours of daylight, only to loom up like a sharp-edged reef from the bottom of the sea at night and rip huge tears in the keel of whatever thought might be occurring to you. And then she would think: Leonor's little girl! What has happened to her? Has she become the target of Leonor's madness? I do have a responsibility; I was the one who helped her come into this world after all.

'We've got to go over there and make sure Leonor's girl is all right,' Daniela said one day to the other women of the village. 'It's been almost eleven years and I've never laid eyes on her, not once.'

The other women nodded. They decided they would go over there one afternoon shortly before Easter. As a pretext for the visit they were going to say they wanted to give Leonor a basket of fruit and nuts. That was hardly customary among them, to be sure, but as one of them said someone else had said, things actually could change over the years. So over there they went: Daniela, Gabriela, Cristina and Julia. The sand was

a dark brown colour that day, strewn across the hinterland
like a burnt scab.

The house looked as desolate as it had that night eleven years
before. Despite its desolation, it was still the grandest house in
the whole of Caudal. Unlike Leonor, Arcadio Maldonado, the
man who had built it to honour Leonor but who had died a
few months before the birth of Lucifer, was popular with the
villagers. In the village they said that he had only improved
with age, just like really good wine. They didn't use the expression applied to the other men of the village who had aged well:
good cocks make good stock!

'I wonder how much money he left,' Daniela said as they
walked across the courtyard.

'Enough to stop Leonor having to get her fingernails dirty,'
Gabriela said.

'I've heard it said he went to the bank and emptied his
account only a day or so before he died,' Cristina interjected.
'He took it all home with him in large bags.'

'There's no end of gossip in our village,' Daniela said.

'She can spend the rest of her life lying on her couch,'
Cristina said.

'No end of gossip,' Daniela repeated.

They knocked on the door and waited. They had to wait
quite a while before they finally heard the sound of someone's
steps on the other side.

'Hello,' said the girl who opened the door. 'Who are you?'

She was darkly angelic as though drawn from a story by
Henry James or a painting in some cool marble chapel in
Toledo. She was tall for her age and had freckles. Her eyes

were bright green. Her jet-black hair fell down behind her shoulders.

Daniela introduced the other women from the village and Luci greeted them guardedly.

'Could we come in for a moment?'

'All right,' Luci said.

They stepped into a hall that led to the central part of the house, which was a garden. A profusion of dark green plants were growing at various heights, and a fountain murmured in the centre of the atrium. The open space gave off a sense of dampness, greenery and shade. The women gasped: never in their wildest dreams could they have imagined something like this existing in Caudal – a leafy garden with water and shade and in the Mexican style in the middle of the house as well. Was this what Leonor had done with the money her husband had left her?

'Do you attend school?' Cristina asked when they had sat down at a table amid the foliage.

'I've got permission to study at home,' said Luci.

'We never see you in the village,' Daniela said.

'Mum isn't that fond of the village.'

'But she hardly knows us really,' said Gabriela. 'You should come down to the village every once in a while. If you don't, people will start talking. There are some people who think Leonor has been keeping you locked up all these years, just to give you an example.'

Luci laughed out loud.

'Mum says if you spend too much time with other people, you end up being like them. You start evaluating yourself by their yardsticks. Because people measure you; they multiply you by unfamiliar denominators and sub-divide you and subtract you, they can make you a stranger to everyone including yourself.'

'You sound like an old book when you talk,' Gabriela said.

Luci picked up an eraser from in front of her and started to pick it apart into small pieces she then pushed around the table.

'That's the only thing there is to do here,' she said. 'Reading old books is all there is to do in this place, that and the watering and looking after the plants.'

She made a sweeping gesture towards the greenery around them.

'Based on what Mum says, things only get worse if you go out. She says there's no end to the number of fools there are, especially in Caudal.'

The women stared at her.

'Only I might come down to the village at some point in any case,' Luci said. 'I need to see if I can find a man.'

'You need to see if you can find a man?' Daniela said in alarm. 'What do you mean by that?'

'I've only met two men in my entire life,' Luci said. 'One is the handyman Mum employs to do things around here, the other is the gardener. They both come up from Madrid once a week. Neither of them likes to talk, and they just do what Mum tells them and then off they go again. I've never had a real talk with them.'

'Well,' Gabriela said. 'I wouldn't bother coming to Caudal if what you want is a real talk with a man. You'll find it's not worth the effort.'

Daniela looked at her in reproach. Wouldn't it be wonderful if Luci did come? And if she did, they could look after her and ensure everything was all right.

'That's Leonor arriving now,' Luci said, and her face cracked into a wicked smile.

The sound of tyres could duly be heard on the gravel in the courtyard. Leonor was soon standing in the doorway behind them.

'What are you all doing here?' she said.

'Hello, Leonor,' Daniela said. 'We wanted to see how you were doing. We're just sitting here having a nice chat with Luci.'

'A nice chat,' Leonor said. 'A lot of blather and self-important nonsense is all there ever is to hear in Caudal. Be off with you, you've no business to be here.'

Cristina pointed to the basket in the corner.

'We just wanted . . . '

'Get out, I say, before I decide to give the pitchfork an airing.'

The women returned to the village.

*

The visit to Leonor's house coincided with the arrival in the village of the new priest. The old one had left a few days before, exhausted with age and by funerals. A black car had come from Madrid to pick him up, and a chauffeur had stuffed a large number of suitcases in the boot while the priest sat gloomily in the backseat, muttering 'little village, big hell'. He ignored the greetings of the villagers standing on parade along the main road as the car rolled out of Caudal.

'It's time we had some new blood here,' they said once the car had driven off. 'He'd served here long enough, and his sermons were long-winded and boring.'

The new priest arrived without any fuss on the bus from Madrid. As he got off, he appeared to observe the view, the dirt on the buildings, the way the shutters were so firmly shut, and a few dogs aimlessly running around and sniffing at a ditch. He began to walk towards the church. Once he had passed the cemetery and gone up the hill, he stopped in front of the white house with the green door where the old priest had lived. He opened the door and went in. It slammed shut behind him, and the murmuring over at Pepe's bar rose in volume. Just how old was he? What part of Spain did he come from? The green door was soon re-opened and Ignacio Reyes stepped out, locked up and started walking down to the village. Once there he walked uncertainly along the street, looking at the pavement and in the gutter as though he were searching for something. The villagers squirmed in their seats. What kind of priest would just walk around like that? Then he stopped in the middle of the little square that merged with the street and looked around until his gaze alighted on Pepe's bar. At that point Pepe started cleaning all the tables with a cloth. The locals sat down in their places, alternating men and women. Some of the men remained at the counter because it was possible Reyes would end up there so as not to be forced to choose a particular table and, by doing so, favour one group more than another.

When he finally entered the bar, they tried to feign an unconcerned murmur. He looked around as the door shut behind him. His hair was sweaty and lay across his forehead. He was thin, and the veins on his hands were swollen.

'A glass of water perhaps?' said Pepe. 'And a cup of coffee?'

Gabriela welcomed him. She stood up and said:

'Welcome, Ignacio Reyes, to our village.'

She raised her glass to him then, and Reyes lifted his hand towards her.

'Thank you,' he said. 'I'm glad to be here.'

He started talking as soon as a glass of coffee was put before him. First he told them how nice it was to get out to the country-side. How he had always felt a stranger in big cities, as if they weren't the right place for him. So why did you move to the city in the first place, Daniela Hernandez wanted to ask, but Ignacio had already moved on and was describing La Mancha as a landscape of old castles, and tracks taken by who knows who, that led who knew where.

'Don Quixote himself might have stepped across the cattle-grids around here,' he said with a laugh and made a sweeping gesture with his hand.

They looked down at the tables.

'*Don Quixote* is a book,' someone finally said, and Reyes laughed again, but then he fell silent as he stirred his spoon while staring into his glass. For a few seconds the sound of the spoon against the sides of the glass was the only sound that could be heard; he put it back on the dish with a clatter. Then his lips moulded themselves around the edge and he drank a quick little sip. He picked up the napkin and wiped his mouth.

'That's true,' he said with a nod. 'And books aren't real life, no matter how much you might want them to be. Believing books could be real life is actually extremely unhealthy.'

He nodded at his own words. Then he looked at them. From left to right: Gabriela, Cristina, Julia, Daniela Hernandez.

'Good coffee,' he said next. 'What sort is it?'

'Bonka,' said Pepe.

*

Ignacio Reyes started cultivating a garden, a little oasis whose only rival in the village might be the interior courtyard of Leonor Albornoz' house. But no one could understand where

Reyes thought he would get the water from. The Arabs, he told Pepe at the bar. They knew everything there was to know about artificial irrigation; they created gardens in the desert and got them to bloom. He had been reading about how they did it and had visited gardens around Granada, and the Alhambra as well. He was going to do the same thing here. Create shade at various levels: the palm trees at the very top, then layers of vegetation and, once he had created enough shade, he would begin cultivating the soil beneath it.

'It's not the idea of a "garden" you should have in mind,' he told the locals. 'You should be thinking "oasis" and then applying the principles of an oasis.'

'The fact it worked somewhere else doesn't mean it can be done here,' they said.

'The fact it worked somewhere else means that the possibility exists,' Ignacio countered.

'Even possibilities dry up when they get to Caudal,' they said.

'But not hope,' Ignacio said.

'Hope is vain and plain stupid.'

'Yes. It is vain and stupid. But it's still so powerful it can grow straight out of a cliff.'

Daniela Hernandez also thought that hopefulness was inappropriate for someone like him. As though he had agreed to put on a hat that didn't suit him and was demeaning to his person. But she couldn't help feeling curious. Just imagine if it was possible to make something grow around here? She walked over to his house one day when the air was gentle and warm. It was spring, and you felt as though you wanted to walk far and wide, as free as the man in the poem who just keeps walking, through the dusk and the evening, as happy and carefree as a gypsy. The poem sounded rather solemn in her head: *Et j'irai loin, bien loin, comme un bohémien, Par la nature, – heureux comme avec une femme.* She walked towards his house and was just about to turn back when he stepped out. He caught sight of her and waved her over. She stepped forward hesitantly.

'Hello,' he said when he saw her. 'I recognise you from church. You live down in the village.'

'That's right,' she said.

'Why don't you come in for a cup of tea? I've made a pot; I was just going to have some.'

'No,' she responded. 'I don't drink tea.'

'I'm sure I could make something else.'

'I don't drink anything else either.'

He looked at her. She kept staring stubbornly at the ground.

'What's your name?' he asked.

'Daniela Hernandez,' she replied.

'Were you born here?'

'Yes.'

'You're not a very talkative lot in Caudal.'

'That's just the way we are. We're like that in Caudal.'

Silence.

'You know what,' he said. 'I've actually been feeling rather lonely since I arrived in this village.'

He laughed, and his laughter sounded hollow.

'I really miss having someone to talk to. Some kind of companionship. You seem to have each other for that down there. Don't you?'

'Yes,' she replied. 'We've always got each other in our village.'

'You've got one another and you aren't very bothered by anyone feeling left out.'

'The other priest never felt left out.'

'But I do.'

'What?'

'Feel left out.'

She had no idea how to respond.

'Over there is where Leonor and Luci live,' she said, pointing to Leonor's house.

She stared down at the ground again, not understanding why she had said that about Leonor and Luci. There was silence. The kind of silence that meant you would say anything at all, just so words could be heard.

'Come in,' he said and walked towards the house.

When she hesitated, he gestured her on.

'I mean it. Come in. Don't stand there.'

She followed him slowly into the little house. There was only one room inside, with a little kitchen attached to it.

'So this is where you live,' she said.

'Yes, this is me,' he replied.

The bed was unmade, and there was an open bottle and a glass on the bedside table. The walls appeared to be damp, and on the floor was a flame-coloured carpet and on the carpet an open writing book and a pen. He has chosen to turn a cave into a sitting room, was what struck Daniela. She thought of her own sitting room. It was bright. Sickness is quick to find a way in where there is no light, her mother used to say when she was little. Ignacio was pottering about in the kitchen. The bottle-green shirt was faded from washing and his jeans looked dirty. You'll get ill if you stay here, she wanted to say. Instead she said:

'I have to go now.'

'Where?'

'To the graves.'

'Anyone in particular?'

She shook her head.

'Just graves. I look after them so they don't fall into ruin. Old friends.'

'So even the dead are treated as part of the community? But you can't be bothered about the living?'

She tried to snort but the snort sounded like a failed sneeze. She immediately took a handkerchief out of her pocket and wiped her nose.

'The way you make things sound,' she said.

Silence fell once more. He had moved in close, and was now right behind her. She could smell his scent, the odour of sweat and old alcohol. She thought of the old priest whose after-shave you could smell even from the pews. She wanted to move, but just stood there as if turned to stone. She thought: He doesn't scare me. I'm going to turn round. I'm going to turn round now and look him straight in the eye. And no matter what those eyes of his are saying, I'm going to stay where I am and look straight at them. That's what I am going to do. I'm turning round. She turned round. In his eyes was something that looked like curiosity. Or was it . . . a sense of triumph?

She remembered the old priest again. He had been there for as long as she could remember. He was the one who did the talking in church throughout her entire childhood. He would never have made a joke about her habit of going to look at the graves. He would have thanked her, and she would have seen genuine joy in his eyes when he did so. She remembered the time he had caught her as a child cutting the legs off frogs in the rain. She had been out there by the watering hole on the plain with a pair of scissors in her hands, and all of a sudden there he was behind her. She gave a start and looked up at him in all his enormity, angry and a bit sombre, the clouds scudding past on the dark sky behind him. Are you cutting the legs off frogs, child? he had asked. So that's what you're up to – cutting the legs off frogs. That's very naughty of you, Daniela. Just how do you suppose they're going to be able to jump about when they don't have any legs? She had replied in an indistinct mumble. To see what would happen, you say, to see what would happen – you have to be very naughty to cut the legs off frogs just to see what would happen, Daniela. I've got to find a punishment for you now, my child. Ten Rosaries and fifteen more Our Fathers, that should do it. And you've got to promise me you won't cut the legs off frogs any more. You've got to promise me that. *Although* if you are going to keep cutting the legs off frogs no matter what, you'd better give them to your mother because no one can prepare frogs' legs the way she can, fried in parsley with garlic and lemon. I don't mind telling you, Daniela, no one can cook frogs' legs like your mother.

She recalled that episode with a stifled laugh and suddenly wanted to tell it to Reyes, to let him know how the old priest had put it, the way he had complimented her mother on how she cooked frogs' legs. She was on the point of telling him, but then she thought someone like Reyes, an educated man from the city who had read Cervantes and talked about irrigation with Arabs, would never understand. He wouldn't think there could be anything harmless about cutting the legs off frogs. He would look down on her, and then start talking about nerve tissues, pain, animals and human beings. He would say: Animals are people too, or possibly: Human beings are animals, too.

She said: 'I'm going now.'

She was just going out the door when she felt him grab hold of her shoulder.

'Wait,' he said.

She turned her face to him again. His lips pressed against hers. She poked him hard in the chest.

'Sorry,' he mumbled. 'I . . . '

She stared at him.

'I'm just so lonely,' he said. 'I'm just so bloody lonely, I . . . you seemed to be so . . . '

'What?'

'I don't know . . . available?'

He looked guiltily at her.

'Did you just say I looked *available*?' she asked.

'Of course you don't,' he mumbled. 'Forgive me, I'm . . . '

'There's nothing to forgive,' she said and turned around. 'It was just a mistake. I'm going to forget it ever happened.'

She moved towards the door.

'I don't understand why you came here,' she said before she closed it behind her. 'You should have gone somewhere else. This isn't a place for people like you. The people in our village are like dogs. Unless you get the whip hand over them, they won't just be using those jaws of theirs for talking.'

Then she left.

*

Caudal:

Like extras who have been asked to have a seat and relax for a bit, they sit there staring straight ahead in the heat. The road is dirty. Every now and then a car comes along. The bus from

Madrid will soon be arriving and its approach can be heard from far off. The sounds of laughter and chatter can be heard from the greengrocer's and from The Laughing Turtle bar. The sign for The Laughing Turtle sways slightly in the breeze. This is a blue turtle that has been carved out of wood. There is a smell of frying coming from the bar.

A lady comes out of the grocer's with a bag of fruit in her hand. A loquat falls out of the bag and rolls across the street. Not one of the people sitting at the bus stop gets up to call out, 'Hey, I think you dropped a loquat.' They all remain seated. No one gets up to run over and pick it up and then run after the woman with it.

They all just sit there and look at the orange loquat lying in the middle of the black roadway. A car comes along. It's a red car, and the driver knows one of the people sitting there waiting because he raises a hand and calls out something through the window that has been wound down. Judging by his smile, he appears not to have any teeth. After he has driven past, the loquat remains on the tarmac. A dog comes running: a stray, a dog without an owner, just looking for a diversion of some kind. It stops and sniffs the loquat and then sticks its tongue out very rapidly to give the fruit the briefest of licks. Then a car can be heard approaching, and the dog leaves the roadway and moves towards the edge. It stops there for a while and looks at the loquat and then turns to look in the opposite direction, where a bitch is coming in fast. The dogs couple in front of everyone. The observers' eyes wander. Some of them look at the dogs; others keep gazing fixedly at the loquat. One of them looks out over the hinterland. Screwing up his eyes to see better, as if something vastly important were occurring on the horizon.

The bus finally arrives. The loquat is crushed beneath one of its front wheels; the dogs stop coupling and run off towards the cemetery. The onlookers enter the bus, and the bus drives off. For a few moments nothing at all happens, apart from the sign for *The Laughing Turtle* continuing to sway in the wind.

*

Green shoots started to appear out of the soil in Ignacio Reyes' garden. He wished he could show them to Daniela Hernandez and that she would come back some day, so he would have an opportunity to rectify the situation and everything that had gone wrong. But Daniela did not come. The girl from the ochre-coloured house turned up instead. One day she was just standing there on the dry gravel path, looking at what he had been growing. And, unlike Daniela and the other villagers, she didn't seem to have anything against talking. She also turned out to know quite a bit about plants. Have you got a spade? she asked and started digging. You can't have that here, she had said. You'll have to replant it and put it over there.

She started turning up more and more often. They dug the soil, talked and sometimes they laughed. The girl appeared not to have the complicated relationship to laughter that the other villagers had, who seemed to think that smiling was a highway to hell. The girl laughed out loud: her mouth open wide, her head thrown back. Sometimes he was forced to look away when she laughed because it was as if she were exposing something of her innermost being in laughter, and that was something he couldn't possibly be meant to see. I have taken every precaution, he thought. And even so it feels as though certain situations are *drawn to me*. Those situations are constantly at my back, sniffing at my heels, and if I stop or drop the pace even for a moment, they will bring me down, like a storm brings down a rotten pine tree. But if this is a test, I am going to withstand it. I am gentle and warm, but I can also be hard and cold. Just talking and laughing is innocent enough, and anyway no one can see us up here in my house.

How little he knew them! Of course they could see him. They were watching him the whole time. And if one of them couldn't see him, another could; if he couldn't be seen face to face then he could be seen with binoculars from a house on the outskirts. And the girl at his side kept talking. About this flower and that one. This insect or that. About Leonor Albornoz and Arcadio Maldonado, and how one day she was going to take the bus to Madrid and then on to Catalonia. She talked about the intrinsic and inescapable ugliness of the villagers. And a kind of calm settled in the air around them while she talked. But calms can be treacherous; they are dark waters you cannot see through and you really shouldn't dip your hand beneath them. Reyes would also talk from time to time. He talked about love, and tried not to think about physical love. But when he talked about God's omnipotent and unconquerable love, confusion got the upper hand and he understood nothing of what he was saying.

*

That day:

The mass began as usual. He read aloud something about love in a confused and prosaic manner, and then fell silent. The doors opened. The sound of the wind outside entered the church, and then the doors slammed shut. It took a few seconds before he could make out who it was standing at the back of the nave. It was Luci. She was dripping wet and her muddy boots had left tracks across the floor. And what was that in her hands? Two plastic bags? *Rubbish bags?* Filled with something.

He put his sermon down on the edge of the pulpit.

'What is the reason for this visit?' he said.

'Nacho,' she said. 'I've got the money in these bags. We can leave now.'

The villagers gaped at them from the pews. She called him *Nacho*. Leonor's daughter called the priest Nacho. You can't call a priest by a nickname. And if you do, that can only mean . . . They kept staring, first at one then the other.

'I don't understand,' Ignacio said, but a blush had already begun to steal across his face. 'I really haven't got the faintest idea what you mean.'

'You said you didn't have any money, didn't you?' the girl said impatiently. 'But I do. In any case Mum is never going to make up her mind what she's going to do with it. We should have it. We should go to Catalonia, you and me.'

Every face turned towards the girl and then back to him.

'The bus is leaving in thirty minutes,' Luci said. 'Are you coming?'

'I don't know what you're talking about,' Reyes said as sweat began to glisten on his forehead. 'I haven't got a clue. Here I am holding mass, and you come in and tell me we should be leaving?'

'But that's what you said,' the girl said and looked at him in disappointment. 'You said we'd get out of here if we had money. Well I've fixed that now. We can go.'

For a moment he was filled with an intense feeling of joy. In his mind's eye he could see himself in slow motion, throwing off his robes and taking the girl's hand; he could see them running down the aisle of the nave, holding the plastic bags full of money while banknotes were whirling around them in the air; he could see them whirling around those idiotically staring faces that had not yet had the time to judge them and were still simply observing, dumbfounded. They threw open the doors and ran over the plain and, in his vision, it was spring and the petals of the flowers were bobbing merrily in the summer breeze, nodding in fervent accompaniment to their movements. He was running beside her, *heureux comme avec une femme*. They were headed towards a new life, towards a new spring, towards the first real summer he had ever known.

Even then he was astonished by the image and that he could actually allow it to break through. In retrospect, he will think that the strangest thing about those seconds the image endured is that he never feared there would be punishment, not for one moment.

His voice sounded strange even to him when he finally said,

'I really have no idea what you are talking about, Luci Maldonado.'

'Look, we said we . . . '

'What I am saying is that I don't understand any of it.'

Luci stood there looking at him for a little while. Then she turned and walked down the aisle. Her head was hanging and the bags were dragging against the floor. She gathered her strength to open the doors and then they had shut behind her.

Reyes returned to his sermon. He couldn't bear to feel his flock staring at him. But when he raised his eyes and looked out over the plain around the church during one of the psalms, he saw the figure of Luci. She was walking dejectedly down towards the village; the wind was mussing her hair and her white boots were dirty. The plastic bags dragged behind her in the mud and a few banknotes were whirling in the wind.

A few hours later and she was gone. They searched for her at Pepe's, by the graves, and then just drove aimlessly back and forth as the people in the car tried to work out where she could have gone. Reyes was among the searchers as well; he walked to the watering hole on the plain as though he took it for granted she would be there, then he wandered around down in the village with his robes flapping around his calves and that unhappy expression on his face.

Daniela remained in the background. She would later regret she had not played a more active role from the start. She might, then, not have had to do so afterwards, when events began to escalate. What was the point of a bunch of extras? She would think at that point. There can be no theatre without actors. This is a lesson you have to learn, along with much else, but you always learn it too late to profit from it.

*

Leonor turned up at Pepe's bar for the first time in many years. Although she didn't talk about Luci but Reyes. Determined and forceful, she stood there facing the villagers, who seemed to have forgotten all those years she had spent alone in her house looking down on them. She was here now and she was one of them and she was strong and she was telling them to their faces what to do.

'You know what you do with paedophiles?' she said. 'You burn them alive. You butcher them like pigs.'

Gabriela nodded.

'That's what you do,' she agreed. 'It's the only way.'

Daniela shook her head.

'Honestly, I just think he was feeling lonely,' she said. 'I don't think he ever intended to . . . '

'You can tell a snake by its spots,' Leonor interrupted. 'And I've never trusted that priest. I can see him in his garden from my house, and I always think that's a man you cannot trust, there's something fishy about him.'

So why didn't you just go over when you saw your daughter there? Daniela thought. Why did you hide in wait like a beast of prey in the long grass?

'And that's why I am proposing that we hold a trial,' Leonor said.

A murmur swept through the bar. A trial, here in Caudal!

'A trial?' Cristina asked. 'Put the priest on trial? You're joking.'

Leonor looked at them, one and all, glassy-eyed.

'Just hold on,' Daniela said. 'What is it we're actually discussing here? We can't hold a trial without a courthouse. And anyway there has to be some suspicion that a real crime has been committed.'

'I do suspect that a real crime was committed,' Leonor said. 'And I am the mother of the victim.'

'Just think about this, Leonor,' Daniela appealed. 'To have a trial you have to have a prosecutor, a lawyer for the defence and a courthouse.'

'True,' said Leonor. 'True. And we've got all that. Prosecutors we've got in plenty, since the whole village, with the possible exception of you, Daniela, thinks he is guilty.'

She looked around the bar just to make sure no one was planning on contradicting what she had said. They were all staring silently into their glasses.

'The only thing we're lacking is a defence,' she went on. 'But then we've got you for that.'

'What?' said Daniela.

The whole thing sounded crazy to her.

'You'll be perfect,' Leonor said. 'You'll be his defence counsel. You were made for the job.'

This is the first time I've seen Leonor outside her home, Daniela thought. This is the first time I've seen her down here, and she looks crazy and dirty. Only nothing matters to her any more. She's not a mother defending her child, she's a captain determined to have her ship. She's come down here to take the helm – over the rest of us.

'All you have to do is convince us,' Leonor said and turned her back on Daniela.

'What am I supposed to convince you of?'

'The innocence of that fucking paedophile.'

Leonor laughed savagely, and the others laughed along with her in disbelief.

Daniela went home and rang Del Pozo. She told him something was about to happen, that someone would have to intervene to stop what had been set in motion otherwise someone might get hurt.

'I never get mixed up in anything that happens in the village,' Del Pozo said in reply. 'I've always said I won't get mixed up in anything going on in the village.'

'They're going to hurt him,' Daniela said. 'At best. I don't even want to think about what the worst case would be. You're the only one who can stop it; you're the only one who can stand up against Leonor.'

Del Pozo sighed.

'That's the way it's always been,' he said then. 'People who come from outside never can fit in with us.'

*

Daniela was the last to enter and sat on a pew at the back. Reyes sat tied fast to a chair in the nave, a little in front of the altar. This isn't happening, she thought. Some things just cannot happen, and this is one of them. One of the windows had been opened and the barking of dogs could be heard, persistent, unrelenting, unsettling. She made an effort not to meet Reyes' eyes. Just before Leonor stepped up to the pulpit, he asked to be allowed to go to the toilet. Leonor shook her head. Daniela could see this from where she was sitting in one of the rear pews, and so she went up to Leonor and whispered to her that she couldn't see the point of that.

'Does his humiliation have to be taken to such extremes?' she asked.

'He'll just have to hold it in,' Leonor answered coldly. 'If he can manage that, it might be considered an extenuating circumstance.'

Daniela went back to her pew. Leonor stepped up into the

pulpit and declared the assembly open. Leonor was the first speaker on the list. Vincent, Pascal and Paco spoke after her. They all simply repeated different versions of what Leonor had already said.

Then it was her turn. She went up into the pulpit. She set out her arguments without losing her composure, without meeting his eyes. He had come out here, after all, to be with them. He had got his garden started and was setting up the irrigation. He was bound to have felt lonely.

'After all, we've got each other, but he had no one and loneliness makes for bad company.'

Some people nodded thoughtfully. Others stared stubbornly out the windows. She went on:

'I remember the first day he arrived. He was standing in Pepe's bar talking about books and castles and tracks across the country. Do you remember that?'

They didn't look as though they remembered. She lost her bearings and had no idea how to get started again.

'When all is said and done,' she said, 'we all gain by his crime because it makes us appear better than we actually are. If there was a crime, that is.'

She tried to come up with a laugh when she had said this, but no one laughed with her. She could feel the cold tickle of a drop of sweat running down her spine.

'Can you really not remember what it was like when he arrived,' she began again. 'When Ignacio came to join us? It was as though a lord got off the bus and began walking around. What is he doing here, we thought, when we watched him go up to the house?'

'A lord,' Leonor exclaimed. 'I've said it before and I'll say it again: you people down here should have realised right from the start that he had something to hide. A priest who wants company! No good could ever come of that.'

The villagers murmured in agreement. Daniela was letting the situation run away from her. Panic grabbed her by the throat.

'I just mean we should give him a chance,' she shouted. 'He hasn't done anything after all; he just did some walking around and he dug the soil with Luci, that isn't a crime.'

'But it can *lead* to a crime,' Leonor responded. 'That's exactly what this is all about. If he just wanted company he could have gone down to the bar and chatted with Pepe. That's what Arcadio always did. That is what any good man would do.'

'Or pop over to the brothel,' someone mumbled.

Leonor giggled loudly.

'But if no crime has been committed then we can't . . . ' Daniela began again.

'Daniela,' Leonor said and moved a step closer to her. 'Isn't it time we stopped mincing words? Because what is all this *really* about? Well, let me tell you that as far as you are concerned this isn't about my little Lucifer or Ignacio. This is about you. Because that old heart of yours is still trotting. That's what your problem is. Your heart is trotting and if it doesn't find a stallion to trot with soon, it's going to start bolting.'

'That's right,' one of the parishioners called. 'Your old heart is still trotting, Daniela. Trotting like a lame old mare.'

'You've been out walking too much,' Leonor went on. 'And when women like you go walking alone, there's no telling what crazy ideas they'll get into their heads. The good wife stays at home, that was what the old priest used to say. Do you remember? The good wife stays at home, and the honest maiden considers virtue to be its own reward.'

'I've never . . . ' Daniela began but Leonor interrupted her.

'Leave now,' she said. 'I'm afraid your old heart might not survive what is going to happen.'

'What do you think is going to happen?' Daniela whispered.

Leonor shrugged her shoulders.

'Nothing. We're just going to burn the bastard, that's all.'

A buzz swept over the pews.

'I'll call the police,' Daniela said shakily.

'You do that,' Leonor laughed. 'When the police get here the ashes will have been swept up and we'll be having our siesta. It will all have gone up in smoke, as they say.'

'You can't do this,' Daniela cried.

'Leave now,' Leonor said and put a hand on her shoulder. 'Go home and forget Ignacio Reyes the same way I have forgotten my vanished Luci. We've all got wounds to bear and no matter what we do something will always gnaw away at them.'

'You never loved that child,' Daniela yelled. 'You never loved her. You never loved your child, and that's why she was lonely as well.'

Pepe stepped towards Daniela who raised her hand to fend him off.

'I'll leave on my own,' she said.

She got up and, without looking Ignacio in the eyes, she walked down the central aisle and out through the heavy doors and started running towards the village.

'Mademoiselle Villalobos,' Madame Moreau said to me one day. 'There's something I would like to speak to you about. Would you mind coming with me to my office, please?'

I followed her along the corridor and into a small, very tidy room situated beside the headmaster's office.

'Please have a seat,' she said and pointed at a chair in front of the desk. She sat on the other side and picked up a pen.

'I'll get straight to the point,' she began. 'It has come to my attention that you are Alba Cambó's neighbour.'

'That's right', I replied.

'I have read the piece she wrote in *Semejanzas*. I would very much like to get to know her. Is she a nice person?'

I wasn't really sure how to reply. Was Alba Cambó a nice person?

'Nice wouldn't exactly be the first word that comes to mind when I think of Alba Cambó,' I said.

Moreau laughed out loud.

'That sounds good. I don't trust nice people. In any case I would very much like to meet your neighbour. When I choose a friend, I do so with great care.'

That last bit must just have slipped out as there was something chilly in her eyes the moment she had said it.

'So I would like to ask you to pass on to her an invitation from me. You would be invited as well.'

I handed the invitation to Alba. She opened it, read it and frowned.

'I see,' she said. 'It isn't the first time this has happened. Anyway tell your teacher I'll come and I'll bring Valentino with me.'

That was how I came to take the commuter train to Sitges along with Alba Cambó and Valentino Coraggioso to have dinner at Madame Moreau's.

All three of us had got dressed up, not overly so, but Alba had heels on and Valentino was wearing dark trousers and a crisply ironed white shirt. It was when we entered Moreau's hallway it dawned on us that the way we were dressed couldn't have been what our hostess had been expecting. The hall hadn't been cleaned and her shoes had been placed just inside the entrance, and it felt as if she had forgotten we were coming. Not that she had, as she was soon walking towards us and when the door to the kitchen was opened we could see that the table had been laid, and there was the smell of food.

'Come on,' she said. 'Don't just stand there. I'll show you round.'

Moreau's flat was on the small side and consisted of a narrow hall, a tiny kitchen, a bedroom and a small sitting room. The bedroom was closed, which got under my skin because bedrooms say something about who you are and some of the bits of the puzzle of who she was would have fallen into place if I had been able to look at it. The bedroom is the place you spend the most time in. It can't help giving away who you are. Was Madame Moreau's bedroom lined in red velvet and was her bed extravagantly decadent and lit by lamps with gilded feet and naked angels? Did it contain a mirror with a broad golden frame and were there lovely underclothes scattered across the back of a chair? I wanted to be surprised, to have to admit that Domingo was right to fight for her. Or put it this way: I wanted to feel that there was a living creature behind that facade – to see Madame Moreau as someone who had simply put bars around her soul, her decadent bedroom, because it was so precious it could never be shown to anyone. Only the door was closed, and Moreau didn't offer to open it during the brief tour she gave us.

The rest of the flat exuded a cultivated and dusty femininity. There were double rows of books on the shelves; they were also spread across the table and formed piles on the floor. Soiled lace curtains that had not been hemmed hung across the windows and sagged to the ground. She appeared to collect seashells and little bits of wood carved into different shapes. Papers were something else she seemed to collect, because there were piles of them more than a metre high made up of nothing but newspapers and periodicals. Narrow corridors for walking wove between the piles. There were two large desks in the living room that were also piled high. There was no television. The lighting was bad throughout the flat, apart from above an armchair on which lay a threadbare blanket. Behind the chair stood a large lamp with a shade shaped like a bluebell, and like the blanket, the shade was worn. The lighting in the kitchen, on the other hand, was far too bright. Moreau had the same type of fluorescent tube people have had in our country ever since Franco, which makes all the diners round the table look like patients in a hospital. That was where we were seated after the tour. Moreau had laid the table with a waxed yellow cloth and white napkins and on the tablecloth was a dish of burnt lasagne and two bottles of wine. Cambó and Coraggioso took their seats, and Valentino had an expression of distaste on his face: this really wasn't the kind of thing you ate in his part of Liguria. And Alba had linen tablecloths and napkin rings and would never have served anything as banal as lasagne.

The roles we had been assigned were obvious right from the start. I had been invited as the connection, and Valentino Coraggioso as the hanger-on, only Cambó had been invited as herself. When Moreau spoke her remarks were addressed solely to her. She asked how Alba was getting on in Barcelona, where she came from originally and how she happened to start writing. Cambó replied in monosyllables. Moreau dished the lasagne onto our plates and poured wine into our glasses. Cambó would ask something about Moreau, and Moreau would reply. The conversation felt laboured right up until the coffee.

Once the plates and the glasses had been cleared away, Moreau suggested we should drink our coffee in 'the drawing room'. We tacked between the piles of books towards a maroon-coloured sofa. Alba and I sat on the sofa. Moreau sat on a chair, ignoring the fact that Valentino remained standing without anywhere to sit. After a moment's indecision he pulled over a pile of books and sat on it. Moreau got up and went over to a cupboard that she opened, getting out three balloon glasses.

'Brandy?' she said in an exaggerated American accent, holding up the glasses.

Alba lifted a hand in a gesture of refusal.

'No thanks. I'd rather smoke this.' She got out a ready-rolled joint from her handbag.

'By all means,' Moreau said and poured brandy for herself and Valentino.

Madame Moreau also lit a cigarette and started talking about the school for interpreters and translators and about the episode with Domingo and the cakes.

'And so I enter the classroom,' she said turned towards Alba. 'And there they all are sitting in their seats, twenty-four faces, expecting me to be pleased. I didn't know what to do. That whippersnapper had bought bubbly and sandwiches to make me happy. It was his new trick, you see, as prayers and presents and notes hadn't worked, he was going to try this out. I could have slapped him, and I should have, except I was surrounded by all the other students and I was obliged to show some kind of gratitude. *Gratitude*, you understand, in a situation like that!'

Alba said nothing. Moreau puffed at her cigarette.

'So I promised to repay them for their kindness. It was completely idiotic of me, but I was just standing there and I had to say something. In any case, I promised them some kind of recompense. And now I haven't got the faintest idea how I am going to get myself out of it.'

Alba looked at her with lidded eyes.

'You'd better take them on a study visit, hadn't you,' she said and shrugged her shoulders apathetically. 'Show them something they've never seen before, something that could offer them a chance. Use your network of contacts.'

'My network of contacts . . . ' Moreau laughed out loud. 'Do I look like a woman with *contacts*? The only people who know who I am in this city are my students and the people who work in the store where I shop. I don't know anyone and I've no desire to get to know people just to help a bunch of daddy's girls get on in life.'

Alba looked at me with a slightly scornful smile.

'I might be able to help you,' she said then to Moreau. 'I've got some contacts of my own.'

'Would you really do that? For me?'

'Of course,' Cambó said. 'I'll help you if I can. Of course I will.'

Moreau gave Alba a little smile; she was sitting there with a joint in her hand, bouncing her foot as though she could hear some kind of music in her head. Valentino had picked up a book from the pile he was sitting on. He turned it over and then back and leafed through it.

'Found anything interesting, Tino?' Alba said to him.

'Yes,' he replied. 'A book by someone called Luce Irigaray. On the back it says she's some kind of feminist ur-mother.'

'That's right,' Moreau said tersely, stubbing her cigarette out in the ashtray on the table.

The smile she had given Alba had disappeared, and the habitually tense expression was back on her face.

'It's certainly the case,' said Valentino and put the book down on the table, 'that feminism is a breath of fresh air in our society.'

'I wouldn't want to buy a second-hand car from you,' said Moreau and shook out a new cigarette.

'How's that?'

'What I mean to say is: why should *you* think that feminism is a breath of fresh air?'

'Why not?' Valentino said and shrugged his shoulders.

'If *I'd* been born a man, I wouldn't think feminism was a breath of fresh air.'

She lit a new cigarette and continued:

'The way I see it: why be a hypocrite? It's the duty of a prisoner to try to escape, but the guards are obliged to do their duty as well and that is to go on keeping the prisoners locked up, to check that the fence is intact and there aren't any holes to crawl through.'

Moreau turned towards Valentino and looked at him in challenge as if she was expecting some riposte. None came. Then she said:

'Being phoney just spoils the fight. We shouldn't pretend. We ought to meet as real enemies.'

She reached out her hand to Valentino, and she actually had a smile on her lips. I had time to think that this was only the second or possibly the third time I had ever seen her smile, before the extraordinary happened. Valentino stood up and was about to go over and take Moreau's hand, and as he stepped towards her he turned his head slightly to catch Alba's eyes (she looked at him with a puzzled expression on her face as if she was saying no, I don't understand any of this either). Then he took another step onto a magazine with a shiny cover (*Semejanzas?*) and the sole of his shoe slipped on its surface and he lost his balance and fell. If you've ever seen a tall body fall in a small space you know how crazy it looks, as though all the proportions have been put out of whack or gone haywire. His long arms were fumbling for something to grab hold of and when he couldn't find anything they windmilled through the air; he put his hands behind his back only to move them quickly to the side but it was no use because all control over his body had been lost. He fell headlong and with the full weight of his body onto the floor; the back of his skull struck the hard cement because, of course, there wasn't a book or pile of magazines that could have lessened the blow on the particular spot where his head came down. At the point of impact Valentino's head encountered only the stone floor of Moreau's flat. The sound of his head striking the stone was muffled and horrible: a person being hurled at the mineral. Alba and I sat motionless throughout the duration of the fall. Moreau was still standing there with her hand extended to Valentino, and the smile vanished from her lips yet again. Once Valentino was on the floor, it felt as though we had frozen in our seats. We stared at him. A moment later Alba was leaping up to get her bag and her telephone, only then Moreau reached her hand out to her and said:

'Wait a bit.'

Alba's hand dropped and she looked at Moreau in confusion.

'Just wait,' Moreau said again. 'Let's just sit here for a bit. He's bound to come round in a little while. I've worked in hospitals and I don't think that was a dangerous fall. Nothing was crushed in on the way down. At the very worst he'll have a swelling.'

They sat down slowly on the sofa. Moreau's hand was on Alba's arm. At first they sat there without moving then Moreau picked up the bottle and poured some brandy into Alba's glass and then into her own. Alba looked blankly at me and I had no idea what to do and responded with a shrug. Alba leant over to her handbag mechanically and took out a fresh joint; Moreau picked up a lighter from the ledge under the table and handed it to Alba.

'But we can't just leave him lying like that,' Alba said.

'Just let him rest. He'll come round soon. I told you I'd worked at a hospital. I've seen this kind of thing before.'

There was complete silence for a few moments.

'We could go out one evening,' Moreau said then. 'I could take you to a nice place here in Sitges. We could drink mojitos and margaritas, smoke joints and have a good time. I go out so rarely nowadays.'

The whole thing just felt completely impossible to take in. Alba was sitting there quietly smoking, and my teacher Moreau was sitting facing her while Valentino lay unconscious on the floor. Moreau was saying: *We could drink mojitos and margaritas. Smoke joints and have a nice time*.

'That's right,' Moreau went on. 'There's a bar I know where we could spend all night dancing. We could just dance like crazy, everyone does. Then we could sit outside the church while the sun rises. You're only four or five metres to the sea from the church in Sitges. It's lovely – you've got the sea and the sky straight ahead. We'd be sitting there as the sun's first rays spread across the sky and the surface of the water. We'd still be half drunk and for a few moments we'll believe we . . . '

'Elaine,' Alba said then. 'We can do that. But there's something I want you to know if you really are entertaining ideas about you and me.'

'Yes,' said Moreau.

'I'm ill and I'm going to die.'

'What?' Moreau cried and her cry sounded hoarse and out-of-control.

'That's the situation: I am ill and I'm going to die. I've got a few months left, and I'm trying to live them as well as I can.'

She looked at Moreau and smiled at her a touch reassuringly, as if she wanted to say that it wasn't as bad as it sounded, that was just the way it had turned out.

'So I'd love margaritas and dancing and anything else Sitges has to offer. But in six months I'll be gone, just so you know.'

Alba smiled resolutely and raised her glass to Moreau. Moreau raised hers a bit hesitantly and they met with a little clink.

'*Santé*,' Alba said. 'Let's drink a toast to the time that remains. Let's drink to the fact that I'm bound to be alive for another two months.'

Moreau adapted rapidly to the new state of affairs.

'I hope you haven't started baking cakes, cleaning the oven and going to church,' she said.

'What do you mean?'

'I hope you won't mind if I speak frankly. All the women I've ever met who've been told they're going to die have started baking cakes and being nice in a way they never were before.'

She paused for a bit.

'Until the pain starts getting serious, that is.'

Alba looked at Moreau uncertainly.

'It's just that what I mean,' she went on, 'is all the women I've met who have been told that have become more accommodating than they ever were at any time in their lives. It's as if that final shutting down of any other option forces us back into the trap. They bake, cook, turn into supermums and superwives, just so they can feel they have done some good, so their lives haven't been entirely in vain. As if showing concern for other people was the only thing that would remain of us when we are gone.'

'But there might be something in that,' Alba said.

'Rubbish,' Moreau exclaimed. 'You ought to be the person you always were – even when you're going to die. It's not that hard. Lots of people have died before us. There are more dead than living in this world, if you want to look at it that way.'

Alba laughed aloud.

'You change when you're dying, Elaine.'

'You change because you've *been given the time* to change. That's what actually happens. As for me, I want to die hard, violently and fast. I'm commanding fate to kill me that way. I don't want to have the time for regrets and for trying to put things right.'

'So you don't want to have time to make sure of the love of your nearest and dearest?' Alba asked.

Only the question seemed redundant as Moreau presumably didn't have any.

'It's as if cancer was something the patriarchy had invented for women,' Moreau asserted. 'We turn into the very thing they want us to be. That is very humiliating, Alba. Don't forget the humiliation and always act proudly when confronted with it.'

Alba laughed again.

'Maybe you think I should kill myself?'

'I really can't say that I do. But if someone like me had been asked, I would have helped someone like you.'

'We ought to have a look at Valentino,' Alba said.

She sat down on the floor and took Valentino's head between her hands.

Coraggioso hadn't died. He hadn't been blinded or paralysed either. He didn't seem to have come to any harm, not anything immediately visible in any case, and after a while he woke up, his head between Alba's hands, and looked at each of us, one after the other. Then he sat up and laughed; he felt around his head with his hand as though he were trying to find a wound.

'Have you got a cushion?' he asked Moreau.

Moreau turned toward me.

'In my bedroom, Araceli. Could you fetch one, please.'

I went to Moreau's bedroom. I opened the door expectantly. I let it swing back cautiously and waited for my eyes to adjust to the dark. Only what I saw inside was not the room I had imagined on arriving. What met my eyes instead was the saddest bedroom I had ever seen. A narrow bed stood along one of the walls, and it was obvious that only one person could sleep in it. There were books inside as well; periodicals and newspapers in piles, and clothes were strewn across the piles. I recognised some of them. There were mounds of clothes by the foot of the bed and a lamp without a shade was placed at its head. Everything that emerged out of the gloom seemed functional and somehow makeshift, and held nothing of what I had been hoping for. The air was stuffy – the way it gets in a room that is never aired but still has to absorb last night's effusions. I grabbed the only cushion I could find off the bed, which was a flat pillow with a dirty case, and returned to Alba, Moreau and Valentino.

Once Valentino had woken up, taken a walk around Moreau's sitting room and drunk a few glasses of water, we got ready to go. Moreau drove us to the station and for the thirty-five minutes of the train journey we passed the villages along the sea until we got to Paseo de Gracia. We walked towards Joaquín Costa and not one of us said a word. I was thinking about the evening we had just spent. About Moreau's small flat, about Alba's cancer as an invention of the patriarchy, and the way they let Valentino lie on the floor.

'There's nothing there,' I would say to Domingo the next day. 'You'll look in vain for those valleys and hidden landscapes. There is nothing behind that facade.'

And even though he was bound to retort, 'You're just judging by appearances, Araceli; you think that the map is the territory,' I would stick by what I had to say:

'There aren't any unexplored ravines behind that facade, Domingo, there's just a vast and grubby nothing.'

Moreau kept her promise about paying us back for the 'kindness' we had shown her. One day when she got to school, she told us she had arranged a study visit for us with the trade association for Catalonia's timber suppliers. They were not insignificant, she said. The timber market was huge, and almost everyone who worked in the timber field was completely ignorant when it came to foreign languages. It would give us a good opportunity to get those first commissions we could then use as a step up the ladder when we applied to interpreting agencies for larger and more important jobs. You can only find real life out in the real world, she said. You have to get out there. Like tadpoles you've got to start swimming with the big fish, and those of you who don't get eaten up are the ones who will survive. I am going to give you this opportunity and I want you to take it. I want you to make a start; mine will be the hand that takes you out of the jar and plops you into real water and there you'll have to swim for your lives. Okay? Okay, we said.

At home I told them about the opportunity Moreau had promised us. Blosom looked sceptical the way she always did when told something new was going to happen. Mum responded by asking why we had to be so negative, after all it was nice of the school to give us a chance, to take us somewhere the real opportunities could be found, wasn't it? That was all very well, Blosom replied, you had to earn money because money was like air; life felt light and easy when you had it but when you didn't just getting around was difficult. I didn't tell them about Moreau's simile of the tadpoles, the jar and the big fish. But Blosom wouldn't take her eyes off me and said, Watch out, Araceli, don't let them sell you like a bag of meat along the chain from one supplier to the next. People like that only think about their commission, about interest rates and deliveries, and I find it hard to see what you little piggies would have to offer them. They're bound to need help understanding one another, aren't they, Mum said, seeing as they do deals with people from other countries? Blosom shook her head and said that people like that were only bothered about the nitty-gritty and the only thing that mattered was whether you were going to buy the goods or not. It was never any more complicated than that. She kept looking at me; I got up and went into the kitchen, and I could feel those eyes like two nails in my back the whole way through the living room.

The trade association lay a bit outside town towards Badalona. It was in an industrial zone along with quite a few other businesses, small factories, each of which seemed to make a particular product while the one next door produced something quite different. Some of the facades had been tiled in various colours. Domingo said it looked as if someone's wife or mum had made an effort to decorate them, only there was obviously something doomed about the attempt because where the tiles had fallen off in places and were lying in pieces on the road in front, no one had bothered to pick any of them up. Moreau had prepared us about every conceivable aspect of the timber trade; we had learnt the names of a great many kinds of wood in four different languages and also read the documentation she had got direct from a contact in customs and which showed you the kinds of timber that were being imported, where they came from and how they were transported. She had also gone on a bit more about the tadpoles. There is no future for most of you, she said laconically, her eyes fixed rather gravely on the floor. We just smiled at her, because none of us felt what she was saying was being addressed to us in particular; the future lay ahead of us like a freshly swept path. We thought all we had to do was start moving.

We took a bus there and had to walk the last bit. The sun was still low in the sky and it was that time of the morning when the smells are not yet at full strength, when a little coolness still lingers and there's a faint odour of oil and gravel along with a hint of detergent, and nothing has been completely taken over by the heat. There was no shade to be had anywhere. It was almost two kilometres from the bus stop to the factory. Madame Moreau went first, and her face was bright red. Domingo walked beside her, carrying a pile of papers she had brought along. Once we got to the trade association, we had to wait outside for almost half an hour while Moreau negotiated with the watchman on duty who then had to go off to get confirmation that someone inside really was expecting a class from the translators' school. Eventually we were let into the entrance, which turned out to be a vast hall in which wooden pallets were piled on top of one another and forklift trucks moved back and forth. Some of the workers were standing in one corner having a smoke. We were shown in through the hall and up a narrow staircase covered in close-fitted blue carpet. Complete silence reigned upstairs. We were in a corridor that had posters on the walls, on the one right in front of us it said *Maderas Del Pozo* and underneath the name was an aerial photograph of an enormous timber yard. *We have the range to meet every need*, it said in italics above the image. A man came out of nowhere to say hello to Madame Moreau; they appeared to know one another, because Moreau looked relaxed and smiled at him several times while looking back at us, as though explaining to him that all she was asking was for us to be taken under his wing for a while. The man gestured to us to follow him. We walked down several long corridors with people sitting along them in little offices that were separated from the corridor by huge panes of glass. There were no windows or other sources of daylight anywhere. We finally came to an auditorium and the man asked us to sit down. We took our seats while the man stood at the front looking at us quizzically, then he began talking about the structure of the Spanish timber market and how much was imported from various places and what was made from the different sorts of timber. Muriel poked her elbow in my side and pointed at a cockroach running across the floor. The talk was over pretty quickly, and Madame Moreau looked slightly embarrassed. Domingo asked several questions of the man who gave the talk, and he responded briefly. It was obvious he wasn't interested in having lengthy discussions with us. In the end the man pulled down a map that showed where the largest concentrations of timber-processing industries were to be found. The map was old and looked as though it had been hanging in a classroom for many, many years. Domingo asked which languages they most often used interpreters for and the man replied that it was mostly Chinese at the moment. Can you speak any Chinese? he asked, and we shook our heads. He finally said he didn't have any more time as he had a meeting to go to. The class got up and followed Madame Moreau out, only Muriel and I went in the opposite direction because Muriel had seen a sign for a toilet and needed to go. I waited for her outside. When she came out, the man who had given the talk was walking towards us along the corridor. Your class has gone down to the lobby, he said, pointing away from us. That turned out to be a short visit, Muriel said. There's not much I can tell you, the man said. I've no idea why you came to us in the first place. Madame Moreau wanted to give us a chance to get out into the real world, Muriel said. The man laughed. We need jobs, Muriel said. We've been staring at those walls for ages, and we've had a whole load of different scenarios staged for us, only none of them were real.

The man looked at us. Then he said:

'Well, in that case . . . if it's the real world you want . . . perhaps you could . . . in that case maybe I could . . . '

We stared at him.

'What do you mean?' Muriel said.

Moreau and Domingo were once again at the front when we walked back to the bus stop, but Domingo must have been ordered to leave the papers at the trade association because he was walking freely and easily while chatting to Moreau; they appeared to be having fun and we could hear them laughing now and then from where we were at the back. Muriel said: Domingo's hair is really incredibly red. I was wondering about how to tell them at home about my day; I wasn't worried about Mum, but Blosom had a sixth sense for anything you were keen to hide. I hadn't picked up on that to begin with, but then I noticed that if you tried telling a lie there would be something odd in the air afterwards. Mum might have swallowed it but the ensuing silence was always just that bit too long, you couldn't talk your way out of it and if you looked round you would find Blosom with her eyes fixed on you as though she was saying: *I'm not going to stop looking at you until you tell your mother the truth.* You could stare right back at her with a look that said: *You can keep staring at me as much as you like but you can't make me say anything at all, and you've got no proof that what I said is a lie.* It usually ended with my turning my back on her and popping out for a bit. When I got back her eyes would be less insistent but they would still be fixed on me – for a few moments longer than felt really okay.

'Have you got the business card?' Muriel whispered when we parted outside the school.

'Yes,' I replied.

'Who's going to go first?' she asked.

'You?' I said.

'Okay. I'll call you tomorrow.'

Did she even hesitate? Or did she just pick up the phone and call? I'd have liked to see her with the card in her hand and the phone to her ear. 'Hello? I'm Muriel Ruiz and I'm ringing because of a business card I was given by a man at the trade association for timber products I've just been visiting with my class.'

If she even dithered at that point, there was no sign of it the next day at school. All she told me was that the agency wasn't your standard agency. I didn't understand exactly what she meant by 'standard agency': she made it sound as if there really was such a thing, but she managed to make clear to me what was different about the agency whose name was on the business card. It dealt with contacts of any and every kind and passed them on to its members. Business contacts, potential customers, data companies, interpreters and translators – the whole lot. But also companions you could hire for various trips or even in the city you lived in. Pure gold if you wanted to earn a bit on the side, the person who answered had told her and added that if Muriel felt like it they could arrange some work for her.

We hesitated. For a few moments we were unsure about what Moreau's real motive had been in arranging the study visit. Was this what she had meant when she said we were tadpoles who had to find deeper waters if they were going to swim and that those who could make their own way would be the ones to survive? Was this a way of getting one foot in the door, a way of starting from the bottom and working your way up? We'll just have to try it and see how it turns out, Muriel said and rang the number again.

The first (and perhaps the only) man Muriel was put in touch with through the agency was not married and not particularly flush either. She described him as completely average overall, so average 'it makes it seem inconceivable he's being exploited'. He wasn't especially well travelled either and he didn't have an exciting past. No hobby to make him stand out. But he has a good heart and a flat right on the seafront in Perellot, Muriel said.

They saw one another once, twice, three times, then they realised that they really did like each other, or enough at least to go on seeing each other, and after that it was a regular thing, and taken for granted sort of, even a bit bourgeois as well. They started going to the cinema together on Wednesdays and to restaurants on Fridays. He drove her to the school sometimes; he had a clapped-out car he used to park on the other side of the street and he would stay inside and keep an eye on her as she crossed the road and went in through the entrance. You couldn't see his face from the window of the classroom but you could make out that there was someone inside, a slightly shrunken shadow that put the car in gear afterwards, accelerated and drove off.

The first time we met Paco Parra together was a day at the beginning of April. A light rain was falling as we walked towards Parque Güell. Muriel said, 'This falling rain is soothing our acne-inflamed noses, Araceli.' She had masked her spots and pimples with some cheap concealer she would soon be exchanging, thanks to Paco Parra's income, for a more upmarket variety, while I made do with what I could get my hands on in Mum's and Blosom's bathroom cupboards. It had stopped raining by the time we got to Parque Güell and so we sat on a park bench placed under a makeshift roof and waited for Paco Parra who was supposed to turn up after a lunch meeting. There was still a kind of dampness to the air and the dust felt sticky against your skin.

'We're eighteen years old,' Muriel said, 'and we're the smart ones and the young ones and the soon-to-be rich ones as well. So life belongs to us.'

'You may be rich already now you're seeing Paco Parra,' I said. 'Second-hand rich.'

'We'll get there someday,' Muriel said then.

'How do you mean we'll get there someday?'

'When we sort the money.'

'Money's not everything, Muriel.'

'Money counts for a lot.'

'There's things you can't buy with money.'

'Don't say that,' Muriel said. 'Money bought me, and I've had the greatest respect for it ever since.'

I laughed.

'I'm never going to sell myself for money,' I said.

'You can sell your body,' Muriel said. 'Selling your soul on the other hand, that's prostitution of a very different character. You've got to make sure you stay hungry, and once you're hungry you're your own master. Not some other bastard who comes along and tells you what to do.'

'It could be like that, I suppose,' I said.

'A day will come when neither you nor I will have to think about money. People like you and me shouldn't have to. We are going to find solutions, Araceli, I promise you.'

It really did feel as if we were going to find those solutions when we were sitting there. Barcelona lay at our feet and Gaudí's merry roofs were shimmering all around us in different colours. There was the scent of resin coming off the pine trees and warmth was rising from the soil.

'When's he turning up?' I asked.

'Soon,' Muriel said.

'It's not polite to keep your lady waiting,' I said.

'He's an important man,' Muriel said.

He did turn up finally. You could see from a distance that he wasn't exactly an intellectual. He wore a grey suit and had rather long, shuttered eyelids. His nose was determined and his skin was large-pored. His lips were thin and a few old nacreous teeth peered out from behind them when he smiled. His hips were narrow and his trousers were draped sadly across them and would have slipped down if it weren't for a brown belt firmly keeping them up. He had thin hair and a receding hairline. There was no way he had the kind of haircut George Clooney had, like Muriel had said.

'That's one sick old lover you've chosen,' I whispered to Muriel.

'Ssh,' she said and put her index finger to her lips.

When he arrived, he spoke with a thick Catalan accent. He appeared to be the silent type: his eyes stayed on you and didn't glide away, as if he was waiting for or even demanding you speak first.

'Paco Parra,' he finally said and offered me his hand.

'Araceli Villalobos,' I responded, shaking his hand which was soft.

We chatted. Paco Parra seemed quiet but well intentioned. It was obvious he wanted me to like him. He must have realised how important it was to be in well with the best friend and even though that didn't entirely redeem him it took the edge of the hostility I had been feeling towards him from the outset. When I asked him what he liked to read, he said he didn't have time to read, he was a senior civil servant. That's how he put it:

'I am a senior civil servant,' while laughing at the same time, as though it was something those around him should obviously forgive him for.

Okay. When we complained about our spots, he said that he thought spots were lovely, that wrinkles were much worse, and that if he got to choose he would much rather walk beside a girl who had spots from being young than an older woman who was wrinkled with age. His words were almost more welcome than the spring rain and our faces felt less inflamed and we were able to smile and laugh. Now the ice was broken, Paco Parra repeated several times that we were really first-rate and had lovely laughs, and Muriel laughed and said 'you old goat'.

Then he talked about the system he worked in. He said he carried out its every whim.

'If the system tells me to get it some coffee, I do. If it tells me to massage its feet, I do that as well. If it asks me to satisfy it in some other way, I do that too, until the slow currents of its turgid thought processes are running through me.'

Muriel looked at him scornfully.

'That's not the kind of thing you should joke about,' she said.

'Life is full of limitations, Muriel. You have to accept the one thing to get another. You give something and you get something back.'

'The dog has spoken!' Muriel yelled.

'The dog?'

Parra looked at her offended.

'Well you're talking just like a dog. You've been indoctrinated into conditional love. Just like a dog, you've learnt from childhood on that love is conditional, that love is something you have to earn, and if you make mistakes you can end up being . . . excluded from it.'

'I think what you're saying is hurtful,' Parra said. 'I'm not a dog.'

'So are you going to withhold my pocket money now?' Muriel asked, giggling

'The things you say,' Parra said and looked at the ground. 'If I'm a dog, then that sharp tongue of yours makes you an adder.'

'Only then there are the cat people,' Muriel said without taking any notice of the adder comment. 'The cat person loves unconditionally without demanding any kind of compensation from his or her beloved. The cat person is a wonderful, if unreliable, kind of human being.'

She stretched out in the sun and remained lying there on the bench between Paco Parra and me with her eyes closed and a smile on her lips. Parra and I glanced at one another, then we sat there looking straight ahead until Muriel sat up again and went on talking as though the issue of dog and cat people had never been brought up.

Muriel used to say that there was the possibility of a father (and not for your children but for you) within every man. And she consumed these fathers almost compulsively, as if men were a perishable commodity with an expiry date. Unlike the others, Paco Parra remained a fixture in her life and that was because money has no expiry date and money was the key to freedom in Muriel's world. The equation was a simple one, as she said. The older, stiffer and more frozen they were, the greater was her added value. The effect was exponential. Exceptional, as well. And when he met Muriel Ruiz, Paco Parra had got his figures burnt more often than almost anyone I had ever met, as I realised that very first afternoon when we met in Parque Güell. He told us about his ex-wives. The first one he had married in order to have sex because both he and she came from strict Catholic families; he married the second because he was in love with her (and that was the biggest mistake he had ever made), the third, because he had become practical and realised he needed someone to take care of him.

'What about Muriel?' I said.

'Muriel is party time,' he replied.

He came out with other stuff as well, Paco Parra. He knew how to twist things around to make them sound good. For instance, he said to Muriel Ruiz that what he longed for was a great tenderness. *That Great Tenderness*, he wrote in a letter to her. *The Great Tenderness that will illuminate the holes in my soul, that will water the chapped surface of my earth.* And as for Muriel herself, he said she was like Bach – beautiful on the surface and even more beautiful the more you listened. Other people were like Mozart – easy listening and fun, but they never had that seriousness you could find in Bach. Muriel clearly believed what he said. That was the way she was – if you said something flattering about her she simply took it as the truth, if it was criticism, she would turn it over and over in her mind until finally discarding it as falsehood. That's true of everyone, by the way.

On the days we didn't go to Parque Güell, we went to the steps in front of the Museum of Contemporary Art. When you sit there above the Plaza de España with La Fira to your left and right and look straight ahead, Tibidabo hits you in the solar plexus, both the church and the amusement park. It is dead ahead of you, as though someone had drawn a line with a ruler through the air from the steps and placed it right in front of you, a few tens of kilometres away and on the other side of town. Paco Parra had brought soft drinks with him and a bag of crisps. He sat down on a bench and loosened his tie. A gypsy was playing a few yards away. People stopped to listen. They stopped and stood still for a while just taking in the music.

'So fucking beautiful,' Muriel said and Paco Parra nodded.

When the man stopped playing Muriel started to cry. She sat there with the sticky bottle of pop in her hands and bits of crisp at the corners of her mouth and the tears flowed across her cheeks. Black trickles of mascara ran into her mouth.

'Why are you crying, Muriel?' Paco Parra asked.

'It's so fucking beautiful. It makes me feel so sad.'

Then she started talking about the sadness that came over her when it was raining or when last winter's leaves rustled on the oak that stood outside her window and 'I just can't work out why those leaves are still on the branches – they should have fallen long ago because they're dead, aren't they, and they keep clinging on all the same to a life that is already over.' Then she talked about the sadness that came over her when she went walking in nature. And how when everything around her was beautiful and untouched, she could fall to the ground and 'dissolve into an intense bout of weeping' that sort of came out of nowhere and just filled her with an enormous melancholy.

Paco Parra put his arm around her.

'You're so sensitive,' he said. 'That's lovely.'

'It's painful,' Muriel said.

He patted her on the head.

'Do you want cigarettes? I could go and buy some.'

She dried her tears and sniffed theatrically while nodding. Paco Parra got up and walked over to the kiosk. He looked pleased. As if he was thinking he had the whole package now – a child who was a precocious and sensitive woman at the same time.

'Watch out, Muriel,' I said when Parra had gone to the kiosk. 'You're throwing your heart on the dungheap.'

'You don't know him,' she replied.

'You're manipulating him.'

She shrugged her shoulders.

'If I don't, someone else will.'

'Only when you're twenty, you'll be too old for him and he'll find someone new, someone who's like you are now. Think about that, and the fact that everyone is replaceable and all he wants is youth – and not you.'

'Don't worry,' she said then. 'When I turn nineteen, Paco Parra will be dead of old age.'

Paco Parra returned with cigarettes for Muriel and a bag of popcorn for me. That was one of the good things about Paco Parra. He never forgot about me and always made sure I was taken care of, having realised that was the smart thing to do. I think he must have felt a certain liking for me as well, because otherwise Muriel Ruiz would not have asked me the next morning at school if I wanted to go with her to the seaside for the summer. Paco Parra had asked her to bring a friend along.

'Is that because I'm going to be set up with someone?' I asked.

'Of course not,' Muriel said. 'It's so I'll have someone to be with when he's working.'

'What am I supposed to tell them at home?' I asked.

'Tell them you're going to the beach with me and my uncle.'

Mum asked if Muriel's uncle was going to be there as well.

'Yes,' I said.

'Then I think it sounds like a really great idea.'

Blosom didn't ask any questions. She probably thought it would be nice to be on her own with Mum so they could watch their soap operas and drink port in the afternoons, discussing the plots during the adverts, and then sit outside in the evenings listening to the conversations between Valentino Coraggluso and Alba Cambó.

A few weeks later when Muriel and I came out of the baggage hall at the airport in Alicante, Paco Parra was there waiting for us. He was wearing a mint-green shirt, and I could see he had sweat rings under the arms when he embraced Muriel. He took my hand and I got the feeling I no longer appealed, or maybe it wasn't that he had anything against me only now I had arrived he didn't like the fact I was there after all, it took something away from Muriel and him, and his smile turned stiff, and was anything but welcoming. He packed our cases into the car and then we drove to his house in Perellot. I got carsick on the last part of the journey because Paco Parra kept driving fast along winding roads beside waterlogged rice plantations. The flies that had come in through the open windows flew stubbornly at the screen once Parra had closed the windows and turned the air conditioning on. Paco Parra kept on talking and right from the start it felt like he only knew how to talk about stupid things. For instance, he told us there had been a long-standing war between the various authorities in the town over who would do the rubbish collecting and that there was a lot of money in rubbish collection.

'There's money to be made in refuse,' he said, nodding.

There was silence in the car after he said that. Then he told us about an article he had read in the paper about Jesus and his disciples actually being castrati. Does that mean we have based our entire civilisation around the morals of a few castrated men? Paco Parra asked. If that was true, he said, he couldn't take it in. It was just too much to swallow, even if it did explain a great deal.

Muriel must finally have realised that Parra could only talk nonsense because somewhere around Valencia she interrupted him to say that she couldn't make up her mind who was the handsomest between Brad Pitt and Leonardo di Caprio. And she couldn't decide either which she liked more, orange or lemon Fanta, or which lip gloss was best, Lancôme's or Clinique's. Paco Parra was silent. For a brief while beads of sweat were pooling on his nose, although he soon wiped them off with a hand-kerchief he kept in the breast pocket of his shirt. He listened to her after that and soon he was nodding at everything she said. The expression on his face when we arrived was enough to make you think that Muriel Ruiz was the smartest chick he had ever met.

He parked in the street. Everything looked shabby and greasy. There were oil stains on the pavement and all the balconies on the building had cleaning things on them. It was unbearably hot with not a breath of wind; it felt like being in hell.

'I thought there'd be a breeze by the sea,' I said.

'It'll feel better up there,' Paco Parra said.

We went up to his flat and Muriel and he installed themselves in Paco Parra's bedroom, which had a large four-poster bed with a shiny red bedspread. He showed me my room as well, which was the smallest room in the flat and barely had enough space for the bed on which a crocheted orange blanket lay. After that he said we were going to celebrate our arrival and he got out wineglasses from a cupboard in the sitting room. We drank a toast and Paco Parra opened the doors toward the beach and the sea. Muriel walked round the flat in the meantime, exclaiming with exaggerated enthusiasm at what a lovely place he had, it was so cosy and, then, what a view over the sea (she would say to me only an hour or two afterwards that a house without a woman's touch was like a body without a soul).

'Chin chin,' Parra said to us.

All three of us looked out over the sea. You could see some sailboats on the horizon.

I realised right from the start that it was going to be a difficult summer. The days were going to be long and stressful; the air would be stagnant with humidity, and the staircase in Parra's building would smell of fried fish and tortillas. I would fall asleep and wake up in the little room Parra had assigned me that was the size of a broom cupboard. It had a small window that looked onto a minimal courtyard and at night the wind used to cause an acoustic phenomenon in that drum-shaped space. It made a sound like a major mechanical catastrophe, and trying to fall asleep to the noise of an airplane engine coming apart was clearly going to get on my nerves, it was going to be a long hard summer, the only thing to do was grit your teeth and bear it.

Only a few days later and I would be proved right about almost all the negative vibes I had got off Paco Parra. By the afternoon of the second day I had realised that the man my best friend was sharing a bed with was nothing but flaws. He ate too quickly and too much and belched loudly when he thought no one could hear him. When he sat at the table he did so with an expression that said where is my food and where is my wine and where is my woman? He talked a lot, but always about petty subjects such as the women who had betrayed him or the money he had never got his hands on for a whole host of reasons. Sometimes it seemed as though the women and the absence of money had ganged up on him, as though they had conspired to do everything they could to knock him out of the game. At those times he had admitted to defeat at the hands of what he said were 'superior forces' and 'circumstances'; that was what you did when you were a good sport like him.

I used to giggle when he said things like that, but then Muriel would look at me angrily and at the same time in appeal as though she were saying, okay, I know he may not be the hippest guy on earth but would it really cost you so much to give him a chance, for god's sake, Araceli?

I kept quiet then, picking crumbs off the rolls and dropping them on the floor and the evening breeze would pick them up and you could watch them rain down in a little waterfall over the neighbour's balcony.

Sometimes Parra walked down to the beach and sat there, all on his own, a hundred metres away, and looked out at the sea. From the terrace where we were sitting you could see sand, sky, the sea and Paco Parra's back.

Muriel might ask:

'What are you gazing at?'

And I would reply:

'Paco Parra's back.'

She used to smile then as if she believed I was seeing the person inside him at last. I was actually thinking that it was incredible that a back, just one human back, could radiate so much loneliness. He never turned round either, which was just as well because the eyes, as they say, are the mirror of the soul.

I think back on him once in a while and feel sad to the bottom of my soul. When you looked him in the face that summer, it sometimes felt as though he was completely naked. The person inside him peeked out all over, like a body that is bursting the seams of the clothes it is wearing, allowing the flesh to pop out, letting it blossom through the hems and bloom like chubby fingers. Loneliness and sleeplessness were etched on his eyelids as was the strain age was starting to inflict on him, and then there was, of course, his total lack of ease. His lips were too narrow, his eyes were too bright, his body too large and pale. When he used to sit in the sun on the terrace he looked like a real porker. It was as if the light had found its way inside him, but couldn't get out. I couldn't work out if he had laughed too little or if he had had too little sex. Muriel said I was cynical and superficial. I retorted that I might be cynical and superficial, but no matter how cynical I was it hadn't stopped me from

174

realising the truth about Paco Parra and the light around him: he absorbed it, mutely and completely, like a foam mattress.

But it was the vulgarity that shone through everything he did that meant I didn't have that much to worry about. Muriel could never really be seriously in love with Paco Parra.

After a week or two there was no avoiding the fact that Paco Parra wanted Muriel all to himself. That was why he recommended a different beach to me, a beach that lay a bit further away; all you had to do was take the bus to the next village. Muriel shrugged her shoulders and said it was only for a few days, then he had to go off on a job and we would be alone again. So each day after breakfast I took the bus for about a kilometre. I had books and magazines with me and there was a bar right by the beach and I really didn't have anything to complain about. I came home in the evening and then we spent a little time together, before Muriel and Parra would go out dancing or to a restaurant. Parra always had the foresight on those occasions to arrange for someone to bring me food from the bar.

Now and then they would ask me if I wanted to go out with them, but I declined.

Only one evening when they got back, everything was different. Muriel came into my room, sat at the furthest end of the bed and said everything had gone wrong and the only thing to do now was pack up and go home tomorrow. It had all turned to shit with Parra and that was the end of the sweet life both for her and for me.

'So what happened?' I asked.

'I haven't got a fucking clue how to boil it all down for you. There are intimate matters involved. The kind of thing you don't talk about to outsiders.'

'Okay,' I said. 'Then would you mind turning off the light when you leave and letting me sleep?'

'Hang on,' she said then. 'I'll tell you.'

It had all begun with her telling Parra about Andrés, her former boyfriend. He couldn't cope when she broke it off with him because of Parra. He went crazy, started beating his fists against the wall and screaming that he couldn't handle being without her. That's what she did to men, Muriel. She warped their frontal lobes for them and they were never quite normal again for the rest of their lives. Andrés was no different.

'Stop it now,' she told him. 'I've found someone else. A fifty-five year old man who is a lot richer than you.'

It was a really stupid thing to say, as she realised afterwards – only everything was excused when you were in love, wasn't it. And she hadn't realised, had she, that Andrés was so deeply in love with her? Or that he had already planned out the whole of their lives together and even been to check out a house in a posh neighbourhood, and in that sense was already living the life he had staked out with Muriel. So that was why he couldn't cope with her saying goodbye. He had jumped her and attacked her. That was a really stupid thing for him to do, Muriel said, though at the same time it was all part of a kind of game they played.

'Hard to explain,' she said. 'Anyway it turned out the way it did. And I didn't think about it that much afterwards.'

But recently one morning she had told Paco Parra about Andrés. What happened when she ended it, how he had attacked her and how it had all gone wrong. Parra had got up (they had been lying on a sand dune on the beach), brushed the sand off his Bermuda shorts and said, Fucking hell, Muriel, fucking hell, I just can't believe what I'm hearing, I can't live with the idea that someone did that to you. That is the lowest of the low, and blah blah blah – a load of moralistic drivel that didn't sit well in a mouth like his – like picking a lovely rose and putting it on top of a rubbish dump or a dungheap, is about how appropriate those words were in Parra's mouth, Muriel said.

'We're going to get through this together,' he said as well. 'You're going to tell me exactly what happened and then we're going to deal with it, we'll get through it together and I will be there to support you all the way, you're going to lean on me and I'm going to make sure you get over this.'

And Muriel started telling him what had happened, how Andrés had gone crazy and hit the walls and then come at her like a blazing torch. And what happened then? Parra said in her ear and his breathing just kept getting faster, what did he do then, how did he do it and in what way, to the point that he was so excited he got on top of Muriel and asked her to keep on telling him about it. And Muriel, who had been pretty shocked at first about how the whole thing was developing, soon stopped telling him exactly what had happened, because as she said she didn't really have anything against Andrés (he was an arsehole just like most men but no better and no worse), and began making things up instead.

So while the toad was lying on top of her, panting in her ear, she invented a new version of the whole thing and added a lot of details she wouldn't want to admit to in the light of day, though maybe later on, until Parra came and he was lying beside her and he told her that that was the best fuck he had ever had.

He had asked all sorts of questions about Andrés. How long they had known one another, where he lived, what he looked like.

'Ok,' Muriel said. 'That I could deal with. It got him off, and that was fine by me. So far so good. I could live with that.'

She shook her head.

'It's what happened afterwards I can't cope with. It was what happened next made me see red.'

The next day when Muriel got out of bed, it turned out that Parra had fixed her this killer breakfast. A load of weird yellow fruits that he peeled and fed to her. Then he dipped his fingers in the vanilla croissants and asked her to lick it off his fingers. Like a cat, he said. Do it like a cat. And Muriel had replied she might be able to do that at some other time of day but not in the morning because mornings were best reserved for your own needs. That was just the way she was. And if he didn't like it, there was nothing she could do about it. In that case he had better put her on the bus and send for someone else. She couldn't compromise on mornings.

'Of course,' said Parra then. 'You're so right, Muriel. You are the most mentally healthy person I have ever met.'

After that he left her in peace the entire morning and Muriel had another sleep, then walked down to the beach and checked out a guy of her own age who had been checking her back and then they had lain there continuing to check each other out until Parra suddenly appeared with a parasol and lilos and those yellow fruits that he had peeled once again and fed to Muriel.

Then he had got out the vanilla croissants and said she could lick it off his fingers now, couldn't she, and she had done it and the guy of her own age she had been checking out while lying there had turned his head away as though he found it disgusting. He hadn't checked her out again after that and she had been feeling pretty pissed off even then, she said. The fact that he revolts me is one thing, she said, but ruining what could be my immediate future is not ok. So she was already feeling a bit annoyed. Then evening fell. Muriel and the toad went home and fucked as per usual. Then they had a shower, brushed their teeth (though that goes without saying, Muriel said to make things clear, sort of), and then they went and had dinner at a posh restaurant that must have been getting financial support from Paco Parra's department to judge by the fuss the waiters made. They ate in peace and quiet, emptied a bottle of wine that Parra ordered and then they drank coffee and ate truffles.

'And then he suddenly announces he's got a surprise for me.'

And Paco had got up, pulled out her chair, and she had gone ahead of him in the direction he was pointing and the waiters had bowed to them even though Parra hadn't even paid. They had gone out the back way and into an old warehouse at the rear.

'What's happening?' Muriel said.

'Don't worry, darling,' the toad had replied. 'Just trust me.'

At that point he had got out a black bandage and tied it across her eyes. Muriel said it felt like being in a gangster film. Then he had let her into a different room and it had smelled of fear, damp and diarrhoea inside.

'Voilà!' he had said finally. 'Voilà, my darling.'

And then he had taken the bandage off from over her eyes and there on the floor, tied up and cowering in one corner, was Andrés.

'I couldn't believe it,' Muriel said. 'I couldn't fucking believe it was him. And so fucking scared. You should have seen his eyes. And it smelled really bad besides. I bet he shat himself.'

And what Muriel was thinking, standing there, was that the toad would force them to fuck each other in front of him. He would sit in a chair, light a cigar and watch. And Muriel said she must have been so unbelievably shocked by the entire situation because all she could think about was that Andrés had shat himself and that the floor which was made of cement would be cold.

'Though,' she said. 'I could have put up with that as well. If Andrés had been allowed to clean himself up and if the toad just wanted a bit of a show, I could have handled that too.'

Unfortunately it wasn't that kind of little show the toad wanted. Because soon he was coming over to her, holding something behind his back and wearing a secretive expression on his face.

'Here,' he said and handed her a baseball bat.

Muriel didn't have a clue. She just stared at the toad.

'What?' she said.

'Here,' said the toad. 'Just let him have it.'

'What?' she said again.

I can just see her standing on that cement floor with the baseball bat in her hand. Her heels and those curls of hers that would have stopped bouncing around. Her obscenely narrow legs and the toad with his permanent erection pressing against the lining of his trousers. Andrés in his leather jacket, scared stiff in the corner.

'You want me to *hit* him?' she said to the toad.

'Depends what you mean,' the toad had said then. 'It's not about what I want, Muriel. It's about what you need.'

'What I need?'

'That little bastard raped you.'

'Yes.'

'He abused you.'

'Okay.'

'You can get your own back now. He can't do anything to you. You should beat him black and blue. That's what you ought to do. I can't do it for you because it's your anger you need to deal with. Only now I am giving you the chance, it's my present to you because I love you so bloody much. I love you so bloody much, Muriel, that some days when I wake up it hurts in my chest. And I am who I am, with all my failings, all the other baggage that being a person entails, but I want to give you this now. If you want to humiliate him in some other way, just say the word. I can ring Vincent and Álvaro and they'll come and help. It's your night, my darling, you decide. Your night, tonight.'

And Muriel stood there looking from Andrés to the toad and back to Andrés again.

'I could have hit him myself,' the toad said again. 'But there are things no one else can do for you, things you have to do on your own.'

That's when Muriel felt the anger. So she said. That's when I felt the anger, and it came burning up from my toes and it was red-hot. It flew up my legs like buckshot. I felt shaky all over and as if I was about to fall over my platform shoes. Then I raised the baseball bat. And I can still see the expression on the toad's face, that self-satisfied toad grin, thinking he's done something right and I'll suck him off again tonight. I can remember that look and how lost and sort of distorted it got when he saw I wasn't walking over to Andrés but towards him. It was so incredibly fucking satisfying, Araceli, to be able to drive that bat into Parra's face. Fuck, it was so bloody satisfying, Ara, let me tell you. And she had thumped him as hard as she could until Vincent and Álvaro ran in and helped their boss get away from her. She must have screamed as well because in the car on the way back Vincent told her she had broken his eardrum and that Parra was legally obliged to pay damages for that.

When she had finished telling me, we lay there in silence. I asked if he was lying in there, all bruised, and if we would be going home tomorrow. Only Muriel didn't answer me. Instead she said she could tell me the deepest and truest truth about men, a sort of open sesame I could carry with me forever. If I swore not to tell anyone, that is. I swore. I lay in bed and she leant over me and I was expecting her to whisper something perverse in my ear. Along with the sea outside that would be one of the most perfect moments of my holiday.

But Muriel didn't whisper anything. Instead she spat in my hair. A big thick gob flowed slowly down my temple.

'You idiot,' I said.

'I was supposed to tell you the big secret about men, wasn't I?' she said. 'That is all there is to say.'

'You idiot,' I said again.

I wish there was nothing more to say about the Paco Parra episode. It would have been nice, desirable even, if that had been the end of the story, but there was one more thing. Something had been going on between Paco Parra and me. The last few days on the beach in Perrellot, Paco Parra had started showing me these little kindnesses. It made me uncomfortable. I became aware of it one day when I was in a cafe on the square and saw him go into an ice-cream parlour. He ordered a tub of ice cream, with pear and coconut (Muriel's favourite flavours) and rum and raisin (which is mine). When the lady in the shop explained that they didn't have any rum and raisin, he asked her where he could get some. The other place will have some, she said then. When we opened the tubs later that evening, he said nothing about having had to drive to the other bar which was several kilometres away to buy that flavour for me. He said nothing at all, just opened it up and served the ice cream. This made me more observant of the way he was behaving towards me and I discovered in him a kindness I hadn't felt from him before, and which I didn't feel he showed even to Muriel. To her he was openly adoring, to me he was secretly kind. I noticed it in the little details, how he seated me at lunch so that I had a view, how the sheets on my bed got changed, or in the little things he put in my lunchbox those days I went to the other beach. I felt confused, not understanding what it was about, and that led in turn to my feeling inhibited in his company. I always thought about what I would say before I said anything, and I was terrified of asking him for something he wouldn't be able to give me. Is he interested in me that way? I turned that idea over in my mind again and again, but always had to reject it as an impossibility. I couldn't work out what he wanted. His good intentions frightened me.

And that was why, more than anything else, it was a relief to get the train back to Barcelona.

HEUREUX,
COMME AVEC UNE FEMME?

My first encounter with Gestiones Commerciales took place that autumn, in October. When I saw the man I was supposed to meet, I realised immediately I wouldn't be able to make love and I can see, as I write this, how the insight of that moment was fitting reward for the naivety I had brought to the role of a professional – not even that summer with Muriel and Paco Parra in Perellot had managed to rid me of the notion that love ought to be a precondition for physical intercourse.

And there was a stiffness to the man in question, a quality that was inhibited and unlovable and didn't fit with the gaiety of the hotel lobby where we met. The lobby had mirrors whose surfaces were blotched with black spots and indulgent in that they made you look hazy and blurred. You were forgiven everything in advance because they made allowances for every defect. The look that Rodrigo Auscias gave me, on the other hand, was searching and remote right from the start. It stole slowly over my face, inspecting every distortion, pore and other blemish that Muriel had failed to conceal with her make-up box, and then moved downward towards my shoulders and my neckline which plunged deeper than usual that evening. A drop of sweat squeezed itself out of the hollow of my knee and ran down into my shoe. This is impossible, I thought, and even considered saying I wasn't who I was. And I wasn't waiting for anyone, and was just about to leave. I closed my book, put it in my bag and stood up. That was when he put out his hand and said:

'My name is Rodrigo Auscias. I have a room on the third floor with a view over the city. You're Araceli, I take it?'

It was Muriel who persuaded me. Not directly, not by saying: 'Araceli, it's time you got out there and sold yourself,' but by her example. Muriel always had money at the time and, although that hadn't been a problem at the beginning, eventually money became a very precise dividing line between the person Muriel was when she was with me and when she was with other people. I was the person she could go for a walk in the park with, have a cup of tea at an outdoor café and then chat with for hours over that cup of tea, which, while it was a source of pleasure and the kind of thing everyone really needed, 'didn't actually change anything'. There were other things that could change you from the inside, other things that could bring you closer to a deeper and genuine sense of being, but all those activities had costs attached. Flying wasn't free, nor was having a wardrobe that expressed who you were and it wasn't free to share the essence of a real night with someone, if you were being continually obliged to measure everything in coin. Muriel came up with the answers: As you make your bed, so you must lie on it, and God helps those who help themselves.

That was something else that was typical of Muriel – all those proverbs, those clichés, she based her communication on. There was always something that would fit the bill. And if one proverb didn't feel right, its opposite would; there was never any one truth you could stick to. For Muriel Ruiz truths were like sheets fluttering in the wind – they kept switching sides and sometimes they got tangled up in themselves. Sometimes they just hung there, heavy and unglamorous and drenched with rain. They weren't something you could respect, in her view. Not the sort of thing you can have any respect for, not in the long term, she said and stubbed out her fag end with her heel.

'The way I see it, Araceli, you've got no choice,' was what she said. 'Whatever you do has to lead somewhere. Otherwise life ends up just being a minor series of meaningless sex acts that don't lead to pregnancy.'

She nodded as though she had said something really clever. Metaphors were not really Muriel's strong point, seeing as despite all her emancipation as a woman she could, comically, sound like a figure from the Old Testament.

I looked at her. Muriel and her moisturised skin, her eye-lashes coated in several layers of expensive mascara, sweetly and gently perfumed, and holding her white cigarette with a gold circle at the base in one hand. At some point you have to decide whether you're going to live or die, she repeated. If you decide to live, all you have to do is make a start. Find sources of income, make the best of what you've got.

'Okay,' I said in the end.

She took out the business card from her pocket, rang the number and spoke in confidence to someone who sounded as if they were writing down my name.

After a few days a lady rang me with a hoarse voice that I thought was a man's at first.

'Hello, Araceli. I've got a client here we could start with.'

The man who had requested the agency's services was a quite ordinary man. 'A perfectly ordinary man,' the voice said. 'No funny business at all.'

'You're meeting at six pm at the Hotel Nouvel; it's on one of the lanes near Puerta del Ángel. Clean and simple, that's our policy, and no funny business.'

The following evening I was walking along Catalunya. The shop windows were large and generous and my reflection made me look like I had been corseted and polished. Muriel had helped, lending me things from her wardrobe and fussing with my face so its distortions ended up looking like exotic features instead. She had drawn in black pencil along the edges of my upper and lower lashes and pressed in where the lines met and then put her little finger into the corner of the eye and pulled straight out. I had put up a fight at first. Then I just settled for her toning it down a bit. She painted my lips with the same shade of crimson she usually wore.

The lobby of the Hotel Nouvel was almost devoid of people. Chandeliers hung from the ceiling, and there were paintings on the walls with baroque frames that, along with the mirrors, lent the hotel an air of decadence and decline – only these were imperfections quite unlike the ones I was used to because in this place they evoked life, adventure and glamour. I took a seat and realised, though not right at that moment, that I had arrived too early. That realisation would take another few minutes. It was only when I had been sitting in one of the velvet-covered chairs in the hotel lobby for almost thirty minutes that I looked at the clock and realised I must have arrived at least a quarter of an hour before I was due. Turning up too early was unforgivable in a business like this. Punctuality cast a shadow of the everyday, a pedestrian boringness, over even the most decadent professional. It was too late now, though, I couldn't back out; I couldn't just quit the field without meeting the person I had come here to see.

I got out a book. I sat there for a long time, staring at the open page in my lap. Then it dawned on me that people who read books tend to turn the pages of the books they are reading, and so I turned the page of the book. And the very moment I was turning the page I got the feeling that the man I was supposed to be meeting was looking at me.

I leant back in the armchair in the lobby. Then I thought that was ridiculous and put the book down in my lap. That was when, exactly twenty minutes after the appointed time, I heard a voice behind me:

'Sorry I'm so late. What are you reading?'

He put out his hand.

'My name is Rodrigo Auscias. I have a room on the third floor with a view over the city. You're Araceli, I take it?'

Rodrigo Auscias' eyes were clear, like shallow water or just like a place where all the water had drained away. We went up to his room, which was small with a large bed in the middle. I felt embarrassed that the bed was so large – it was as if it was obvious right from the outset that that was the place where our time together would be spent. Auscias invited me to sit in one of the chairs. I sat down and tried to hold my knees in so they wouldn't touch the bed. He sat in the chair beside me and gave me a glass of something bubbly, acidic and cheap.

'Why are you doing this?' he said.

'Because I need money.'

'Isn't there anything else you could do?'

'Like what?'

With that I assumed that the obligatory pause for conversation was over. Muriel had warned me about it and advised me to get it over with as soon as possible, because if you got bogged down it was like stepping on chewing gum that would be stuck to your foot for the rest of the walk. We could now proceed to the next part of our encounter. Rodrigo Auscias was sitting stiffly in his chair, observing me while I was wondering how to go about it. Were you supposed to remain seated, waiting for him to take the initiative, or move closer to him and unbutton the top button of his shirt? Or start undoing your own instead?

'Is this the first time you've done this?' he said.

'Yes,' I replied.

'I can see that.'

'Does it show? How?'

Rodrigo Auscias scratched his scalp while thinking.

'You ought to go in for a different line of work,' he said then.

I shrugged my shoulders. Auscias drained his glass.

'It's just I didn't think people like you really existed,' he said.

I cleared my throat.

'As long as there are people like you, there'll be people like me. Shall we get started?'

I stood up and took one of my shoes off.

'Do you know that the skin disease scabies is caused by a tiny spider that burrows under the skin?' Rodrigo Auscias said then.

He was looking directly behind me, out the window, and in that light his irises shone yellow like beer in sunlight.

'What?' I said.

'That's right. I read it in the paper on the way here. The itching afterwards is a complete nightmare.'

He stared at the empty air and seemed to forget that I was there for a brief moment. I sat on the bedspread.

'Araceli,' he said then and put his wineglass on the bedside table. 'Couldn't we just lie here on the bed? Just lie here and not say anything of any consequence at all?'

I had heard about johns like him. Who really just want to talk. It made Muriel furious. Selling your body was one thing – but your mind, that was prostitution on an unparalleled scale.

'There's a different rate for talking,' I said, without meeting his eyes.

'How much?'

'Double. At the very least.'

'Okay then,' he said. 'Let's say that. You'll get double the rate if you can put up with listening to me for a bit.'

I lay down next to Rodrigo Auscias with my hands across my chest. Our shoulders touched. Rodrigo Auscias continued talking for a bit about the article he had read in the paper, about the spider and scabies and some other skin diseases he had also read about. Then he talked about lice that had become resistant to delousing treatments. Then he talked about a treatment for obesity that consisted of a substance that was extracted from bulls' testicles. I said he seemed to be obsessed by illnesses and asked if he was a doctor. He didn't reply to that. Instead he told me that he had a tendency to gain weight, particularly at certain times of the year like Christmas and summer. At that point I dozed off for a bit. I woke up when he said that his wife was as thin as a stick, on the other hand, and had never had any problems with her weight. So you have got a wife as well, you bastard, was what I wanted to say to that, but my throat felt thick with sleep and my mouth refused to open. There was total silence then. After that Rodrigo Auscias lit a cigarette and lay there blowing smoke rings at the ceiling. We watched the smoke rings slowly changing shape and getting tangled up in one another. I thought about Muriel Ruiz' sheets. I had a sip from the glass on the bedside table and then mentioned them to him, Muriel Ruiz' truths that changed shape all the time like his smoke rings. Like sheets hung out to dry on a line. They weren't something you could rely on, or even lean against. I thought he would ask who Muriel Ruiz was but he didn't. Instead all he said was:

'The only person you ever have is yourself.'

Then his breathing changed. It became quieter, and I thought he had fallen asleep. We lay there like that, and I was wondering what would happen now. Only suddenly I heard him say:

'Araceli. Let me be completely honest. Coming here wasn't my idea.'

He lay on his side, looking at me as if he were going to say something very important.

'What?' I said.

'I was sent here.'

'Who by?'

'Alba Cambó.'

'What? What's she got to do with this?'

'When she found out you'd got in touch with the agency, she rang me and arranged for . . . She set this up. So it would be me, and not someone who might hurt you.'

'How does she know about it?'

'No idea. Someone tattled, I suppose. Your mother, maybe?'

I remembered Blosom's silence. Fuck. I was forced to look away because my face was on fire and it felt like there were tears in my eyes. I had thought I was going to be working. I had got Muriel involved, I had worried, I had worked up the courage, and then sat there like a lady and forgot to turn the pages of the book. I had actually got involved in the business of being a professional. And then a john comes along who isn't a john, but a hired babysitter.

'I bet you're having a good laugh at me,' I said and got up. 'On the inside I mean.'

'I'm not laughing at anyone,' Auscias said sadly. 'You were just someone who thought this is how things work. It's all part of it, trying things out, taking the paths you find ahead of you. It's nothing to be ashamed of.'

'I'm not ashamed,' I said and immediately regretted the sharpness of my tone.

He looked at the floor.

'Are you a virgin?' he said after a while.

'Maybe,' I said.

'And . . . perhaps you think you're a bit too old to still be one?'

'Yes,' I said. 'I thought this might be an opportunity to . . . well.'

'You mustn't think that way. You've got to promise me. You may think it doesn't matter how you do it, only it really will matter later on when you get older and think back. You mustn't give yourself to someone you don't want.'

'I thought maybe you didn't seem that bad.'

Auscias laughed aloud.

'You may not be very good at selling yourself, Araceli, but you're even worse at lying. That kind of thing grows on you; the attraction has to take its time. You see the person. You start fantasising about them. Then suddenly one day you've got there, and it's all wonderful.'

It sounded cool when he said that. 'Then suddenly one day you've got there and it's all wonderful.'

'That doesn't sound very likely,' I said.

Auscias shrugged his shoulders.

'That's what I'm saying. You've got to find the right person.'

'I already found one person,' I said. 'A person who would do. His name is Benicio Mercader and he lives in Perpignan.'

'In that case you should have looked him up instead of coming here,' Auscias said.

'I've no idea how to find someone like him.'

'I might be able to help you at some point,' said Auscias. 'I'm good at finding people.'

The idea of finding Benicio Mercader felt suddenly exhilarating. I laughed to myself. The thought of seeing him ten years on and being able to tell him, I have thought about you the whole time and now I am here. Have you longed for me as much as I have longed for you? And Benicio Mercader wouldn't just be some sick, old lover. Benicio Mercader would have answered yes. Even if it wasn't true, because it wouldn't have been. He would have answered yes, and I would have believed him because men like him are good at lying. Men like him would never want to see a woman trying to give him something of her own fall apart in front of their eyes, and if a lie was the price for their concern, they wouldn't hesitate to tell one.

'Maybe,' I said. Maybe one day.

I started putting on my shoes.

'Is it all right if I take off now then?' I said. 'Now we both know this is a sham, we could go our separate ways.'

'Araceli,' he said and looked distressed. 'I would appreciate it if you could stay with me tonight all the same.'

'Now I really don't get it,' I said.

'I need to talk,' he said. 'I felt really glad about the turn of events when you mentioned the double rate. I was thinking this girl is clever, and I can benefit from that. I was looking forward to just lying here and having someone to listen to me. I'll pay what we agreed.'

'Haven't you got a wife who'll listen to you?' I asked.

'A wife who'll listen to me!' Auscias cried. 'That shows you don't know anything about being married.'

'Or a dad, or a mate then,' I said. 'Someone who knows you. You don't know me after all.'

'I have spoken to friends and psychologists. And it all felt so pointless, not one of them understood and I don't even understand myself. So that's why it occurred to me that if only I got the chance to tell someone the whole thing from the very beginning in the course of a single night, to go through it all over again and assemble the bits one by one, the bit that came before and the bit after, to create a kind of sequence, then maybe I would be able to see the logic of it all. And that even if things don't have a meaning, maybe they have a context at least.'

'Not a meaning but a context?'

I didn't understand what he meant.

'Exactly,' he said.

I looked at the clock. It was ten. Muriel was bound to have already finalised her plans for the evening, and there wouldn't have been any point going round the bars looking for her. So I might just as well lie here and earn a packet.

'Okay,' I said. 'Let's do it.'

'Would you mind if I read you a poem?' Auscias said.

'That's fine,' I said. 'We're on your time now. I'm just the listener.'

He smiled at me, and although his eyes were still beer-coloured, they looked happy. He got out of bed and went over to his bag. He got out a thin volume and sat in one of the chairs. Then he opened the book, cleared his throat and started reading:

> *I am dying of sadness and alcohol*
> *he said to me over the bottle*
> *on a soft Thursday afternoon*
> *in an old hotel room by the train depot.*

'To be perfectly honest,' I interrupted him. 'I've never really liked poems that much. I've been to a few readings together with my friend Muriel who knows a fair bit about that sort of thing. And we've watched poets at those events reading from their books while people sit around them having a sleep, and the ones who weren't asleep didn't understand a thing. Only no one ever gets up and shouts: Hang on. What is it you're really trying to say?'

'Poems can be a bit like that,' Auscias said. 'But it's really about habit. If you try to get inside them and understand them properly, they can become a light that illuminates your entire existence. Just listen to this:

> *meat is cut as roses are cut*
> *men die as dogs die*
> *love dies like dogs die,*
> *he said.*

And then this:

> *Love needs too much help, he said.*
> *hate takes care of itself.*

'Do you see? Love needs too much help, but hate takes care of itself. That's exactly the way it is. Exactly like that. That is so well put.'

'Yes,' I said.

'And then this:

> *stick with the thorn*
> *stick with the bottle*
> *stick with the voices of old men in hotel rooms.*

I was fit to burst with laughter. That was exactly what I was doing right then after all. I was sitting in a hotel room with a glass in my hand together with Rodrigo Auscias. Only I didn't want to point that out to him. I assumed we were hearing different things in those words, and maybe he didn't think of himself as old in any case.

'And so to the finish,' he went on, 'it's so dead right.'

> *is that what all the noise is, I said,*
> *my god shit.*

'So that's how it ends? Like that?' I said.

'Just that. Nothing else. Just *my god shit*, a door slamming shut in the reader's face.'

'Right.'

'It's by Bukowski,' he said and closed the book.

'Oh, right,' I said.

'But it wasn't Bukowski we were going to talk about,' he said.

'No,' I said.

Auscias sat in silence for a bit. Then he began his story.

'There had always been an attraction between Alba Cambó and me. A tension we never allowed to get the upper hand because we always behaved as we were supposed to and only met every six months or so, mostly when we ran into each other in the street. We would go into a café then and talk about what was going on at work and in our lives in general. More often than not it was about what was going on at work rather than our lives in general. Although on one occasion I had moved, on another she had bought a boat, and on a third she had resigned from her job and started freelancing. And once she put me in touch with someone, a man with a timber yard from her village. That contact turned out to be very profitable for me, and only a few months later the owner of the timber yard in question had become my biggest customer. I kept feeling I should repay her for that. Even though I had no idea how, I used to think about it every so often: how I could make it up to Alba Cambó for giving me that contact in the timber trade. But no good opportunity ever arose. I just tried to be nice to her in general to make her feel she could turn to me if she ever needed to. There was this one time she arrived at our meeting, her eyes hollow and red with weeping, and told me that her mother had died. She also told me she had inherited a house in a small town and wanted to sell it. I put my hand on her shoulder at that point. Apart from that we never touched one another in all that time.

If ever I said anything about my private life, it would be to mention the courses Bret and I went on, and, if Bret had won a competition, I used to show her whatever picture I had on my mobile. She was always polite on those occasions and would say "like master, like dog" and while that should really be treated as a compliment, we never dwelt on half-baked things like that. We just looked away instead and maybe asked for more coffee or said something completely unrelated. When I talked about my work, I used to tell her mostly about the stuff I did with young people in my spare time. I must have thought that was the part of my life that would interest an outsider most and that it was easiest to find common denominators with people you don't know very well in books and through reading. Although I did sometimes talk about the timber trade and then I found it impossible not to mention the timber market and its regressive structure. I thought having to listen to all the details would bore her to death. I could hear my own voice, after all, and it often used to strike me that I sounded far too worked up, and I was very aware of the contrast between my own angrily impassioned patter and that cool and kindly way she had of listening. I would sometimes feel extremely uncomfortable in those situations, as though I had been exposed or caught out, it's hard to pin down, in any case I kept going back to the subject of books.

Eventually I worked out that my attempts to impress Alba Cambó with the books I had read and the writers I was familiar with were completely pointless as few people are as genuinely un-literary as she is. That might sound slightly daft in retrospect given that she actually had some things published in *Semejanzas*, but even then she had read nothing, although she never seemed to suffer from the sense of inferiority that can afflict some people who have never read anything. She just smiled, and was always interested and friendly, and said she didn't read books. If I asked why, her facial expression would change, and she could look genuinely concerned when she explained the reasons, like a person who has tried to climb a rock wall and failed and now finds herself back at the base coming up with explanations for her failure such as the incline was such-and-such, the weather conditions were unfavourable, or some other assertion about circumstances that were beyond anyone's control. She had grown up in a home without any books; she had never experienced their appeal as a child. Her father had died before she was born; her mother's nerves were weak and she never went out of the house. All I learnt as a child were simple pleasures, Alba said. I imagined her when very young, walking in parks or having a boyfriend of her own she spent the afternoons with. Sometimes when I took Bret out for a walk through one of the parks in Barcelona and the soil was wet with rain and giving off heady scents the way it does in the evenings, I would see young couples entwined on the benches and oblivious of the world around them. I used to think then that that must have been how Alba Cambó spent the hours she devoted to 'simple pleasures'. But when I asked her she laughed and said it wasn't like that at all. She had smoked on the sly, necked in churchyards, driven round in cars with people she didn't know. "Lived, just lived."

I soon gave up any ambition I had to talk to her about literature. I continued talking about my timber goods. Alba always listened attentively and also asked questions that made me sometimes think she was genuinely interested in what I did.

I never talked about Encarnación.

We had known one another in this rather superficial way for almost three years when I got a message from her on my mobile one morning at the beginning of the holidays. *It's odd,* she wrote, *that you live so nearby but we never get to see each other at home. Why don't you come over today and Ilich and I will light the grill? Let me know if you can't come, otherwise we'll expect you at nine.*

I thought about it for a while before responding. During the time we had known one another there had been a tacit agreement between us that we would not involve anyone else. Whoever her partners might be, my dog, my family, these were other spaces we might mention to one another *en passant* but would never enter together. And until now everything had remained pleasantly undefined. There had been a great sense of ease in our relationship despite the thoughts I have just described. And now she wanted me to join her partner and her to grill some chops? A partner I had never heard her say a word about besides. Although she had just mentioned him as if it were the most natural thing in the world: *and Ilich and I will light the grill.*

I racked my brains. Was I making too much of it? What harm could there be in a barbecue on a June evening? And as for her having a partner she had never mentioned, maybe that was the very thing she was trying to do now. And maybe meeting like this would be a way of getting closer, of really getting to know one another's worlds? It shouldn't be making me recoil. It was the natural evolution any relationship is bound to follow. Over time you get closer to one another – that's the way things work and that is how it is supposed to be. And ultimately you could say that is the only positive function time has – it gives people the opportunity to deepen relationships and get to know one another better. That is what I was thinking, along with one or two other things. And I felt disappointed when I arrived at the conclusion that I wasn't keen on accepting her invitation to deepen our friendship, and that it was making me tired and uncomfortable. Had I been infected by my wife's introversion? Encarnación liked to say that people were, in essence, like the stock for a sauce, like the stuff you can buy in a bottle in a store. You could dilute it any number of ways, you could add port, cream and herbs, you could jazz it up however you liked, but the stock always remained the same, and sooner or later the taste would force its way through like a nauseating odour from the underworld. It made no difference how much enthusiasm you entered a relationship with, or what blinders you put on, or the kind of games you were intending to play. Sooner or later those fumes would force their way through.

"I like having acquaintances," she would say. "But God preserve me from friends."

It was, in all probability, the abysmal nature of this reasoning together with the sight of my wife sitting bent over her crossword that made me accept Alba's invitation in the end.

Of course I'll come, I wrote back. *Should I bring anything in particular?*

A good mood . . . she replied with a smiley.

I wondered what those three dots meant. I couldn't help thinking that they felt like an insinuation. But then again, what possible importance could someone who never reads attach to three dots?

Encarnación was still sitting on the balcony solving crossword puzzles when I came out to tell her about Alba's invitation.

"Wouldn't you know it, I've been invited to dinner tonight," I said.

"Oh yes?" she said and looked up.

"A superficial acquaintance I've known for several years. She lives in the city."

Encarnación nodded at me. I told her that the superficial acquaintance was called Alba and that I had got to know her on a business trip a few years ago.

"She's a friend of a friend," I explained. "She came up with a business contact for me in Caudal."

"You don't have to explain anything to me," Encarnación said putting her pen down. "If you want to go to dinner at the house of someone you know, you obviously should. I'm not running a kennel. You are a free man, Rodrigo Auscias."

What did that mean? Was she pulling my leg? *Rodrigo Auscias. I'm not running a kennel.* What a bizarre way of putting it. She's on her own too much, I thought. Her thoughts are starting to go round in circles; they end up going nowhere and then get themselves tied in knots. She is suffocating. I have to get out. Spend time with superficial and uneducated people, people who don't think, people who won't distress you. People who aren't bitter and ugly, people who . . .

Eventually I found myself facing the mirror in the hallway, persuading myself that something was going to become more profound; I would be getting closer to another person and at the same time further away from myself. Two birds with one stone. I smiled at myself in the mirror. My teeth were disagreeably even.

Like someone who has to sell baby wipes and needs to make an impeccable impression on mothers mechanically changing nappies. My hair looked exaggeratedly neat as well. My eyebrows were perfectly arranged as was the collar of my shirt. How the hell did I turn out like this? I thought. In the mirror I could make out our tidy hall, the kitchen and then the living room and the window furthest away. In the corner of the mirror that reflected the sitting room I could see Encarnación's figure bent slightly over the balcony table concentrating on her crossword. The plants looked splendidly restrained in their pots. Several sharpened pencils with nibs that created sharp little silhouettes were positioned in a container in front of her.

"Town in Italy four letters?" she said.

"Pisa," I answered.

A little bird was perched on the balcony rail. Encarnación looked up for a moment, staring at the bird. The bird looked at her. They sat like that for a second or two before Encarnación looked down at the table again and the pencil started moving. The bird flew off. She remained where she was. She would soon get up, at the same moment perhaps that the door closed behind me. Maybe she would heave a sigh of relief, go into the kitchen and put the coffee on. Maybe she would open and close the cupboards. I had seen her do that. She would go into the kitchen, open doors and then close them. Not to get anything, just to stare at the shelves inside with their glasses and plates, farting sometimes when she thought no one could hear. Then she might get out a cookbook, browse through it and then put it away. Then back to the sofa by the television where someone would keep talking, all predigested stuff handed to you on a plate, and she would be sitting there, sometimes dozing, sometimes commenting on what was happening on the screen. And

I would be there beside her. With her boredom like a shackle around my ankle, a dead weight dragging me to the bottom of the sea, filling me with a tepid idleness that made any life outside our four walls an impossibility.

I laughed at the face in the mirror. Alba Cambó! I thought and walked to the door.

A few days before, Encarnación had told me about a dream she had had. She told me about it over breakfast. In the dream she had put an advert about wanting a room in the paper. A woman who introduced herself as an accountant had rung her to say that she had a room to let. Encarnación had gone to see the room and agreed to rent it. The accountant had shown her the rest of the flat. They would have to share a kitchen and sitting room, and there was a cage with two rabbits in on the balcony. They would have to feed one each, the accountant said. Encarnación had thought it would have been better to split the routine and feed them both every other day, but the accountant had insisted they each feed their respective rabbit daily. There was another flat next door, and Encarnación had tried to look into it from the balcony. Inside she could see parts of red sofas reflected in a lot of mirrors that broke up the view and made it impossible to get any sense of the room as a whole. Only she could see parts of people in some of the mirrors. Faces sitting on the red sofas and staring straight ahead. There are people in there, Encarnación had said to the accountant. It's a mental hospital, the accountant replied. The people sitting in there are catatonic, but they have to be tied down anyway. They wake up suddenly and then they go mad. The dream continued. Encarnación fed one of the rabbits, and the accountant fed the other. One day

Encarnación's rabbit escaped and she ran after it trying to catch it but could only get hold of one of its back legs. She could feel the leg jerking as the rabbit struggled to get free but she lugged it home and put it back in the cage. On another day the accountant said she needed to carry out a test on Encarnación, who answered all the questions the accountant put to her, and they were silly and ridiculous questions such as which of two skirts did she think was best, or which of two lipsticks did she think was prettiest. Completely silly things, Encarnación said when she told me the dream. Why are you asking me? she said in the end. I don't care, the accountant replied. It's him up there who wants to know. She pointed towards the roof of the opposite building and up there was a man. He was too far away for Encarnación to see his face, but she could make out that he had his arms crossed over his chest and his face was dark. What does he want to know about me? Everything, the accountant had replied. Although Encarnación felt angry, she answered the questions as best she could. She was also trying to make a good impression on the man with her answers. She was ashamed of this in the dream, she said when she told me, and I'm still ashamed of it now that I'm telling you about it but I'm telling you anyway, it is just a dream.

I had a lot of questions once she had finished. Why had she put an advert in the paper for a room? (Where was I in the dream? That question was impossible to ask.) And what did the sofas look like? Were they covered in pale red leather or dark red velvet? There is an enormous difference. Just saying a 'red sofa' is not saying anything at all. What did the man on the roof of the building opposite look like? Like me? Like some other man? I wanted to ask her all this when she had finished but she didn't seem to want to talk about the dream any more.

So I said that the dream was easy to interpret, that the red room was her unconscious, that the man on the roof was her superego and that the rabbit was her desire for freedom. Then she asked why the people on the red sofas were catatonic. I had no idea how to answer that and we said nothing more about the dream.

I was not unhappy with Encarnación. I may have been bored from time to time, but I wasn't unhappy. We were not at the brink of despair like so many other couples. We hadn't allowed ourselves to be put through the mangle of therapy like many of our friends. We hadn't learnt to trot out, tiredly and with dull eyes, those rote phrases about it not being a question of happiness but of balance and it wasn't about desire but about satisfaction, and that as long as you have your lists of things you're supposed to do and you have sex three times a week and two kids then everything is under control. I have got many friends like that and I know that they will never be happy, nor will they find the balance or joy they talk about. They have been thinking the wrong thoughts for too long. Give them the slightest bit to drink and without fail they will start talking about meaninglessness; they will explore it from every angle and aspect. They believe the fact that it sometimes troubles them is a huge mistake, a misunderstanding, a delusion, but that is not the case at all. The sense of meaninglessness that many of my friends suffer from is the truest part of their experience. But they can never get at it, because they spend all their time explaining it away, trying to relieve the symptoms. They are what we call in the trade "damaged goods". I once said that at a dinner. They looked at me as if I were a terrorist. Then they

filled their glasses and continued talking about meaninglessness and an automatic mower that someone had just bought.

Once, when I was with my family at the beach at Salou during
my teenage years I saw a couple walking along the beach. A man
and a woman who must have been at least sixty. The woman
wore an emerald-green bathing costume and had shoulder-
length grey hair, and the man was wearing an unbuttoned
beach shirt that fluttered behind his hips in the wind. They
both had large dark sunglasses on and were attractively tanned.
The evening sun had cloaked everything in a golden light, and
their shadows extended far out over the water. It was a beautiful
sight in purely visual terms but what fascinated me most was
that they were *talking* to each other. They were so involved in a
conversation that they had to stop every now and then to look
at one another while they continued gesticulating passionately
and amicably. I didn't let them out of my sight. It was as though
I had seen the incarnation of a happy relationship – although
not between young, beautiful and sturdy people but between
people who had shared their everyday existence for almost a
whole lifetime, who had settled into it and realised that it was
a protection and not a threat.

Even if I wasn't quite there yet (to say that Encarnación and I
were as happy as the couple I saw on the beach as a child would
have been an exaggeration), I managed to persuade myself that
we had come a good bit along the way. I could still be filled
with tenderness when looking at her, more frequently in fact
than when we first met. Encarnación used to sit outside on the

terrace of the flat we lived in; sometimes she solved crossword puzzles and sometimes she would look at the terraces on the other side of the street. The woman who lived on the ground floor of the building opposite had a home help who came to clean her flat, and Encarnación could sit looking in fascination at that woman as she cleaned with the doors open to the sitting room. I could never understand what was so exciting about a person doing the cleaning, but Encarnación had soon learnt which days the woman came and then she would put her chair on the terrace and sit there until the other woman had finished, following her with her eyes while the crossword or the book lay untouched on the table in front of her. Sometimes a slight unconscious smile would appear on her face. I have no idea what she was thinking but something would catch in my throat, and I would think *I love her so much*.

I explained the sadness that came over me in waves as a natural event. I didn't spend a lot of time reflecting on the fact that at times Encarnación seemed closed off and out of sorts. Everything comes in cycles, I thought. It will soon be spring, and everything will feel different again, or we will make a trip to the mountains in a bit and return with our batteries recharged. It will all turn out right in the end, it always does.

The building Alba lived in was grander than I expected. There were ornaments all over the facade and the tops of flowering shrubs could be seen behind a high wall. A bored-looking concierge who sat in a little cabin just inside the entrance raised his chin at me in what I took to be a greeting. A long, wide and dusty staircase led up to Alba's flat. There was an air of decay about the landing. Dried flowers stood in pots outside her door and there were spiderwebs in the window that gave on to the street. A withered apricot sat on the window ledge and when I inspected it more closely I could see that someone had taken a bite out of it. I rang the bell, and it was Ilich who opened the door. He looked like a builder. Short and stocky, not a hair on his head, and eyes that were slightly cloudy as though covered in a film of dust. He put out his hand. I put out mine too and felt his, which was cool and limp. He must have thought the opposite, because he put on an expression of pain when I gripped his hand. Easy does it, he said and I didn't care for his tone. Alba came towards us down the hall. Come in, she said. This is Ilich. Ilich said nothing. Why don't we sit out here, said Alba and we went out onto the balcony. Ilich was silent for almost the entire first part of the evening, and Alba wasn't particularly talkative either. I felt pretty uncomfortable with the situation and kept talking; I told them about a book I had bought and hadn't finished and that was still lying half-read on the table next to my bed. Then I said something about your right as the reader to put down books that failed to grip you. Ilich and Alba kept nodding but their eyes were glassy as though they were thinking about something entirely different. Alba poured more wine into my glass. The food that was served wasn't up to much. A few overcooked steaks that Ilich shoved rather sloppily onto our plates, accompanied by some endive with blue cheese. The silence remained heavy and oppressive the whole time; the conversation never got going and I kept drinking, hoping the time would pass and I could go back home. I must have got drunk quite quickly because I was soon telling them about something I had read in the paper that morning, an item about a man who had tried to balance on some logs in a harbour. He had fallen into the water and been sucked out by the current. His body was found floating face down a few hours later. I see, said Alba when I had finished. What's the point of telling a bloody awful story like that? Ilich said and wiped his mouth. He reached for the bread and broke off a bit he swiped across his plate and that turned brown from the burnt food and the fat. What? I said. I couldn't understand how I had offended him by telling the story about the man who drowned in the harbour. Alba smiled at Ilich and then at me. I raised my shoulders. You may be thinking it's odd that I brought the two of you together like this, Alba said. Only the thing is, you both work in the same business. Well more or less. In any case you both work in the same industry and I think you could both gain something by getting to know one another. Rodrigo, you know the timber trade in this country and Ilich is trying to get ahead in it too, although without any real success so far. But, she added, I think Ilich has got the right grain. (She laughed at her own expression.) Then she started talking about the things I had told her. With a richness of detail entirely alien to Alba Cambó, she reproduced my metaphor about Maderas Del Pozo as a huge turd that was blocking any progress in the intestine that was the Spanish market. Then she described the manoeuvring by the old guard, who were doing all they could to keep new ideas at bay. She used the exact words I had used when I described them as "toads" and "blocks of wood". I tried to interrupt her – what I had told her had been said in confidence, or maybe not even in confidence: they were the kind of thing you confide in someone you believe you can trust absolutely. They were not the sort of thing anyone else in the timber trade was ever supposed to hear, particularly not someone like Ilich, an opportunist upstart, who was trying to get ahead and was bound to use the same information either to make an impression at some event or for purely practical ends. I was too drunk by then to have any clear understanding of how what Alba had been saying could be directed against me, but I had some sense of how useful it might be. Ilich grinned at me from the sofa. The Confessions of a Successful Gentleman, said Ilich when Alba had finished talking. That was a really juicy titbit. Really great. He nodded to himself. Well it's not really like that, I said. You've blown the whole thing out of all proportion, Alba. I'm only using your very own words, Don Rodrigo," she said then, and she and Ilich laughed loudly at the "Don Rodrigo".

Suddenly I was longing for Encarnación sitting by the balcony rail looking at the little bird. How tainted everything is, I thought.

Alba got up from the sofa. Rodrigo, she said, could you come with me into the kitchen and help serve the dessert? I got up and followed her. Out of the corner of my eye I saw Ilich pick up the remote from the coffee table and put the television on. I closed the door behind us when we went into the kitchen. The room was small and smelled of fried food. There was a hatrack on one of the walls, and plaits of garlic, baskets of herbs and eggs and a teapot were hanging from the hooks. Besides the smell of burnt meat, the kitchen was untidy in a casual way, not at all orderly and antiseptic the way Encarnación liked it. Alba got out a chopping board and started slicing a watermelon. Have you known one another long? I asked. Alba shook her head. Not at all, no. I've known him for a few weeks. Two months at the most. I had imagined your boyfriend would be different, I said. Different in what way? Alba asked. I'm not sure, I said. Someone more like us. Someone with a proper job in any case. Just a bit more normal, I don't know how to put it. Ilich seems so . . . I was looking for the right word. He's a huge mistake, Alba said, turning towards me. A huge bloody mistake from start to finish is what he is. She put down the knife and dried her hands on a towel hanging on the oven door. The worst thing is, she went on, I knew he would be a mistake from the very beginning. So why did you start seeing him then? I asked. She turned her back to me and started putting the melon slices onto a large dish. You're probably not going to believe this, she began, but the answer is he could boss me around. He'd say to me, "This is what you're going to do," or "Pull yourself together, for God's sake." He was ironic and sarcastic when I did things wrong. He was exotic, that's all it was. No one who knows me properly would dare do that. I thought that was incredibly sexy. I see, I said. Alba nodded to herself. The problem, she said then, when you begin a relationship with someone rough and ready like that is that there's no getting rid of them afterwards. Ilich believes there's something between us and I'm starting to think he's already imagining us having a future together. It's a feature of the simple mind that it believes in simple solutions of the "since we've been getting on well for a while, we're bound to go on doing so for the rest of our lives" type. That's the way Ilich sees our shared future: a landing strip already laid out and covered in asphalt. She held her arms (and the knife) out straight in front of her as if to create an image of the landing strip. And now I've got to deal with the hangover. Because how am I going to get rid of him? She turned round and threw her arms in the air. And that was what made me think of you. What? I said. I stared at her. Everything she was saying felt impossible to take in. That's right, you see I thought you could give him a helping hand. You've got contacts after all, you're a success. That was why I suggested we invite you here to see what you might be able to do for him, if you could find some common ground. Common ground, I said. What do you mean by that? You know, however you want to put it, Alba said. We'll just have to see if it'll work out. It would be nice if we could avoid coming to blows. What? I said again. And what do you mean "we"? Let's go, Alba said then and picked up the plate of fruit. We really should stop getting bogged down in analysing everything. Let's have some fun. That's what it's all about in the end, isn't it? To try and have a bit of fun in this vale of tears.

Confused, I followed Alba back into the sitting room. Alba sat next to Ilich on the sofa. I sat there in silence, thinking about what Alba had said in the kitchen. I thought about how ridiculous it was of me to have stood in front of the mirror at home wondering if I wanted our friendship "to get deeper", and a load of other drivel. Nothing is ever about what you think it will be. Nothing can ever be elevated to a purely theoretical, conceptual level. Everything is always and inexorably practical and shabby. Ilich chewed the melon and the juice ran down over his chin, which he wiped with the back of his hand. He chucked the rinds on the table and Alba picked them up and put them back on the plate. After a while they started kissing. Ilich's hand was resting on Alba's thigh. I got up and started to walk towards the hall. Thanks very much, I called. Hang on, Alba called after me. Don't be in such a hurry. Come back, Ilich said. I came back and Alba made room for me on the sofa while she said in an affected voice that the night, like her, was still warm and expectant.

I have always thought that there are three things I love about my life: Encarnación in particular, and women and wood in general. I have no political convictions. I don't give a damn about politics. People with political convictions frighten me. People who are willing to sacrifice themselves for an idea are also willing to sacrifice other people for the same idea. That applies to people who have been the victims of injustice as well. They are the most dangerous people of all because they believe themselves entitled to revenge. As for me I am totally spineless. I would never go to extremes for a point of view because there is nothing playful, sexual or pleasurable about points of view. That is what I have always thought: that I love three things in life and I don't give a damn about the rest.

But the evening with Alba and Ilich made me re-evaluate my image of myself. Maybe I was coming apart at the seams; maybe I was beginning to have views. I didn't like Ilich. Not his old revolutionary name, not his German appearance, not the sense of the rebel manqué he positively exuded. And I didn't appreciate either the ménage à trois being arranged on the sofa. I found watching Alba in the arms of another man – and one she didn't have any feelings for according to what she had just told me – disgusting. Seeing Ilich's young and muscular body moving in harmony with Alba's made me feel that I didn't fit into the sexual constellation now forming before my eyes, and that in turn made me think about what sexual constellations I did fit into, and that what I was watching was a scene from some pathetic porn film I once saw by mistake when travelling across Spain on timber agency business and in which a very old man was being satisfied by two very young women. When I watched that film I was filled with a powerful sense of revulsion. It was a scene staged solely to earn money from the target group; no real young woman would prefer a man like that. The other possibility my sexual self envisaged at that moment was even more depressing: Encarnación and me naked in our marriage bed.

I put my hand on Alba's breast, and Ilich said, Now then, Don Rodrigo, why don't you undo that tie of yours and let's have a good time.

After some time on the sofa, we went into Alba's bedroom and continued. Ilich appeared not to be sober; at several points he started laughing, or even giggling, while Alba seemed to be parodying a porn star with cries and groans that were much too loud. As for me I managed to convince myself I shouldn't think, just do. That might have worked if I hadn't at one point looked up at the mirror that was stuck to the ceiling above Alba's bed. The sight that met my eyes drained me of what little desire I had managed to conjure up so far. I could see Alba lying on top of Ilich and the muscles playing under her skin as they moved together. Ilich's powerful arms were embracing her. I was at the bottom of the bed next to their entangled legs. Compared with their bodies, mine looked like a plant that had been through a period of severe drought. My shoulders were the colour of ivory; my collar bone was very pronounced and surrounded by dark shadows; my sex appeared to be some kind of growth, or a bolt, and my hands looked helpless as though they had no idea how to behave in order to become part of the situation beside them. But the worst thing of all was my face. With my mouth half-open and lips that were far too narrow, a searching gaze and my hair plastered to my scalp, I looked like a martyr in a war scene who has turned his face up to heaven to ask God for help. Good Lord, is that me, I had time to think before I heard a giggle from Alba and Ilich, who were also looking upwards. Someone's got to go, Ilich said and grinned while he stroked Alba across her back. Don Rodrigo, Alba giggled. She laughed so hard I could see her gums. Then I looked up again and broke out in a cold sweat. How are you feeling? Ilich said and sat up on the bed. You're sweating like a swamp. Nothing's wrong, I said.

I went to the toilet, had a shower and got dressed. While Alba and Ilich lay there chatting, I sat in the sitting room. I lit a cigarette and looked out the window. Pla del Born was down there, and the cafes had put out tables and chairs. A bird sitting on the guttering in front of me dipped its head and had a quick drink; it then looked watchfully at me on the other side of the window. It was beginning to get light. Alba went into the kitchen and there was the sound of dishes being clattered. The coffee-maker hissed and the aroma spread throughout the flat. Shortly afterward she came out with a tray that she put on the table. One cup for you, she said to me, one for me and one for Ilich. Ilich, she called. Ilich came in and sat on the sofa and drank the coffee. Alba asked what we were going to do today. Ilich said he wanted to do something different. I laughed out loud.

"Something different? Isn't that what we were doing all night?"

The moment I uttered the words I could hear how desperately ancient I must sound in their ears.

"How old are you?" Ilich asked, bringing the cup to his lips.

"Fifty-three," I replied.

"So it's too late then," Ilich said.

"For what?" I asked.

"To off yourself," Ilich answered.

"What do you mean?" I said.

"I mean that all the brightest people kill themselves when they reach fifty – at the very latest," Ilich said. "Because it's all over after fifty; after that it's all about trying to hold on to what you've got."

"Hold on in what sense?"

"To the territory you've managed to piss out for yourself, I suppose," he said.

He told us of a man he had heard about who spent his whole life researching the work of an author who had inspired him in his youth. The man had written articles, essays and dissertations about the writer, and his deepest wish was that all the people who came across the author's work would associate the writer with himself.

"A bit vain it has to be said," Ilich said, "but that's what makes a lot of people tick."

Then one day the academic in question discovered a flaw. He had been granted access –because of the research he was doing – to an archive containing writings the author had left as his legacy, and he would be the first person to explore the archive before it was opened up to the general public. What the man discovered there turned his blood to ice. In one letter the highly respected author expressed a range of socially unacceptable opinions. As though he were having an intimate conversation with himself, or confessing his true self in a poem, he gave vent to the anti-Semitic, racist and misogynistic views he couldn't express openly but which he felt had nourished him throughout his life, filling him with the hatred that could provide him with the vital energy he required to get out of bed, begin his day and start work.

"The necessary enemies," Ilich said, nodding to himself. "The ones we need to carry on living, so we can go on believing that one day we are going to blow those bastards out of the water and put a pistol to their temples."

"What are you saying?" Alba said, looking scared.

"In any case," Ilich said, without paying Alba any mind, "the academic smuggled out the notes in his briefcase. He went home, shaking and in a cold sweat. He made a fire in the open grate and burnt the sheets of paper. And so began a new era in his life, because from the moment he read those lines the author had written, all his energy and all his efforts were devoted to concealing what he had previously dedicated his life to discovering. Just as his own image was supposed to be elevated by that of the author, it would have fallen apart if people discovered he had spent his whole life on the work of a Nazi, a racist and a misogynist. Some nights he tried to calm himself with the idea he had burnt the only proof and on others he just lay awake afraid there could be other evidence. He was dragged down by the curse."

Ilich grinned.

"The curse of turning fifty. The people who fail to off themselves before they reach fifty can never manage it after that. I could give you other examples."

He went on tell me about a Catalan poet who decided when he was thirty that he would kill himself when he got to fifty. No one believed him then but when he reached fifty he proved them wrong and took his own life, all calm and collected and without any fuss. His friends were astonished by how diabolically stubborn he had proved, but they admired him as well. When they subsequently turned sixty and seventy, and even older, and were transformed into vegetables slurping porridge in homes whose walls were painted the same colour as the insides of a fly, many of them would think: suppose I had done what the poet did? But by then it was too late.

"If you hesitate, you're lost," Ilich said.

"I have to go now," I said and got up.

The palms of my hands were damp and I was feeling dizzy.

"I'll give you a call," Ilich said to my back.

"Why would you ring me?"

I turned round.

"So we can be timber pals," Ilich replied.

"We're not going to be timber pals," I said.

"Aren't we?" Ilich said. "Check this out then."

He came over to me, and out of the corner of my eye I could see Alba sitting stiff as a post on the sofa. He held up his mobile phone.

"That's you, Alba and me," he said.

He stood beside me and pointed at the mobile's screen. On it I could see myself on top of Alba's body with her feet around my shoulders.

"What the hell?" I said.

Ilich slapped the mobile shut.

"So I'll be ringing you," he said.

"Give me that," I said. "That's illegal for Christ's sake."

"All's fair . . ." Ilich said. "Although really, all I need is the one job. If you can help me with that, mum's the word. Then I'll keep this little love token to myself."

I walked home to Encarnación. She was sitting in the same spot as when I left. Once again she was on the terrace solving crossword puzzles, and the woman was cleaning in the flat in the building opposite. A wind had risen off the sea, bringing with it a smell that had to be oil and tar from the harbour. She didn't ask me where I had been and, remembering what she had said the evening before about not running a kennel, I didn't come up with an explanation off the top of my head either. I sat next to her and helped with the crossword. After a while I went into the kitchen and made lunch. We ate and then we returned to the crossword. Alba rang in the afternoon. I could hear from her voice that she was jumpy. What have I got you mixed up in? she kept saying. He's a criminal, through and through. It's fine, I kept saying, to calm her down. We'll fix it. I'll sort out a timber contact for Ilich and then you break things off with him. It'll all work out. Ilich isn't someone to mess with, Alba said. I've had to deal with worse, I replied. You've got to be careful, Alba said. Yes, yes, I said, it'll be all right. We just need to keep our cool. It'll all turn out fine in the end. I'll give him the number of a chair factory in Albacete, I said. A little shed out in the wilds of La Mancha. I laughed. He can spread his nets there. It'll have to be the real deal, Alba said. You've got to come up with someone with real power. Ilich isn't the kind of person you mess with. Why don't you ring Del Pozo? My ears pricked up. Del Pozo? I'd heard about him through Alba, after all, and over time Del Pozo had become my most important customer, and in fact my only regular: his orders rolled in on a monthly basis and he was the only one I could continue to rely on while the others came and went. But asking for favours was risky in this business. I hadn't cracked all the codes yet despite several years as a timber agent but even so I knew that even a single conversation could prove disastrous if not handled correctly. Bringing along a tyro like Ilich to see Del Pozo . . . he might very well consider that an insult. The idea of having to get in touch with Del Pozo about all this brought my palms out in a cold sweat again. I replied that Del Pozo wasn't someone you just turned up to see. He was the spider at the centre of the web. All the threads ran through his hands. I don't think we've got any choice, Alba said. I'll see what I can do, I replied. We hung up.

Over the next few days I tried to persuade myself that I had been too easily intimidated by Ilich. And that he was the kind of person who was always spreading his nets among the people around him just to see what he might catch. An opportunist, pure and simple. But the thought of that bloody film gave me diarrhoea in the mornings. I looked up my name on the internet almost daily and heaved a sigh of relief when there was no sign of the film. I realised though that all this madness had to be brought to an end and that if I did help Ilich get a meeting with Del Pozo, a resolution of some kind might be possible.

In the end I rang Del Pozo. I began by asking after his wife Dolores, and Pozo replied that she had a liver disease that was turning her skin yellow and they were eating unsalted vegetable purée every night. And how is your daughter Nieves? I asked then. I don't see anything of her, Del Pozo said. She's gone and got a boyfriend, so I don't see anything of her any more. He went on talking about his wife's liver disease and seemed to have no interest in whatever my errand might be. I kept listening, because I knew that's what you had to do with Del Pozo: being forced to listen to his drivel for half an hour before you got to say why you were ringing was a way for him to show who was in charge. All you could do was accept it for what it was; you had to just accept it, you always have to accept the structures of power. After twenty minutes of chatting about liver disease, he said he was sorry but he couldn't talk any more, he had a meeting to attend. I got in quickly that I had a matter to discuss.

It's about a friend of mine, he needs a job. I see, said Del Pozo. You can come on Friday, the two of you, he said then. I can see you on Friday morning. I said thank you and we hung up.

I was at pains to point out to Ilich how incredibly lucky he was that Del Pozo had agreed to meet him. We drove in my car. He sat in the passenger seat with the window open. I asked him to close the window on account of the air conditioning. Ilich pretended not to hear and hot air continued pouring into the car. What a great time we had the other evening, he said after a while. I looked at him and he waved his mobile with a smile on his lips. We said not another word to each other for the rest of the entire journey. We stopped at a motorway restaurant and both had a sausage with chips. When we drove into Caudal de la Ribera, Ilich said that the cemetery was twice as large as the village. More dead people than live ones here, he said, grinning again. When we passed El Sultan de Oro, he said: Have you had a fuck at that club?

"No," I lied.

Though I had, very definitely, had a fuck at that club. I couldn't stop myself; I had pulled up outside one day out of sheer curiosity while driving to Del Pozo's. As I entered I could smell the stagnant air, see the worn red sofas, the tables that hadn't been wiped clean. I was about to turn round in the doorway but Encarnación and I hadn't had sex in ages. I stood there, and the place reeked of smoke and bodies. A woman came towards me with open arms. She wore a broad smile in which I glimpsed a row of ochre-coloured teeth. Come in, she said. She took my hand and led me over to the register which lay open on the counter in reception. I've just come to sleep, I said. Once again her red-painted mouth formed a huge smile. Of course, she said. Everyone does.

We parked on the courtyard in front of Del Pozo's office. It smelled of resin and gravel as we got out of the car. The heat buffeted us. Ilich said, An industry in the hinterland – what a fucking nightmare. Yes, I said. Absolute shade or absolute light. There are no grey zones here. Ilich spat on the ground and mumbled something I couldn't hear. I don't understand how a dump like this can have the kind of incredible turnover you said, he said. It's just a fucking shed. Don't judge a book by its cover, I said. So where's the bloody book then? he retorted. It's just a saying, I said, and he grinned.

I rang the bell, and we were welcomed by a secretary who put us in an extremely chilly waiting room. The sweat turned cold beneath our shirts, and Ilich shivered. After a few minutes the secretary came in to announce that Del Pozo would see us. We went up a flight of stairs and in through the door the secretary held open with a smile. Would you like some coffee? she asked. No thanks, we said.

"Come in, come in," said a voice from the other side of the room.

The room that stretched out before us was the largest office on the entire Spanish altiplano, and maybe in all of Spain. The flooring was parqueted in a tropical redwood and the walls were covered with panels in very select timber. Above the panelling hung portrait paintings that recalled those you see when you visit the castles or estates of noble families, although these had been badly painted and the frames were much too garish. It was obvious that the individuals portrayed were related to the man now facing us, seated behind an enormous desk on the other side of the room. He was short of stature, thick-necked, and had a rectangular head with drooping, flabby skin. He had no hair at all and was wearing rimless spectacles with thick lenses.

"Rodrigo Auscias," he said with a drawl. "It's been a while."

I went over and took his outstretched hand. I clasped it, and it was spongy and cold. I asked after his wife and her liver disease.

"Those vegetable purées will be the death of me," Del Pozo said in his nasal drawl. "I've always loathed vegetables."

He talked about his wife's illness for a bit. Then he told me that his daughter Nieves had met a guy from Madrid. So he hadn't seen hide nor hair of her recently. Suddenly he stopped talking; he fixed his eyes on Ilich while folding his hands across his stomach and said:

"And this would be . . . ?"

I explained what brought me here. I told him that Ilich was a family friend and he had been trying to get into the timber trade, but was on the point of giving up because the task seemed overwhelming.

"Well," Del Pozo said and laughed slowly. "Those of us holding the reins are an old fraternity, and nothing is going to change while we're still around. Nothing has changed as long as any of us have been alive."

He made a gesture towards the faces in the paintings behind him.

"On the other hand," he continued and raised a finger in the air, "it is time to start considering what the market of tomorrow will be like."

He nodded slowly while talking and paused.

"The market of tomorrow?" I asked.

"That's right. Tomorrow. Either we give in to Europe's demand for transparency or we continue in the same vein. And if you ask me (he held up his hands as though in apology)

I would prefer us to continue doing things the way we always have done."

"Europe, Europe, Europe," Ilich said. "It's always Europe. What about Spain?"

Del Pozo nodded.

"Exactly," he said. "That's what I've always wondered. What about Spain? We're just expected to follow them around, like monkeys in a circus. Only Europe's not worth it. There are quite a few things I would prefer not to have introduced here."

"Right," said Ilich. "They've got higher taxes."

"Oh, the tax doesn't make any difference, I don't give a damn about taxes, I've never paid any. No, I'm thinking about other things. More important things. The balance of power, for instance."

"Okay?" Ilich said sounding interested.

"Women have already started climbing the ladder in Europe."

"Climbing the ladder in what way?" asked Ilich.

"I'm not sure exactly. But my contacts up there are saying we need to hold on to our trousers. Hold on to your trousers, they tell me. Hold on to your trousers, whatever you do."

Ilich laughed aloud and said:

"Wanting things to remain the same is all part of belonging to the old guard. Only I don't think there's any point in holding on to our pants."

Ilich laughed again and looked at me as though asking for confirmation.

"One thing I can tell you," Del Pozo said and leant over the desk. "And this might be useful for you to know as you're still young and unspoilt but you're going to be stuck with it soon enough. Women are never satisfied. No matter how much you give them, they always want more. If you give them a car, they want a different one. If you pay them a compliment, then it was the wrong one. If you give them a vegetable purée, it will have the wrong vegetables in. Nothing is good enough for a real woman – that's the very definition of what a real woman is: nothing is good enough and she is never satisfied, because she always deserves something better. There's a rope around our necks and a knife is being pressed even harder to our throats. And that's why I'll tell you again: make sure you hold on to your trousers, otherwise you'll be for it and your entire generation along with you. Don't let them take your manhood away, because they still won't want you once they've taken it. They'll throw you in the wastepaper basket, like a spent cartridge, depleted capital, a used condom."

Ilich opened his mouth as though he was about to say something, but closed it again, put his arms over his chest and leant back in the chair. There was total silence. The door opened and in came the secretary holding a tray of coffee cups. I thought it wisest not to repeat that I didn't want any, and accepted the cup, brought it to my lips and drank. The coffee was hot and bitter.

"Although it wasn't women we were going to talk about," I said, "but timber."

"Then there's this business with the cities as well," Del Pozo said. "People who live in cities haven't got the faintest idea about timber."

Ilich nodded reflectively while he sipped his coffee. "You're better off listening to someone in the know," he said. "The people with experience."

"The cobbler should stick to his last," Del Pozo said.

"Each to his own," Ilich agreed.

Ilich told us about his grandfather who was a Communist and had been executed during the Civil War. His grandfather had lived in Ciudad Real and worked at a little factory that made bedsteads. It was owing to his grandfather that Ilich had decided to focus his efforts on the timber trade.

"I've got it in my blood," he said. "Trust me, I have."

Del Pozo nodded. Then he said that as for the Left in the war, the Right had never been needed to beat them. They did a fine job of killing themselves on their own. Ilich made no reply to that comment but repeated that as far as the timber trade was concerned he had it in his blood. Del Pozo stared at him for a bit. Then his face split in a smile and he looked like a rat suddenly and unexpectedly baring all its teeth. Then he turned serious again and looked at the clock.

"This is what we'll do," he said getting up. "In about an hour I've got a meeting at which I'm supposed to try to sell a load of mould-damaged planks to a furniture manufacturer. You'll tag along, and Ilich will be in charge of the negotiations. If you pull it off, you can work for me. If you can't you'll drive back home and you will never call again asking for another chance. Okay?"

"Shouldn't I know a bit about what I'm supposed to be selling?" Ilich asked.

"All you need to know is this: the main thing is to get their attention. Don't let them tell you that this or that person will deal with you, oh no, you have to talk to the person who owns the place. If it's Maderas Benicio, there's no point in talking to Gonzalo. If it's Maderas Hernandez, don't bother talking to Rubinetta with a mop in one hand and a duster in the other."

Ilich laughed aloud.

"You may think I'm joking," Del Pozo said. "But it's like anything else. Nothing is ever complicated for someone with a bit of intuition. All you need is to be confident and capable of feeling your way along the walls of a darkened room. Everything is always incredibly simple, much simpler than you think."

Del Pozo scratched his bare scalp.

"A darkened room is exactly the same as a lit room," he went on with a pompous expression on his face. "It's just that the light has been turned off. Never have any doubt about that, and when you're selling timber never have any doubt in yourself, for God's sake. People in general, and timber buyers in particular, can sniff out the first whiff of doubt like dogs, and that's when they attack."

"Okay," Ilich said. "That I can do. I'm good at handling animals."

"What a great guy," Ilich said when we were back out on the car park. "Nowhere near as constipated as Alba said you said he was."

I didn't reply. I started the car and then we drove behind Del Pozo's BMW through Caudal de la Ribera, which was completely empty at that time of day. The streets looked abandoned.

Afterwards they told me how they had handled the buyers. Del Pozo half a yard behind and Ilich in front. The buyers had listened for a good while. They had leant back in their seats like police detectives, inspecting Ilich, amused at first but then with more seriousness. Ilich had kept talking about new strategies.

"We are going to reshape the market. We're going to remove all the middlemen and only Del Pozo will remain. We will be the only player and we will guarantee to sell on low commission. We'll even be taking only three per cent instead of our usual fifteen on our very next delivery."

The boss and his son looked at him with raised eyebrows. They nodded and exchanged glances.

"Feel free," Ilich said at the end. "Please take a good look at the samples."

They lifted up the samples he had put out. They inspected them from various angles and ran their fingers over them. The boss had the knack of an old hand and seemed to experience an almost sensual pleasure when he touched the raw material. For a moment it was as though something shone out of his face, like a ray of sunlight or the light from a lamp. The little factory was humming along around them as usual, you could hear the workers shouting to one another and there was the smell of glue in the air.

Their pens were busy scratching away. They excused themselves for a moment, left the room and went into another right next door. They consulted while Ilich and Del Pozo watched them through a large pane of glass. Three wretched per cent, *three wretched per cent*, what's there to consult about? Del Pozo whispered and leant back. Ilich crossed one leg over the other. He looked out the window at where Del Pozo's car was standing. You had to have signed a lot of successful contracts to have a car like that.

That was when inspiration struck. He had no idea why, because on the surface at least there was no obvious reason not to let everything proceed as usual. Maybe he was just in that lit room where someone had turned off the light, maybe he was just feeling his way along by his fingertips with unusual success. But he stood up, smoothed out the creases in his trousers and walked over to the pane of glass. He raised his hand and knocked carefully on the glass.

"Hello?"

"Yes?"

The faces of the buyers turned towards him. The sweat was shining on their foreheads and the boss had a cigarette in his hand.

"If I could just say one thing?"

"Yes?"

"Would you mind coming out of there then?"

They came out, dragging their feet and looking at him suspiciously.

"The sales process, and also the process of buying, can actually be reduced to a single sentence," he said. "And I am now going to say it."

"What is it?"

They were listening. It seemed as though the workers had gone on a break because there was suddenly total silence throughout the factory.

"Do you like the wood, or do you not like the wood?"

While uttering the question, he kept looking them straight in the eye. As though they were actually talking about a war. About the towns on a map to be obliterated, or spared. Destroy or save? It's all in our hands now, and it's of the utmost importance. We have the power; we are the people making the decision here. You, and me as well. Do you like the wood, or do you not like the wood?

He repeated the question. And added.

"I haven't got all day."

There are times when you manage to apply the exact amount of force required to get what you want. That might sound simple and straightforward but it involves a very precise balancing act between the force applied and the method employed. If he could close this deal, his life would take a new turn. He would become someone else. But the silence was so dense it was almost humming. A fluorescent tube in the ceiling was blinking irritatingly. There was a feeling that something fateful was about to occur and there was no escaping it. He started packing up the samples.

"We accept the offer," they said then.

He's a natural, no two ways about it, was Del Pozo's only comment when they came out of the factory. Del Pozo was very, very pleased. He put his arm around Ilich and announced we were going to La Tortuga Feliz to have a slap-up dinner. Once we had got there, Del Pozo took out his white- and red-gold biro and had Ilich sign a contract. So where did you find this complete natural? Del Pozo asked me, and I felt there was a new coldness to his voice.

They talked about how they were going to work together. I sat on the other side of them in silence, eating the *crema fría* of courgettes set before me. I also ate some tapas that consisted of asparagus spears wrapped in ham. I thought the ham had a faint hint of dog and soon pushed it away. We'll have to get you out to Caudal de la Ribera now and then, Del Pozo said to Ilich. Every other week here, and every other week at your place in Barcelona. Have you got a girlfriend? Yes, Ilich answered. I've got a girlfriend who comes from this village. Is that right? Del Pozo said. Who's that then? Alba Cambó, Ilich replied, sounding rather proud. Oh, so that's how you know one another, Del Pozo said nodding. That little lass. Right. I remember her all right. Her father had seven thousand sheep; her mother went mad. One day she just up and vanished. Got on the bus and disappeared, she's never been seen since.

He ate a spoonful of the cold courgette cream and took a bite of the ham-wrapped asparagus. Anyway, Ilich. Don't bring Alba Cambó down here; she never liked this place and it didn't like her either. You can't be a prophet in your home town, Ilich said with a shrug of his shoulders. Your home town knows who you are, Del Pozo replied. Your home town knows the grain of your timber; there's no pulling the wool over its eyes. But don't you worry, Ilich, we've got a place here that is going to make sure you won't be missing Alba Cambó or any other girlfriend for that matter. He laughed aloud. El Sultan de Oro? I wondered. The food rose in my gorge straightaway. I told them I wasn't feeling well, and that I needed to lie down. The car's the best spot for that, Del Pozo said. It's the only place that's cool.

I went out and sat in the car. I couldn't sleep but I folded the back seat down and lay flat. I closed my eyes but all I could see was that bloody club. The drapes, the greasy tables, the red sofas and a little man who walked round bare-chested with a floral spray and a rag in his hand. I disinfect everything here twice a day, he said, turning towards me. It smells of bodies is what I was thinking. Body fluids? the man asked. Body fluids are like salt. Too little and you don't taste it, too much makes it inedible. Just what are you saying? I asked. He grinned and repeated that he disinfected everything twice a day and that the people who came here were genuine couples who really did talk to each other and that everything here was clean and proper. He sprayed a mist of fluid into the room and the drops fell in a fine, slow rain onto the carpet. I shook my head. Maybe I had got a touch of sunstroke. Voices kept finding their way into my head. I tried to fend them off but it was as if they left behind a lingering echo. I tried ringing Encarnación but she wasn't answering. I could see her sitting at the round table on the terrace solving her crossword puzzles with the bird looking at her while the mobile phone on the table kept ringing.

I remembered that Alba had given me an issue of *Semejanzas* that had one of her stories in it. I had rolled it up and stuffed it in the glove compartment. So I got it out and read it while I was waiting for Ilich and Del Pozo to finish eating their meal. The story was about a young girl in Caudal who fell in love with the village priest. The piece ended with the priest, who had been accused of paedophilia, being burnt to death in the village church. I felt sick the whole time I was reading it. Then I opened the car door and got out. The heat had died down and there was a coolness to the air. I looked back towards the village, trying to see if anyone was about but everything looked empty and abandoned even though it was nine in the evening and people should have been outside eating dinner or just sitting at a bar. The church looked a bit smug where it stood in the village square. As if it were saying, here I am, still standing despite it all. I thought about Cambó's story. My shirt was sticking to my back and I chided myself for not having brought another to change into. A timber agent's rule number one: always have a change of clothes with you, you never know what might happen and if you suddenly find yourself in La Mancha, all you can do is deal with it. How long were they going to stay in there? How much could they have to talk about? A consignment of mould-damaged planks and a successful transaction. Just how much could there possibly be to say about that? I tried to ring Encarnación again. Then I dialled Alba's number. She picked up, and I felt relieved at the sound of her voice, at hearing a human voice in the midst of all that silence. I told her how things had worked out with Del Pozo and Ilich. I went into great detail; I may even have exaggerated my own contribution. I wanted to make her happy; I wanted to get her to say that everything was all right now and that my job was done, just so I could savour that feeling.

"Brilliant," Alba said. "That's brilliant. Ilich will be pleased and grateful. So now we've done our bit, you and me. He's got a foot in the door and that was the deal. He'll have to leave us alone now."

"Yes," I said. "I just want to get all this over with now. I've got a marriage to save at home and a company I've got to get back on its feet."

"Sure," Alba said. "We've all got things we have to get sorted. I'm not really all that well actually."

"What's the matter with you?" I asked.

There was silence on the other end.

"It's not something I'll be asking you to help me with," she said. "This time no one can help me."

"Oh dear," I said. "So this is a rogue of a different order then?"

She pretended to ignore the dig.

"You've done enough," was all she said. "Just see that Ilich gets home okay, save your marriage and your company, and everything will be all right again. We could go back to the way we were before. Having coffee now and then, we could get together just like we used to?"

I could picture the way it used to be. That all seemed remote and impossible.

I fell asleep in the car and woke up several times with the evening sun in my face; even semi-comatose, I could feel how the skin was stretched and burnt across it. I slipped back into sleep and dreamed brief, uneasy dreams. In one of them I was walking behind Ilich and Del Pozo along the endless corridors of the timber yard. Del Pozo was talking about the different qualities of timber, gesticulating all over the place and walking over to the planks and profiles every now and then to run his hand over them, spellbound and silent, the way a horse trainer runs his hand over a particularly beautiful stallion or the way a goldsmith can suddenly feel a violent desire for his own material. Ilich seemed fascinated as well; he was standing beside Del Pozo with a wry smile and he, too, was drawing his fingers over some of the wood profiles, looking as though it made him shiver with pleasure. That's the kind of person who should be dealing in wood, I thought in my dream. People who can feel it in their fingertips. Who can fall in love with a lifeless plank of timber, who would die for a cubic metre of soft Brazilian rosewood. Around us hung paintings of Del Pozo's ancestors. They were staring at us from the walls like great apes, superior and reserved. I just don't have a vocation for this, I thought. It's not me. I have to get out of here. At one point Del Pozo looked over his shoulder to check that I was with them and that was when I caught sight of the lobe of his ear. It was narrow, creased and orange-coloured. It looked flabby and loose. As though in a trance I moved closer, put my hand on Del Pozo's shoulder and bit his earlobe. The flesh was tender and sweet on my tongue. What am I doing? I thought in my dream. Have I lost my mind? Then Del Pozo turned his face towards me and without paying any attention to the bitten-off lobe that was now in my mouth he smiled at me, gently and slowly, almost kindly.

The night continued with one fevered dream succeeding another. The next one was about women's bodies and feathers. The women were white, large and smooth, walking across a beach in front of me. I stared at their powerful legs, at the fat and the muscle tensing under their skin, and I felt a sudden desire. But just as I started to sense the heat rising in my loins, the women's bodies changed shape. They still came walking along but the ones that now appeared on the beach had no backs. Some of them appeared to have been chopped off in the lumbar region, others were more like stalagmites: they finished above the hips in what looked like a little curl. Hello! I called in my dream. Hello. No one answered. You could thread them on a pole, I thought in spite of myself, as though they were hangers. I pictured it in my mind for perhaps a tenth of a second: a pole hung with white meaty women's bodies that ended in little hooks that slipped around the clothes rail. Even though the vision was grotesque I laughed out loud. The women were hanging in a line right before my eyes. I could go up to them, reach out my hand, and skim through them the way you browse among clothes in a shop, looking for something in my own size. I tried to end that thought in the dream. But the idea was so grossly comical, it refused to be shut down. Stop thinking that women's bodies can be suspended like hangers, I thought to myself. Although I continued to peruse the bodies. My size, I thought while my fingers worked through rows of powerful women's backs. My size. There was a sudden smell of apricots. A woman was coming towards me from the interior of the shop with a large basket of warm, steaming apricots. Help yourself, she said smiling at me. I tried to make out her teeth but could only see darkness. I was just about to reach out for an apricot when I realised that they weren't apricots in the basket but women's ears. Hot, steamed women's ears. Some still had earrings in, while on others they appeared to have been ripped off. I screamed. The smell of apricots? Ears? No, it wasn't anything like that – it was, what it was was . . . skin. Sweet, warm, sweat-scented skin . . . Good Christ, I really am losing it, I thought, as I woke up.

It was Ilich's smell. I woke up, sat upright and moved my tongue around my mouth, coated as it was from thirst like a rough and sticky carpet. Ilich thudded down into the seat beside me, smelling of smoke and alcohol. His face was flushed.

"So here you are having a howl all on your own," he said.

"I was dreaming about . . . this horde of women's bodies that . . . "

He wasn't listening. He folded the seat back and undid the top button of his trousers.

"Been checking out the porn, have you?" he said and picked up the issue of *Semejanzas* that was lying on the dashboard. "You old goat."

"There's a short story by Alba inside. Why don't you read it while I grab some fresh air?"

A half hour or so later and we were on our way out of Caudal. Ilich had read the story in *Semejanzas* and said, "That's my girl, torch the fucking bastard, she's got her head screwed on alright, no coddling, just set fire to them."

"Haven't you got anything else for me to read?" he said then. "I have to admit I didn't entirely dislike the experience. It gives you this feeling of being cultivated, if I can put it like that."

I sighed while Ilich opened the glove box and had a rummage inside it.

"I think I've found something," he said and took out a book.

I glanced at the cover. It was Houellebecq's *Platform*.

"Ilich," I said. "Trust me, that book is not right for a beginner."

"I think I can decide for myself if something is right for me or not, Don Rodrigo."

He turned the pages at random for a bit. Then he stopped at one of them and started reading. He laughed out loud.

"Is this really the kind of book you read when you're on your own?"

He laughed again. Then he said he couldn't believe I read this kind of thing; and wasn't that revealing, he said. He started reading out loud the passage where Houellebecq, or Houellebecq's alter ego or Houellebecq's narrator at least, jerks off while reading about half-naked mixed-race girls on a beach. The narrator ejaculates on the pages and then says never mind, I won't be reading that particular book again anyway. Ilich shook his head and looked at me with an incredulous grin on his face. "Do you seriously believe that kind of thing leaves people any the wiser, Don Rodrigo?" I remembered the episode. It's when the main character reads *The Firm* by John Grisham. Taken out of context it did sound rather pitiful, the way almost anything taken out of context does.

"It's not a bad episode when you read it in context," I said.

Ilich laughed again and struck the book against the dashboard.

"You've really gone and disappointed me now," he said. "So this is what literature is all about? A bunch of wankers who stick pages together with their own sperm? Ha! It's enough to make you weep."

I didn't have the energy to listen to him any more but stared instead at the road while I was thinking about timber. Cubic metres and letters of credit and containers. People who inspected planed surfaces with a critical eye. Ilich yawned and said we ought to maybe think about spending the night in Caudal. I had no desire to stay at El Sultan de Oro and there was little likelihood of there being anywhere else to sleep around here so I dismissed the whole idea and said I wasn't tired at all and liked driving through the night, it gave me time to think.

"And you can sleep in the meanwhile," I said.

"Yup," he said. "That's what I am going to do. Cos I'm tired as fuck and drunk as a skunk."

His head drooped towards his shoulder and I thought for a moment he had fallen asleep. Then he stuck his thumb in the air.

"The whole thing went without a hitch. Thanks to you – it all went without a hitch. I owe you a huge fucking thank you, Don Rodrigo, a thank you as big as those bags hanging off Del Pozo's chops."

He laughed at his own phrase and belched loudly. A minute or so later and he was asleep.

I drove out of Caudal de la Ribera. The houses turned unnaturally white in the light of the headlamps; they whipped past us like vacant-eyed statues. As we drove out of the village I saw the club, which looked abandoned as well. Then we passed the church and I slowed down and inspected it more carefully. I was trying to make out whether the roof was new or if there were soot stains around the windows: anything to indicate there was an ounce of truth to Alba's story. Only it was too dark and I couldn't see anything. I felt a huge sense of relief when we finally left the village behind and drove out onto the main road.

I had the radio on for a while to stop myself falling asleep then I turned it off and drove in silence. We passed Cañaveruelas, Guadalajara, and continued on towards Zaragoza. There was almost no traffic on the road at that time of night, and the mountains of Aragon slipped past outside the car window: grey, mute and impregnable. I stopped at a lay-by for a while. I got out and sat on a bench. I just sat there with a cigarette in my hand, but it never occurred to me to light it. The moon had risen and was shining on the slopes of the mountains; their jagged edges cast grotesque shadows. Everything was utterly silent, and it all felt so dead. But the chill in the air was lovely and cool against the burnt skin of my face. I got out my mobile again and rang Encarnación's number but there was still no answer. I lit the cigarette and smoked it slowly; I could feel myself winding down and recapturing a certain calm. My thoughts wandered freely, and for some reason I happened to think about a hamster that Encarnación and I had bought right after we met. Apart from Bret, the dog who came on the scene a bit later, the hamster had been the only creature we'd had in common. We must have seemed odd when we arrived at the pet shop to buy it. Normally the people who buy hamsters have got kids. They buy the hamster because the kid keeps nagging them to. I got the feeling the shop owner thought we wanted it to feed to a snake because he gave us a searching look when he took it out of the cage. I couldn't be bothered denying anything, and we were given the hamster wrapped in a little yellow box with tiny balloons on. What are we going to call it? Encarnación asked on the way home in the car and I immediately thought we should give it a literary name like Orlando, Sancho or Julien Sorel. Then I thought that was ridiculous and suggested we call the hamster The Hamster. The first few weeks there was no smell from The Hamster. Then something happened. Presumably it became sexually mature and the acids in its urine were composed differently. After a few more months the urine had a strong smell. We cleaned out the cage every day and every morning the smell was back. He's marking out his territory with his piss, Encarnación said. But the smell of rotten Chinese food hit us in the face every time we came in the door to the flat. It's hard to believe the little bastard can make such a bloody stink, said Encarnación. One day she stepped on it. By mistake, she said. The Hamster had been out of the cage; she had forgotten she had let him out, and he had been scampering across the floor while she was carrying the laundry basket. By the time she felt that soft body being crushed under her foot, it was too late. The Hamster lay dead where she had stepped on it. I picked it up and the next day we drove out to Estrella del Mar where we planned to bury it. The whole thing felt pathetic. Encarnación kept repeating that it had been an accident, and I played along but I knew it had been no accident, because when we buried it and stood there in silence for a minute or two, we weren't the slightest bit sad, not even melancholy. We walked beside each other along the beach, a little like the couple from Salou I had seen when I was a child. We said not a word about The Hamster but talked instead about where we would go, what we would drink, and what a lovely evening it was. We talked solely about ourselves. Then we had a drink and forgot about The Hamster. And we have never mentioned him since.

The episode with The Hamster hadn't entirely robbed Encarnación of the desire to have a pet, however. It did cross my mind now and then that it might not really have been a pet she wanted when it came down to it, but a child. The animal would have been the first step, part of a gradual approach. I have always wanted a child myself (though not a pet) and I felt that if Encarnación's desire were given a chance to grow in peace and quiet we might one day arrive at that long-awaited moment when she announced she had stopped taking her pills. She might have been wanting to assure herself that there was someone suited to being a father within me before she got down to business. It wouldn't have been entirely unreasonable on her part to want to make sure. And so I was persuaded to accept the idea of having a dog. We were not very well off at that point and that was why I remembered the brothel (which I had only visited that one time), the one that had a kennel. I told Encarnación there was a kennel in Caudal and on my next visit to Del Pozo I could ask if they had a puppy to spare. Encarnación thought it was a good idea and said something as well about the genetic superiority of the fortunate cross-breed over the pedigreed animal. So the next time I drove to Caudal I stopped at the brothel again. I entered the place and found myself in the same musty room with the red sofas where I'd been the first time. The woman with the crescent-shaped mouth was once again at the register. Hello, she said. I see you've come back. That startled me a bit because it would have been several years since I visited them. I had no idea anyone would remember me, I said. It was so long ago after all. Wasn't it — — you saw? (At this point she said a woman's name I no longer recall.) I can see she's free now as well, she said then with a smile. Would you like to have her? I shook my head. No thanks, I said. I'm not here on that sort of errand this time. I'm looking for a dog. The woman looked quizzically at me. A dog? Yes, I've promised my wife a puppy. I was going to ask you if you had any you didn't . . . need? The woman stared at me for several moments; then she shut the register with a bang. Of course we do, Mr Auscias. We've got everything you could ever want in this place. Girls, drinks, cold cuts, a sympathetic ear or a sofa to sit on. Even dogs. We've got it all. She walked straight-backed along the corridor, which was flanked by a row of rooms with numbers mounted on the doors. I walked behind her. I had been thinking of a bitch, I said. My wife would prefer a bitch. They're said to be calmer and more receptive. That was when she came to a halt. We don't have any bitches, she said. There are only women here, and no bitches.

She stood there in silence for a bit before she went on:

"The dogs are all male. Bitches are not something we provide."

I wondered how they could have puppies when they didn't have any bitches. But when she opened the door to the kennel I realised that any notion of puppies was wide of the mark. A bunch of shaggy curs were throwing themselves raucously against the fence. A few younger dogs were pacing rather nervously to and fro behind them. I remembered what the woman I'd spent the night with the first time I was here had told me. We've got a kennel and the dogs in it are all named after famous male writers, she had said. Whenever some guy pays us a visit and is nasty to us, we give the dogs rotten meat. I couldn't help laughing at the whole idea at the time. Passive rebellion is what they call that, I informed her. When you're powerless, *passive* rebellion is what you come up with. It's also called projection. You make the dogs suffer for what the men have done to you because the dogs are weaker than you. It's like a father who abuses his children because the factory owner has forced him to work too hard. It's not a very nice thing to do. Pretty despicable really. That's what you think, is it? she said. It's just we've got to have somewhere to vent our anger too. Of course you do, I said and didn't know what to say next. Only where did you get the idea from? I asked. We had a visit from this feminist once, she said then. An intellectual feminist from the city. She wore high heels and smelled chic. She had these long conversations with us, one on one to begin with, and then with all of us together. She said she wanted to help us, though the truth is she looked down on us. She talked about the power of language; she told us that language had been created by men and that we didn't have a language of our own and if we were going to learn our own language, first we had to learn to talk theirs fluently. We just sat there listening to her. So tell me about yourselves, she said, and she used to look sternly at us over the rim of her glasses while she talked. I'm completely fucking appalled that you're all so bloody ignorant about everything, she said in the end as she stuffed her fountain pen into its case. She had realised there was nothing to be done, not for us and not about the club or the men who visited it, and she was thinking she had been casting pearls before swine in coming here (though perhaps you'd have to say sows). We hadn't turned out to be the kind of people who could serve as research material for her report, not by a long way. She furrowed her brow gloomily while she was collecting her papers and was about to set off home again. Only on the way out she caught sight of the kennel. What are the dogs called? she asked. They don't have names, we said. They're just called The Dogs. Alright then, she said. So let's get something done here in any case. We can make a start with the little things. Even though you can't leave this place and break free, we can start small and work with what we've got. Passive aggression – that's the term for what we're going to do now. We're going to call this little pup Dante. Let's call the mangy old cur over there Chaucer. The canary bird hanging on the wall is going to be known as Harold Bloom. She had a good laugh then and wrote out these little name tags she handed to us. Put them on their collars, she said, before jumping into her car with a chuckle and driving out onto the main road. She left us there with the bits of paper and the dogs. We didn't like the idea at all to begin with. But all the same every time we got a new dog we tried to come up with the name of a male author. It turned into a way to entertain ourselves. Only we didn't know the names of that many male authors. Not male ones or female ones for that matter. Anyway some of our clients are readers and they help us out from time to time.

The woman from reception was standing there with her hand raised towards the dogs.

"You can take that one," she said pointing at a grey dog. "He's called Bret. Bret Easton Ellis. Named after a book someone found one morning on the bedside table."

I picked up Bret Easton Ellis, packed him into a box in the car and drove home to Encarnación. I honestly believe we have made a proper dog of him now, I was thinking as I sat there in the night.

I had finished smoking my cigarette. I chucked the stub on the ground and got back into the car.

We had passed Zaragoza when Ilich woke up. He had a stretch and then just sat there for a while looking out the window; he lit a cigarette and had a smoke and wasn't bothered that I was coughing pointedly beside him.

"What a fucking dump," he said.

"Which one?" I asked.

"Caudal de la Ribera," Ilich said. "And what a fucking asshole that Del Pozo is."

"I thought you liked each other," I said.

"He wanted us to spend the night at that club. 'The best club for swingers in the country', he said. He said they were about to close and it was now or never. He talked about all the fine whores they had working there. The average age was like forty-eight but it was top-notch stuff."

He laughed. I said nothing.

"It's just I've been to quite a few clubs like that," he went on to say. "They're fucking revolting. All these men walking round with shaggy nipples and the women are so past their sell-by date it's enough to make you cry."

"So what were you doing at that kind of club, seeing as you find them so unpleasant?" I asked.

Ilich looked out the window. Then he told me about a film he had seen once about a man suffering from extreme starvation. He had been walking round the streets of some city, emaciated and all but unconscious, crawling along the walls like the living dead. Then he had come to a butcher's. Give me a bit of meat, he had begged, I am starving. Just give me a bit of meat. The butcher had laughed at him, and so had everyone else in the butcher's shop. In the end he had been given a bag. He had gone into an alleyway and opened it. The bag had scraps in it and a rancid smell was coming off them. It's rotten, the man had time to think before hunger overwhelmed him. He started eating the meat, he couldn't help gulping it down, feeling it move around his mouth and then down his gullet. He suppressed the waves of nausea, and ate more. The rotten meat made him feel like shit, Ilich said. It made him vomit. But he couldn't stop eating it, that's how hungry he was.

Ilich took off his shoes and put his feet up on the dashboard.

"Only you know what I think sometimes?" he asked. "The best fucks you ever have are the ones you have with yourself."

"Okay?" I said.

"I mean you never get to fuck the way you can in your imagination."

"Do you have to say fuck the whole time?" I said.

"What else am I supposed to say?"

"I don't know. Make love maybe. Or have sex."

"That's not the same," Ilich said. "That's not the same thing at all, Don Rodrigo. What I was trying to say is that the best fucks I've had are the ones I've had in my mind. There's no smell of bodies, and everyone is perfect. You can fuck people's wives in there and people's waitresses, and if you want to you can fuck all the ones who are fucking other people's wives and maids as well."

"Is that something you usually do?" I said.

"What?"

"Fuck other men, in your imagination?"

"Yeah, that's something I do," said Ilich. "Do you want to try it out?"

"In fantasy?" I said.

"Or in real life?" Ilich said.

"Give it a rest, for Christ's sake," I said,

We drove on for a bit. Suddenly Ilich said:

"Sorry."

"What?" I asked.

"I'm provoking you."

All of a sudden I felt deadly tired.

"I'm not with you," I said.

"Don't play dumb," Ilich said. "I'm trying to be unpleasant to you, to make the trip unpleasant for you. Only when I think about it, I can't understand why, because I really only want to make you feel good. You've done more for me than anyone else has in a long time. You believed in me, you took me to see your contact in the timber industry and did your best to see that I got a job. You get kudos for that, because there's no one else who'd do something like that for me."

I cleared my throat.

"Not to put too fine a point on it, but you did have a hold over me," I said.

It wasn't that I had any desire to diminish what I had done for Ilich, but it would have been pathetic to sit there and just pretend I had done what I had done out of some general feeling of charity or from a desire to come to the rescue of people like him. But Ilich took no notice.

"Fuck it, Rodrigo," he said. "I really do want to make you feel good. I want to make you feel really fucking happy, Rodrigo. As thanks for being such a great old guy."

"Old guy?" I said.

"Gentleman," Ilich corrected himself and pinched my cheek. "As thanks for being such a stand-up older gentleman. I've just got to come up with something. Let me think about it."

He looked out the window for a bit, and I thought that might be the right moment to suggest he erase the bloody film from his mobile. But my throat felt clogged and I didn't dare say anything because even though I didn't know Ilich that well I felt it was safe to conclude he was the kind of person who goes for the jugular at the first sign of uncertainty. You have to possess everything with some people. Walk down the street and think: I own all of this, you too, so keep your trap shut or you won't know what hit you.

"I just thought of it!" Ilich exclaimed. "Now I know how to make you really fucking happy, Don Rodrigo."

"Oh yes?" I said.

He moved to put his back against the window and looked at me with a broad smile across his face.

"Alba said you're a literary person. You like reading, you run study groups for young people and you believe that people are improved by reading. It makes you happy when people read books. Doesn't it?"

I squirmed.

"I don't know about happy exactly," I said. "It's true though that I think it's a good thing for young people to read good literature. It gets them to see a different side of things and . . . "

"Exactly," Ilich said. "You are an altruist, someone who cares about people and you want them to be happy and well-read and content. So I am going to read a book."

He smiled as though he had said he was going to give me a million or a house on the beach.

"Ilich," I began. "In all seriousness, I really couldn't care less whether you . . . "

"Say a book I should read," he said. "You can choose it, Don Rodrigo. Only don't pick one that's too thick because I'll never read it to the end if you do. And not one of those wanking books either like the one you've got in the glove compartment. A book that's just the right thinness and one that's really good. And I will read it for your sake, and I will read it slowly when everything is quiet around me so each word will sort of sink in and put forth lovely little buds in this ignorant head of mine."

He laughed, pleased with his phrase. I did some thinking for a bit.

"*The Old Man and the Sea*," I said then.

"*The Old Man and the Sea*," Ilich repeated.

The old man and the sea, he said as though he had never

heard the title before and needed to make an effort to commit it to memory. And then:

"The old man, that's you, is it?"

We drove on through the darkness. I was thinking about Encarnación. Ilich took his socks off. He crumpled them into rags and rubbed them between his toes. Little flakes of skin rained down on the dashboard. I opened the window a smidgen to allow the chill night air to enter the car. The revulsion I had started feeling for Ilich, for all of him, was only adding fuel to the longing I was feeling for Encarnación. I could see her before me, remote and focused, the way she would be sitting there with her crossword. There was something beautiful about her detachment. It may not have been that easily perceived, not by a stranger in any case and not even by someone like me who had lived with her so closely for many years, because it was more as though she were simply being elusive and quiet when you first encountered it. But if you were where I was, driving through the Aragonese night with mountains on all sides and everything feeling so desolate and stark, and with someone like Ilich beside you, it was as though that image of Encarnación completely enclosed in her own world was the only clear and logical response to it all. The world wasn't something you could be turned towards. You had to turn away from it. *Sauve qui peut*, as it were. There might be lots of wonderful things out there, you might want to bring up beauty, say; not to believe in beauty would be idiotic in the circumstances: all you had to do was look out the window from where I was sitting right this moment. It's just that it ends up jumbled together; you can never separate out the different layers and that kind of beauty can never remain intact. The mountains could be where they are and you could be on a bench at night bathing in the moonlight with the smoke from your cigarette slowly dissipating in front of you. You might have a sense of being in balance with everything around you and you might feel that power that comes from solitude, silence and beauty, but you will still think of a hamster that smelled of rotting Chinese food and there will still be someone like Ilich in the car only a few metres away, someone who has barely even read a single book and who has a film on his mobile in which you are playing a porn star and who will soon be cleaning the spaces between his toes with a smelly sock. Everything is so undistilled that you can never get a proper grip around whatever the essence might be; it slips away from you and gets diluted with other fluids, like water, or urine. But not Encarnación. Not Encarnación. Just let me get home, I kept thinking. Home to Encarnación. I had to acknowledge she was right in her theories about humanity. Her pessimism was the only conceivable viewpoint. I might even be able to tell her about it. About everything that had happened, about Alba and Ilich. She would forgive me my infidelity if she understood that I regretted it. Did I regret it? Yes, I did. Nothing I had gained from it had been worth what I had sacrificed. What had I in fact sacrificed? A day with Ilich in Caudal? What else? Having the runs on a couple of mornings? Was that a sacrifice? Wasn't that something you could offer up for someone else? For Alba? For Ilich? I felt slightly cheered by the thought. I've just got to finish this now, I thought. Put a full stop after the last letter and then lick the seal on the envelope. One last effort and it will all be over.

"Ilich," I said. "Have you got a girlfriend?"

He looked at me in astonishment.

"Of course I have," he said. "I've got Alba, haven't I?"

"I see," I said. "It's just the two of you didn't really strike me that way."

"How do you mean?"

"Like a couple."

"Well we are," Ilich said. "We're just taking a break. The sex between us is good. We'll get together again."

We sat in silence for a while.

"Ilich," I said then. "Leave Alba alone."

"What?" he asked.

"Just leave her be," I said. "The fact that it has been good as you said doesn't mean anything. Real love is quite different."

"Oh, and that's something you're an expert on, is it, Don Rodrigo?" Ilich said contemptuously. "The man who goes in for threesomes while his wife stays at home and does the crossword. And who ends up in a film he has to get rid of so she won't leave him if she ever sees it. Is that what you call real love?"

I felt incredibly tired but managed nevertheless to stay calm and say, "That's right, the film, the one you were supposed to get rid of now that I've helped you."

"Right, I will," Ilich said and got his mobile out.

He was busy pushing buttons.

"That's it. It's gone," he said then.

"Thanks."

I didn't have the energy to wonder if the film really was gone; I gave myself the benefit of simply trusting him.

"No, thank you," Ilich said. "I can't thank you enough. I'd never have got this chance without you. Sorry about having to use the film but I'd never have got anywhere without it."

We looked at one another for a moment. I thought there was something in the way he was looking at me, something honest maybe.

"People don't help someone like me, not unless you put them under a bit of pressure," Ilich said.

"In any case I hope the pressure is off for good as far as I am concerned," I said. "The whole thing has been making me feel pretty ill."

Ilich laughed.

"So *the whole thing has been making you feel pretty ill*, has it? You're fucking priceless, Don Rodrigo. The whole thing has been making you feel pretty ill. Good thing it's over then, and you can go home to the little woman and to real love."

Before we got to Barcelona I had told him again that he should let Alba alone, and Ilich said he would think about it, maybe she wasn't his type in any case. I dropped him off in front of a large grey apartment building.

"We'll be in touch," he said as he got out of the car. "I'll take you out for a beer to say thanks."

"Not at all," I said.

Ilich banged on the car with his hand, and then he got a key out of his pocket and went in the entrance.

"And I will read *The Old Man and the Sea*!" he yelled. "I'll ring you afterwards and tell you what I think."

I put the car in gear and drove home.

It was almost morning of the following day by the time I made my way into our hall. A soft dawn light was stealing into the flat. Everything was silent. I closed the door behind me, I put my briefcase on the floor and then I stood there in the hall and just savoured the feeling of being home. I looked at myself in the same mirror I had looked at myself in a few weeks earlier, before leaving for dinner at Alba Cambó's. I had looked far too proper at the time and that image of myself had irritated me. The man I was seeing now looked entirely different. My hair was anything but neat and lay in damp, frayed wisps across the crown of my head and there was less of it, or so it seemed to me. I was white in the face. It looked like I had got thinner as well; my head seemed big in relation to my shoulders. My shirt was dirty; I was dirty all over. My trousers looked too long or badly hemmed and they were filthy too, as if everything had been coated in a film of dust from the road.

I took a look around the flat. Everything was as usual. Spotless and neat like no one had been living there since I left home. Encarnación's little chair and table were on the terrace with a pile of newspapers and pencils. There was a scent of Encarnación in the flat, a blend of her skin and the perfume she usually wore. What perfume does she usually wear? I asked myself. I didn't even know what perfume my own wife put on. I've got a long way to go, I thought. Might as well start now. Things go in cycles, you go down but then you come up again. You hit a thermal and the upwards motion is completely natural. I am just going to sleep. Just sleep. Then I will start afresh, and everything is going to be fine. I lay down beside Encarnación in the bed. She was lying with her back towards me and her breathing was calm and regular. I fell asleep with my arm around her and I felt the warmth of her back against my chest.

Over the next few months I forgot almost entirely about Ilich. I was in regular contact with Del Pozo, but Ilich was never mentioned. I didn't hear from Alba either, and I presumed she was happy and didn't need me for anything. As for Ilich, I assumed that was how people like him behaved. Their lives happen to them in waves; they mosey along as best they can, doing this for a bit, and then that for a while. They are not the kind of people who tackle things head-on, who eventually manage to really find a rhythm and a constancy in what they do.

Some of the rumours circulating among us timber agents were rather worrying. In terms of both the general state of the economy, which was on the downturn with cuts being made everywhere, and the pressures being exerted on the market by Europe, and by the Chinese. There was a long feature in the trade magazine on how to survive as an "intermediary" (a word I loathe: it deprives you of any justification for your existence), and how a stitch in time will help you grow stronger. The gist of the whole piece was you have to accelerate and slow down at the same time, to put your house in order and make sure you are protected by healthy finances and a good skill set, the usual platitudes you hear when money is tight and everyone's trying to get by as best they can. Over the phone Del Pozo confided in me that he had plans to expand: he was developing strategies to "break the competition down into separate molecules". I tried to get him to understand that my imports of ethically sourced timber were well placed to stave off the competition and that they provided added value, which was a positive factor in times like these. I thought everything I said sounded hollow, but I reiterated that my goods were transported on trucks fuelled by sunflower oil and that I only traded with countries that worked with the motto "a new tree is planted for every one felled". I talked about the importance of standing out from the crowd and that this could be achieved by creating a strong ethical brand; in this way, the distribution chain in our land would appear "ethical" as well. Del Pozo sounded positive, he chuckled and said people like me really were really essential, and even though my goods were a tiny bit more expensive that was offset by the fact that when he bought from me he could sleep like a baby, a clear conscience was the best pillow you could have. He insisted that he flew the flag for my products whenever he got the chance – I was his environmental badge of honour. But no orders arrived. Normally one fax would rustle in every month from one of his secretaries, and these were often fairly large deliveries, several hundred cubic metres, frequently with a high reprocessing value as the countries in northern Europe have chains that can produce practically anything from bedsteads to carved chair legs and a whole load of other things you can sell at whatever DIY centre you choose. I rang him several times but it was the same old song on each occasion: I had all the cred in the trade anyone could want, and if I asked straight out why didn't he put in an order in that case, he would reply that he had something on the go and that one of these days Milagros would be sending over a fax.

The feeling that Encarnación was the one pure and unsullied thing in my world persisted; it wasn't transient and it wasn't dulled by resting, eating, and spending time together, the way I expected it would be. Something still caught in my throat when I looked at her and I used to take my computer with me into the sitting room so I could watch her sitting on the terrace. For long periods I did no work at all but just sat there watching her; I know it sounds silly, but it was as if I was getting a proper look at exactly what I loved about my wife for the first time. She seemed so impregnable. Unattainable. Only how could she be unattainable, it would sometimes occur to me, she's my wife after all. But even though she was always perfectly amiable towards me (we even made love to one another on a few occasions), I couldn't help getting that impression of unattainability. She does love me, I had to repeat to myself sometimes. Of course she loves me, she definitely does, I can feel utterly calm about her love; everything is the way it's supposed to be and all is well.

But despite the fact that we were physically close and despite the fact that after fifteen years of marriage my love had suddenly started to grow stronger than ever, the silence between us was growing as well. It was as if we had been distilling certain aspects of ourselves that were now becoming dominant – I became increasingly fixated on getting the business back on its feet, and she was slipping more and more inside herself. We spent our days in entirely different spheres as a result, which meant we found ourselves faced with a void whenever we tried to find things in common to talk about. There were suppers when we conversed only in monosyllables about entirely trivial matters. Something we had read in the paper, or heard on the radio, repetitions of an already repeated recycling of uninteresting news. Increasingly, Encarnación began to withdraw inside the flat as well. On some days she didn't even open the terrace doors but stayed inside her bedroom, lying on a mattress, surrounded by a sea of ashtrays, cigarette packs, books, newspapers, records and dirty wine glasses. The wine glasses worried me and I always picked them up and took them out into the kitchen and put them in the dishwasher or I washed them up by hand and dried them and then put them back in the cupboard. I didn't like the air of decay it lent the whole apartment when you got up on a Monday morning to see a half-empty bottle on the dining table and then a knocked-over glass beside Encarnación's bed, stained with dark spots from the tannins and smeared with lipstick. Encarnación had always been a very tidy woman, but something was clearly changing.

And all that was just the beginning. Soon she was asking me not just to buy wine for dinner but stronger drinks as well, "to help pass the time". I asked how things were going with her crosswords, and she just stared at me as though she had never solved a crossword puzzle in her life; then she said that that period was over. I talked to a friend about it. I told him about the onset of her drinking habit and how she had suddenly stopped doing the crosswords she had previously devoted almost all her spare time to, and he replied that that had to be a pretty positive development, didn't it? What with Encarnación no longer staring at boxed-in letters like a pupa in its cocoon for days on end? Wasn't she actually doing something different and showing signs of wanting to spread her wings and really start living? The same friend thought I was setting too much store by her drinking habit, in his view a few glasses every now and then couldn't really hurt. Encarnación hasn't had problems with drinking before, has she, she doesn't seem like the type, he said. Have a glass along with her, and relax a bit, try and forget your business worries, he counselled me.

I remember one dreadful day right about that time. I was supposed to visit some potential customers in Lleida, and Encarnación was also going to be gone for the day to visit a girlfriend in Girona and needed a car. I was happy she was actually going to be doing something, getting out of the flat and out of the city, so I went off to hire a car for myself from the rental company so she could take ours. Encarnación left home a bit before me. I got myself ready, did a bit of tidying up in the flat and then went downstairs and got in the car I had rented. I started driving towards the motorway; the traffic was heavy at that time of morning and I had to stop at almost every traffic light. At one of them I thought I saw someone I knew out of the corner of my eye. I turned my head and saw that the person sitting in the car alongside me was sobbing. I was able to make out the heartbreaking shape of a person weeping floods of tears before I realised who it was. A woman is crying in the car alongside me was the thought that suddenly flickered across my brain. Then I grasped the incomprehensible: the woman in the car was Encarnación. She was crying so hard snot was running down her face, and I could see it hanging in a long strand from her upper lip down over her chin and towards her chest. Her face was crumpled in a spasm, squeezing out the tears. They ran across her face, which was pulpy and red. She had both hands on the upper part of the steering wheel and was resting her forehead against them as she sobbed. I had never seen her cry that way; I don't think I had ever seen anyone cry like that. It felt as if the blood had stopped flowing through my veins. I managed to remain sufficiently cool-headed to put the car in gear when the light turned green, and then accelerate and drive off. I stopped in the next lay-by for buses. I sat there for a long time, trying to get myself under control. That evening I wanted to ask her why she had been crying in the car but I had no idea how to ask the question; coming across her in the midst of her pain felt like an intrusion. So I said nothing, but that image of her remains burnt into my brain and hurts as much now, talking about it, as it did then.

The insight I would have needed to make at that moment was no doubt too huge and too painful for me to get anywhere near it. Because what Encarnación was making clear in the car was that she was deeply unhappy and maybe she wasn't driving to see a girlfriend at all but could even have been on her way to kill herself. The idea didn't occur to me then, only now when I look back and understand everything more clearly, her courage must have failed her. I get goosebumps whenever I think about that. It may have been out of some kind of crass instinct for self-preservation that I looked the other way, like someone standing on the edge of a cliff looking in the wrong direction, I just don't know.

I tried to hold on to something. Instead of turning everything upside down I took her drinking habit with a pinch of salt and decided to join her (perhaps that episode of hers in the car had been the result of loneliness?). And slowly we established a new routine. When I stopped work each evening at seven, I went into the kitchen and uncorked a bottle of chilled white wine or cava, knocked on the door to her room and held out the glass to her and then she would look up and smile at me and her smile was entirely genuine. We sat on the sofa and under the influence of the alcohol we talked about the day that had passed, what we had done in our respective spheres, and all I can say is that we were happy then or at least that is how it felt. We talked and talked, about what we had said and written and who we had been working with and how things had gone in general, and all the while we kept drinking and feeling increasingly exhilarated. If we occasionally reminded ourselves that we had actually been drinking on the sofa for the fourth evening in a row, even if it was only a quiet and harmless tipple, we would immediately come up with the excuse that in our case all the alcohol did was serve as a dividing line between what was hard work and our own private world. We needed that gilded boundary in the shape of cava or a viscous Martini in order to feel we were entering a different realm. And after we had said that, we might stagger for a bit between the stove and the kitchen table and on to the fridge to get out the Martini bottle and then on to the freezer to get out more ice and pour in more Martini.

Eventually I found it difficult to wake up in the mornings, so I scaled back my consumption, and you can't turn up at clients with your breath smelling of old dog, but Encarnación kept at it. Once I had got out of the habit of drinking, or was at least drinking more moderately than we had been doing, it became easier to see that her drinking no longer marked that subtle dividing line between work and private life but was something else, something more profound, which could no longer be ignored. I confronted her about it and the answer I got was yes, of course – it wasn't any longer about a dividing line or another glass for the cook but was an inevitable consequence of that old familiar pain of just being alive.

"What?" I said.

Her cheeks lushly covered in roses, she said with a smile that she drank to make herself happy. It was simply an attempt to have a break from the pain of living and a bit of fresh air in the shape of pure joy wasn't really anything I could reproach her with, was it?

"Of course not," I replied. "You're just drinking to make yourself feel happy, the way people who drink do. Cheers, Encarnación."

As I recall the bottles we bought were always expensive and I kept them out of sight of whatever friends and acquaintances came to pay us a visit. I suppose that was an attempt to hide our distress.

In any case the inevitable occurred one day. Because "one for the cook" or "the medicine against the pain of living" or whatever we chose to call it had shifted further and further away from dinner and sometimes started as early as the morning. That remoteness of hers I had found so attractive started to disappear a little, some days she went out several times, in the morning to buy bread and the paper and in the afternoon to walk around window-shopping. Once she was supposed to do the shopping after the siesta and went off to Mercadona where she had some difficulty walking along the aisles. One of the neighbours had seen her. So soon the entire staircase was talking about Encarnación wobbling around the store, reeking of cirrhosis. I made no bones about confronting Encarnación and said she was getting a reputation as an alky and it was dragging us down, all the respect we had spent so much time acquiring would be totally lost if we continued like this. She put her hand on my shoulder at that point as though she was trying to calm me, called me darling, and then told me it was like Leonard Cohen says, that we're all cracked, that each one of us is broken in some way or another, that light enters through our flaws.

I nodded and looked away. I felt offended. She was glossing song lyrics, easily digested and universally applicable lines, sufficiently universal, I supposed that even a stranger outside that bubble of hers could understand them.

"But what if that crack gets deeper?" I said. "What about if it gets so wide you can see the shape of something straight out of a nightmare?"

"Cheers, Rodrigo," was her reply.

I toasted her back and kept on refusing to take seriously the onset of that nightmare vision. I kept on working long hours; I continued accepting her habits. Because where exactly, I asked myself rhetorically once again, does the dividing line run between a glass of wine for the chef, a glass of wine with food, and alcoholism pure and simple?

For several weeks we felt acutely embarrassed whenever we took the rubbish out, but then Encarnación stopped going shopping or showing herself to the neighbours in any way at all. As her introversion had now become absolute, that episode was over and done with for the most part. But some aspect of it lingered on all the same, a kind of festering pus that made our lives feel stagnant.

In any case one day I asked her, just like that and without any fuss, to stop drinking and to behave decently. She had a dreadful fit of rage in response. She was standing in front of me on the sitting-room floor; behind her were the suite of sofas and the potted plants we had placed in the various corners.

"Where is the poetry in you, for Christ's sake?" she shouted. "You behave as if you were a motorway whose only function is to connect point A and point B."

She probably didn't put it like that exactly, they may not have been her very words, she may not have used the complex construction "whose only function is" but that was the gist of her outburst in any case. She also said that all the sympathetic people she had ever known had died of an overdose of heroin.

"So all the sympathetic people you know have died of an overdose of heroin, have they?" I shouted back.

She nodded stubbornly.

"So give me one example then," I said. "Give me one example of a single sympathetic person in your world who died of an overdose of heroin."

She hesitated, but after a while she said that was how Robinson Jeffers had died.

"Robinson Jeffers!" I yelled. "Robinson Jeffers! First I doubt whether Robinson Jeffers died of a heroin overdose. Second he is a writer, and dead. You never knew him."

"I did know him," Encarnación shouted. "I have never known anyone as well as I know Robinson Jeffers."

We continued to shout at each other for a long time, while being stared at by the furniture surrounding us. The gilt handles of the doors were gleaming in the evening sunshine and it was if they were promising us they would continue to exist there for many decades to come. They were, of course, completely indifferent to whether we continued to live there or not.

One day in May I was telephoned by Alba Cambó.

"Hi," she said sounding cheerful. "It's been ages."

"Hasn't it," I replied. "How are you doing?"

"Good," she responded. "Summer's here."

I replied that yes it was. I asked what she had been doing of late.

"Loads of things. I've moved and I've been travelling."

"Where?"

"To Italy."

She had been to Italy for several weeks and got to know a former actor, and they had fallen in love and he had just moved in with her.

"What about Ilich?" I asked.

"I haven't heard from him," Alba said. "I think he's met someone else."

"That's good," I said.

"Yes," she said.

There was silence for a while at the other end.

"Do you want to meet up?" she said then. "Maybe we could get a room at a hotel for an afternoon? Just to chill?"

I laughed.

"What about your Italian?"

"Not with him there. He'll have to stay at home."

"And do the dishes I suppose?"

"That's right," she laughed. "Do the dishes. That would serve him right. I gave up Blosom for him. I had Blosom, who was a friend and who helped me here at home besides, and I swapped her for Valentino who just lies on the sofa like a bag of dead meat and never lifts a finger."

"How silly of you, Alba," I said ironically. "It was silly to make a sacrifice like that for love."

"Wasn't it," she laughed again. "Anyway I just happened to think of you. Do you want to come and rescue me for a couple of hours?"

I sighed.

"No," I replied. "I don't do that kind of thing any more."

"Whoops," she said. "Have you gone and got religion?"

"It's not that. But I'm fighting to save my marriage. You know. My wife. Encarnación."

"The crossword solver?"

The crossword solver? Had I referred to her that way?

"Or my wife, as she also happens to be," I said.

"Okay," said Alba. "I get it. It's just that I want you to know how grateful I am for everything you have done for me. I got you involved in that business with Ilich. That could have turned out badly but it didn't."

"We had a bit of luck," I said.

"Not luck," she said. "Skill, patience and love. On your part."

I assumed that was a compliment but I felt disturbed by her remark.

"I really don't know," I said. "I've really no idea, Alba. I just feel I have to get . . . "

There was a pause.

"What?" she asked.

"I really haven't a clue," I said. "I just don't know. But I'd like to hang up now as long as it doesn't upset you."

"Okay. Keep well. We'll be in touch."

We hung up. I think I heaved a sigh of relief, thinking that would be the last time I heard from her.

I made one final attempt to rebuild things with Encarnación a few days before Ilich came back on the scene. In retrospect that attempt feels patently ludicrous, which is the way of things when you look back and are forced to confront your own unremitting naivety, even though you realise perfectly well that feelings of dismay may be a sign that you've evolved to some extent, that you can look back at yourself and think, Rodrigo, how gullible and romantic you were then. Only what are you supposed to do with that insight? It's all too late anyway, and the insight is about as useful as a dead person winning the lottery.

I was thinking: I'll buy her some roses. Red roses are romantic, maybe a bit old-fashioned and overly traditional, but why not, aren't they beautiful as well? I walked down to the florist's and bought red roses for my wife, and the man who tied them together winked at me and said that roses were still the best bet if you were trying to seduce a woman.

"That's right," I said.

I went back up to the flat with the roses, handed them to Encarnación who said how happy she was to be given them, they were gorgeous, it must have been years since she was last given red roses by anyone. She put them in a large vase and walked round with them for a while to find the right place. Finally she plumped for a spot outside on the terrace, in a corner, perhaps the least visible point in the entire apartment. I said, and presumably I couldn't hide my disappointment, that I had been picturing them blazing red and free beside her as she was sitting on the terrace doing her crossword puzzles (as if a fissure to the past might suddenly open and we could just slip into it and find our way back), that was what I had in mind when I bought them, I said, and that she would want to keep them close to her as a reminder that her husband loved her and that that was something she would want to be reminded of almost all the time.

"Too much sun," she said.

The same night I dreamed about Ilich when he told me about the man who ate the rotting meat. I could hear it clear as a bell in my dream, the whole story from the very beginning, the man who ate the rotting meat and had to force it into his mouth. I woke up in a sweat, I got up and brushed my teeth, and then I went back to bed and had a vision of that man again, standing in front of the butcher's shop digging into the bag of meat scraps he was holding with emaciated fingers, his eyes ravenous. The next morning I felt so dejected that I looked up the number for a psychologist. I got an appointment a few days later and met with a kindly man who listened to me while sitting in a chair opposite. I told him about all the ideas that had been spinning round inside me like clothes in a tumble dryer run amok: about what Ilich had told me of the fifty-year curse, about Del Pozo, about the starving man and his bag of scraps and about the swingers' club. I also told him about the roses and the alcohol, and I could hear how confused and disconnected it all sounded but I went on, nevertheless, to describe how I was starting to feel downright panic more and more frequently. Then I said, maybe to remove the sting of how dramatic it might have sounded to the psychologist (although you imagine a psychologist has actually heard it all, you can be overcome with shame when you openly reveal your confusion) that I was surprised by how familiar I was with the feeling of panic, it was as if I had always carried it around inside me waiting for it to blossom and take over, and it was almost a relief that it had become as pronounced as it had. And it was odd that I knew it so well because I had never really experienced any particular feelings of anxiety previously, I said. Nor could it be said that I had been exposed to any significant trauma. The psychologist said nothing, and I kept on talking. I said that my astonishment went deeper than that. It happened, for instance, that some nights when I lay awake I became convinced I knew exactly what it would be like to die. I could see the flicker of accident scenes, scenes I couldn't remember seeing in real life but that were now perfectly clear. And as I was lying there trying to fall asleep I might also see objects rushing towards me at high speed in the semi-darkness. The psychologist then asked what kind of objects they were and I said that sometimes they were pieces of metal, and at other times rocks and gravel and sometimes they were . . . pieces of flesh. The psychologist made notes and nodded.

When he looked up afterwards, he said that wasn't something to be surprised about at all because the sense of danger and death was an ancient inheritance inside every human being.

"A bit like imagining we have a collective memory card in our spines," he said.

It was logical, he went on, to think that natural selection was based on the principle that those who felt panic, a fear of death, and had sufficient imagination to sense danger at an early stage, were the most likely to survive because they were more inclined to avoid life-threatening situations in a natural environment. All the good-natured and gullible ones who watched the sunsets in silence had been devoured by sabre-toothed tigers long ago. That's one explanation for anxiety and how inheriting it could serve the surviving sections of humanity.

Once he had said this, he looked down at his papers for a long time. I was waiting for him to say something else, for him to relate the collective aspect he had been talking about to my own situation as an individual, but he didn't. Instead he let another minute pass and then looked at the clock and said that the session was over for today.

Three months passed between leaving Ilich outside his building on the outskirts of Barcelona and meeting him again, this time in my own sitting room. I had been on a visit to a client in Ciudad Real for the day; it had been hot and I was longing for a cool shower and a cold beer. I remember entering the hall we shared and how I could feel that something was different the moment I came in. There was no stuffy smell. The shoes were neatly arranged. Encarnación's thin poplin coat had not been thrown on the footstool but had been put on a hanger. I let the door slide shut behind me and pricked up my ears to anything going on in the flat. There was the sound of soft murmurs. I took off my shoes and put them in a row with the others. Then I went into the guest toilet and took off my shirt. It was clean and tidy in there too. I washed my armpits, hands and face. I went into the kitchen and poured water from the fridge into a glass. Then I moved into the sitting room and there they were: Encarnación and Ilich. Sitting opposite one another in the armchairs, and with glasses of mineral water in front of them. Bret was sleeping at Encarnación's feet. Everything around them was clean and neat. None of the signs of the sloppiness of the last few months were visible in the room. There were no empty wineglasses anywhere. Even the television screen was free of dust. Encarnación gestured towards the sofa.

"Have a seat," she said. "You must have had an exhausting day. Your friend Ilich dropped by."

I looked at Ilich and he was holding his hands in front of him as though in apology. I could feel my guts clenching. Was he here to show Encarnación the film? Had he already done so? Was the die already cast and had disaster struck? I drank my water and looked from Ilich to Encarnación, trying to work out exactly what had happened before I came through the door. It was impossible. Their faces gave nothing away; instead they were looking at me with friendly and open smiles I could not understand at all.

"I just happened to be passing," Ilich said. "I thought I'd look you up just to say hello. And to let you know about the book I read."

He leant forward and picked up a book off the table, holding it out to me the way an umpire holds up a red card to a player at a football match. *The Old Man and the Sea.*

"Right," I said and looked at Encarnación.

"I was having a sleep when Ilich arrived," she said. "Only of course I'd forgotten to lock the door."

She rolled up her eyes at being so scatterbrained.

"So Ilich came in. And guess what he did?"

"What did he do?" I asked.

She looked at me as secretively as a seven-year-old, before exclaiming:

"He did the cleaning!"

I leant back in the armchair. I stared at Ilich.

"You did the cleaning?" I said. "*Here*?"

"I just thought," Ilich began, "someone must be lying down having a sleep. Maybe Don Rodrigo, and if not Don Rodrigo then Rodrigo's lovely wife."

He winked at Encarnación who laughed out loud.

"So I started picking things up. Putting things to rights. And begging your pardon, Rodrigo, but the place looked bloody awful. Like a pigsty. You ought to have got someone in to give your wife a hand. If she is suffering from depression like she just confided in me then she shouldn't have to deal with all the crap. A husband ought to take better care of his wife, if he really loves her that is."

He sounded like he was giving me a lecture. It was pathetic, considering what a loser he was. And it was completely ridiculous for him to sit there telling me off in front of my own wife, given that I had helped him and how grateful he had been. I had no idea what to say. I sipped my glass of water.

"It was so clean when I got up," Encarnación said and ran a hand through her hair. "I felt so happy. He'd even cleaned the bathroom. I had a cool bath, and Ilich went down to buy fruit and water. We've been sitting here the whole afternoon, talking about literature and eating pineapple."

Right. So Ilich had walked in, a stranger, obviously, because even though we had met before he could only be described as a stranger in my home, and like the stranger he was he had begun to clean up. Then he had gone and got the shopping. They had talked literature and eaten pineapple.

"I see," I said. "That sounds nice."

"It was," Encarnación said. "And we were waiting for you. Ilich kept repeating that he didn't want to intrude and that he ought to go and come back another day when you were home, but I insisted he stay on, that you would be turning up at any minute."

Encarnación got up and picked up her glass of water.

"And now I've said that," she said, "I'm going to go and lie down again and leave you two to talk about your stuff which I'm sure doesn't concern me and wouldn't interest me either."

She lifted a hand towards Ilich, who raised his own towards her (I thought his eyes were roving appreciatively over her body). Encarnación left the sitting room and closed the door behind her. There was silence in the room apart from the air conditioning humming in the background.

"I'm really sorry if you think I just barged in," said Ilich, and now that the woman was out of the room both the tone of his voice and his appearance were quite different.

"No problem," I said and tried to radiate the strength and self-control I supposed this conversation would require. "I'm just a bit tired. I've been travelling on business all day."

"I get it," Ilich said. "If you want I could leave and come back another day."

The idea of Ilich coming back another day felt even less appealing if that were possible than his staying on.

"What was it you wanted to talk about?" I asked.

"First off I wanted to say something about the book," he said. "The one I promised to read."

"Honestly," I said, "I couldn't care less whether you read it or not. I'm not such a fan of the human race that I'm bothered one way or another if people read *The Old Man and the Sea*."

"So that was all just an act?"

"What was an act?"

"All that stuff about young people and reading groups?"

I drank from my glass.

"I don't know that it was an act," I said with a sigh. "I just didn't really have you in mind when I said it. Get to the point, would you? Like I said, I'm pretty tired after what has been a long day."

"Okay," Ilich began. "In that case I just want to say first off that the book is really okay."

I couldn't hold back a laugh.

"Okay? You're holding one of the greatest books in all of literature in your hands and all you can say is it's really okay?"

"That's just my way of saying it," Ilich said and looked blackly at me. "That's not something to diss me for. I may not have read all your fancy highbrow books, Don Rodrigo, but I have read this one and I read it my way and now I plan on saying something about it. Then I will go out that door over there, so you can have a shower, drink your beer and fuck your wife or whatever you feel you've got to do."

"There's no need to talk about Encarnación that way," I said.

"Okay," Ilich said. "You're right. She's a real woman. Maybe too much woman."

"Too much woman for what?"

He shrugged his shoulders.

"For you, or for life in general maybe."

"Okay," I said and did my best to swallow the insult. "What was it you wanted to say about the book?"

"That it's good, but the best thing is it's pretty thin."

"Okay."

"I like the bit about the fish. It's exciting when he goes hunting it."

"Okay."

"After that it's a bit up and down. There are bits you can skip without missing anything."

"Okay."

"Then I like the moral of the story."

"The moral?"

"Yes. All books have a moral."

"Okay," I said and couldn't help laughing again. "That's something you've read somewhere, is it?"

"Yes."

"Okay. And?"

"And the moral of this book is 'it's just sour grapes', or 'covet all, lose all'. Like a mixture between the two you could say."

He looked at me in satisfaction.

"Okay, Ilich," I said. "So if I've got this right, you've just reduced one of the greatest works in world literature to a hotchpotch of two catchphrases?"

Ilich looked at me blankly. You fucking bastard, I thought. I couldn't keep that thought at bay; it surged up through my limbs and into my head with the force of a wave. I could see Ilich fawning over Del Pozo in my mind, Ilich and the bag of scraps, Ilich and his dirty fingers on the cover of *The Old Man and the Sea*, his cretinous, uneducated little brain that sullied all it came in contact with. Sour grapes covets all. The way little people, bewildered people, try and explain art and life using a couple of proverbs designed for the illiterate. I shouldn't have let him anywhere near that book, I thought. If you want to keep something safe, keep it to yourself, you should never let vulgar and simple-minded people anywhere near it. They turn everything into mincemeat; they can transform a diamond into filthy snow just by looking at it. Calm down, Rodrigo, I was thinking as well, but it was as if that thought never got through. Everything was flickering and turning white before my eyes.

"Ilich," I said and leant toward him. "You turned up here and you cleaned our flat. I appreciate that. It was intrusive, but kind of you anyway. Encarnación is depressed and doesn't have the energy to clean or to look after herself. She did look happier just now and I really appreciate that. It makes me feel happy and so I feel grateful to you."

Ilich nodded, his eyes were riveted on me in his confusion.

"And you've taken the trouble to read *The Old Man and the Sea*. I bet you had to get the bus from your flat on the outskirts to find a bookshop in town, and you must have wandered around in there with a lost expression on your face searching for the book without any idea of who wrote it and what shelf it could be on. That's perfectly normal for people like you because people like you just aren't used to doing that kind of thing. You must have wandered around looking blank, and then you probably had to ask a bookseller for help and the bookseller came to your aid, reluctantly and rather scornfully no doubt, while looking down at you because you've read nothing and know nothing."

"Don Rodrigo . . . " Ilich said and put his hands up in front of him. "I think maybe you should . . . "

"Then you would have taken the bus back to where you live and sat on a chair in your flat and that is where you read the pages, one by one, with a lot of effort and without any real pleasure, but you kept thinking, I'm going to get my act together and read something good, and this is something good, that's what someone who knows a bit about this business told me. When you finished reading it, you put the book down, relieved at being able to return to your porn mags, your games, to Facebook and your feeble attempts to become someone in the timber sector. All of that is perfectly okay, and I understand it and I realise that things have to be a certain way."

I drank from my glass again, but there was no water left and just a tiny, inadequate drop ran into my mouth.

"But what drains the life out of me, Ilich, or not so much drains the life out of me as makes me absolutely furious, not to say what makes me see red, is that you then come here, sit yourself down in an armchair in my sitting room and try to tell me with those ignorant little fingers of yours still filthy from that bag of meat scraps that this book can be boiled down to some moronic proverb. I am doing my best to understand you. I really am. Trying to see you as the person you are in the situation you find yourself in but right now it is bloody hard, Ilich, bloody hard, for the simple reason that you're making it bloody hard for me."

"Right," I heard Ilich say. "And?"

"And what I want is for you to just take your book and disappear through that door and never come back. Never set foot in this place again."

For the first time since starting to speak, I looked straight at Ilich. The face I was looking at was quite different from Ilich's usual face. I could see that, I registered the fact, and yet it was as though that realisation failed to sink in, as though I failed to understand that what I had said really had changed the situation entirely and that it was going to lead to something new.

"So can you tell me," Ilich said slowly, "what exactly is the idea behind *The Old Man and the Sea*? Because I'm guessing you've understood it?

"Yes," I said. "Of course I have."

I paused for a bit and wiped my forehead with a handkerchief I had in my pocket.

"*The Old Man and the Sea*," I said, "is about what it is like to catch a really big fish, *a big fish, Il-ich* (I said it like that, emphatically, with his name, though as I'm recounting this I can't see why, it must have sounded ridiculous). Two champions meet. The fisherman is a champion, and the fish is another. It takes them days to get started, the fish cannot be sure that the fisherman is a worthy champion. But then the battle gets going. The battle between champions. The battle against the deeps, Ilich."

Ilich grinned uncertainly.

"The fisherman wins the fight, catches the big fish and ties it to the boat. It is dead, captured, his trophy. Only then all the others arrive, and none of them will allow the fisherman to keep his fish. Do you get it? Do you get it, Ilich? That it's all about that struggle. Landing the big fish that no one will let you keep. As soon as you return to the real world, it is diminished and a load of little fish eat it up, chew it apart. There are only scraps left of what was supposed to be your trophy, your work. It has all been in vain because of all the stupidity. That's what it is about, Ilich."

I took out my handkerchief from my pocket and wiped it over the nape of my neck.

"You're sick, you are," I heard Ilich mumble. "Fucking sick in the head, mental, that's what you are."

I couldn't put up with any more of it.

"Okay Ilich," I said exhausted. "I may be sick and mental and whatever else you like. But I know what I'm talking about. And I think this is about as close as you and I are ever going to get. Can't you just leave now? Just have the kindness to leave right now?"

"I suppose," he said getting up, "that that fisherman is you. And all the noble intentions, *the big fish*, are a pathetic attempt on your part to get people to read, or something else maybe, something to do with your job."

He laughed icily while walking towards the hallway.

"Yeah, I see it now," he said and turned towards me. "Your fish is the calling you feel to create an environmentally friendly world. To promote your kinds of timber, which are superior to all the others."

He paused for a bit.

"And in that case you're right, Don Rodrigo. The rest of us, the small fry, the vulgar little fish swimming in your wake, who go to swingers' clubs and eat rotting meat out of bags, are going to turn your big fish into scraps. I promise you that. We are going to make mincemeat of you and your whole fishy ideal. Your time is up, Rodrigo Auscias."

He walked to the door, opened it and then slammed it behind him.

"Encarnación!" I called out when he had left.

I felt terribly alone, and I needed someone to talk to about this. But Encarnación must have fallen asleep because no one answered and my call echoed hollowly between the walls.

Obviously I had to ring him up and apologise. The next day I told Encarnación about my outburst, and she got me to see how foolishly I had behaved. I let a week or two pass so the entire episode would have lost its edge and, one day, when I felt rested and in a good mood, I rang him. After a few minutes of lofty disdain, Ilich accepted my apology.

"It's fine," he said guardedly. "Forget it."

During the second part of the conversation he sounded friendlier than he usually did, even getting in before me with several expressions of politeness I had no idea how to reply to. When I asked about Del Pozo he hesitated before answering. I was expecting something cynical about Del Pozo's cheeks or his nasal and inbred way of speaking, his antediluvian way of doing business, something that might elicit some feeling of consensus between us.

"His wife is ill with liver disease," Ilich said finally, "and his daughter has left home."

Even though Ilich's visit had had an anxiety-provoking effect on me (it lingered in my body for several weeks afterwards), its effect on Encarnación was to make her bloom. During the months that followed she was happier, lovelier, and somehow freer, and she seemed to be making an effort to maintain the order Ilich had re-imposed on the flat. Our home looked nice and was tidy now. And the fact that she spent some afternoons outside the flat also seemed to have an enlivening effect. When she came home in the evening she had colour in her cheeks and would drink one glass of chilled cava but no more; she didn't top the glass up but drank only what she had poured out and then pushed the glass away. She started sitting on the terrace again, although not with crossword puzzles but with books and a small radio plugged into headphones. Sometimes she laughed out loud while listening and now and again I would even see her waving at the neighbour opposite. We went on a trip to Casablanca, another to Helsinki, and I was beginning to rediscover the feeling of firm ground beneath my feet. It was a good time.

Until she mentioned the "fifty-year curse" to me one day. I couldn't remember where I had heard the expression at first, and it wasn't until she told me about the academic who was doing research on a writer who was an anti-Semite, a racist and a misogynist that I realised where she must have got it from.

"Who told you that?" I said when she had finished.

"What?"

"What you just told me."

"A friend," she said blushing. "A girlfriend. Pamela Pons."

I made feverish attempts to solve the puzzle in my head. There had to be a ten-year age difference between Ilich and Encarnación. They were completely different as individuals and had nothing in common. Or did they? I tried to imagine them together, tried to imagine what they would talk about, and even worse – what it would be like if their bodies were truly joined. I could picture Ilich moving rhythmically on top of Alba Cambó, that fit body of his, and I felt a pain in my chest when I imagined that the woman with him might not be just Cambó but Encarnación. I tried to keep my suspicions at bay and to persuade myself I was being paranoid, I was seeing things that weren't there and my brain was spinning so fast I was imagining conspiracies on all sides. I started to go through Encarnación's pockets like a suspicious housewife. And I didn't have to wait long before I found a receipt with Ilich's telephone number on the back. Under it was written:

> *Carmosin, ring me.*

He had even given her a nickname. I felt dizzy when I thought of the speed at which the whole thing was progressing.

That day:

I found the sheet of paper in her room. I'm not one to pry but desperation had led me to prying, I'll admit I pried, even if I didn't see the act coming from me so much as the situation. Only what's the use of self-justification at this point? I simply found the piece of paper and on it was written:

> *Rodrigo says dreadful things like, 'You just have to keep going, Encarnación. You may not understand why right now but some-times you just have to keep walking for no other reason than the path is there beneath your feet. The path is beckoning you on, saying take one step, then another, and then one more. And do you know what? The wonderful thing about walking is that as long as you walk far enough, you end up getting somewhere.' I don't know anyone else who would say: if you walk far enough, you end up getting somewhere. I don't know anyone else who walks for the sake of walking, and it feels like the muscles of my face are going to let go and fall off whenever I hear him say things like that. He doesn't understand that something in me has died. I feel no tenderness. I loathe him, but I loathe myself most for being able to go on living in this loveless state. I am going to ring Ilich.*

I am going to fall in love, and falling in love will give me energy.
Or I am going to die. I can't quite make up my mind. Ring Ilich
or die. Ring Ilich or die. Ring Ilich or die. Either I ring Ilich. Or I
say that's all, folks! and get off the bus.

I stood there with the letter in my hand, feeling numb. Trembling, I walked into the room where she was sitting.

"Everything all right?" she asked.

"Everything's fine," I said.

I had never seen Encarnación giggle. I have seen her guffaw, smile, laugh up her sleeve, even grin, but I have never seen her giggle. During the almost two decades of our cohabitation I had never seen her nose contract and tiny, fine wrinkles form over the bridge. I had never seen the expression in her eyes before, which I was to see one day when I returned from what had turned out to be yet another in a series of unsuccessful visits to clients.

I parked the car, and everything was normal. I unlocked the door and went inside and everything was normal in the hall as well. It even smelled slightly of floor cleaner and freshly ironed laundry. Encarnación was sitting out on the terrace, only this time she didn't have a book or a crossword puzzle with her but just a cup of coffee. Her chair had been positioned differently. Instead of being placed so that an observer from the sitting room could see her in semi-profile, it was now on the other side of the table so she was looking straight inside. Behind her I could see the facade of the building on the other side of the street. The pile of papers that was usually lying on a little side table was gone and all there was instead was a little bowl of water with a severed rosebud in it. I said hello and put my briefcase on the floor. Encarnación said hello back and her voice sounded more attentive and warmer than it had for ages.

"Could you come and sit out here for a bit, please," she said.

She got up, pulled a chair over and placed it on the other side of the table.

"How was your day?" I said when I had sat down.

"There's something I've got to tell you before we talk about anything else," she said.

I got the feeling that she was steeling herself, that she was determined to say whatever it was before the courage deserted her.

"Something that's very likely to change everything," she went on.

"Yes?" I said.

"I've met a man," she said then. "I've fallen in love."

"Ilich?" I asked.

"Yes," she said. "I suspected you knew once I noticed the piece of paper was gone. Why didn't you say anything?"

"You're asking me why I didn't say anything?"

She waved her hand in the air dismissively.

"That doesn't matter. What matters is we've been having a passionate affair for the last three weeks."

Passionate? I thought. *So you and Ilich have been having a passionate affair for the last three weeks, have you?* Friendship I could have imagined, maybe even a friendship with erotic overtones, but *passionate*? Encarnación wasn't a passionate woman. Or was she? The image of her being naughty and passionate slowly came together in my mind's eye. And suddenly I could see, as it were, the possibility of that person inside her, and it was as if everything had been shifted out of alignment: her eyes were someone else's eyes, her mouth belonged to a different person, and even her hair was different. As though a building I had been living in for most of my life and whose every nook and cranny I thought I knew and believed I had seen, explored, and even felt shut in by from time to time, suddenly unveiled a set of alternate rooms, as though a secret door had been opened and was showing me a wing decorated completely differently from the rest of the house, using paints and materials that appeared to have been borrowed from a decadent film. That was where she was now.

"What do you know about him?" I asked.

"Only that his name is Ilich and he works in the timber trade," she said.

"You've no idea how old he is, where he comes from . . . "

"And no idea where he lives or who his mother was," she filled in, completely unconcerned.

Her hair was dancing in the light reflected in the windows of the front of the building opposite. Although the skin under her chin sagged a bit, she looked young, young in a way she never had looked before, beautiful. That's right, beautiful and exhilarated and uninhibited. I leant back and closed my eyes. Our house was all around us; its walls may have protected us, but perhaps they were burying us as well. That's right, they were. I can see that now: the walls were burying us and that is what they had been doing the whole time.

"You'd better explain, Encarnación."

"There's nothing to say," she said. "For once there's nothing to say. For once it's all perfectly straightforward and uncomplicated."

But what about me, I wanted to shout. What about me!

After the episode with my wife and Ilich I thought that the game was up. I had lost a large part of my business and I had lost Encarnación. It felt as though I had reached absolute zero and there was nothing left any more. So it may seem rather surprising, if considered, I mean, as part of the larger whole, that I should have been called up a couple of months later, a week or so ago to be more precise, by Alba Cambó.

"I've got to see you," she said. "Is this about Ilich?" I asked, feeling incredibly tired.

"No, it's about you and me," she replied.

We met in Parque Güell. We sat on a stone bench beneath the asymmetric vaults. Alba looked the way she normally did, a bit thinner maybe and her hair seemed more faded. She told me about the agency and you; she asked me to do her a favour and come here today. I said that would be fine, and then we sat there in silence.

"You've lost weight," I said.

"I've got an evil dragon inside me," she said.

She told me she had been given the diagnosis a few months ago, but that the tumours had now spread to her brain.

"Three months left," she said. "Max."

We sat in silence and looked out over Barcelona. I thought about what I should say, only at that moment everything felt so extraordinarily sad I couldn't utter a word. The only thing I wanted to say was: "I see." I could picture how life would simply continue, even though Alba would be gone in three months' time. People would be walking round Parque Güell the way they were doing now; the traffic would be just as it was now, a distant murmur. At the very moment Alba took her last breath, everything would be exactly the same as it was now, Ilich and Encarnación would be walking hand in hand somewhere, smiling and oblivious. I would be somewhere as well but I had no idea where and with whom. I might be alone in an isolated spot.

"How fucking sad," was all I said. "How unbelievably fucking sad."

"It is sad," Alba said.. "All the same there is this one thing that keeps me going."

"What's that?" I asked.

"The idea I have done some good."

"The idea you've done some good?" I said.

"Yes, that I've had some kind of positive impact on the people closest to me. If I have managed to make them feel happiness, my life won't have been in vain. It will all have been worth it in that case. And I can die in peace."

I nodded. A small child was walking slowly in front of us and the mother was walking behind it carrying a red three-wheeler in her hands.

"So that's why I asked you to come here today," she said. "I just wanted to make sure that I had done some good in your life as well."

I turned my head and stared into her eyes. I felt the laughter rising from my belly. I tried to repress it but it forced its way up through my throat and hurled itself out of my mouth. I could see how crushed she looked when it erupted like an avalanche, and I could hear my own voice saying that fuck no, whatever she might believe, she hadn't been a positive force in my life. A curse is what she had been, an absolute curse and nothing else.'

When I woke the next morning, Rodrigo Auscias was gone. His side of the bed had been neatly made; it was as if he had never been there apart from a whiff of the scent he wore. I went into the bathroom and found some rolled-up banknotes in a toothbrush glass for the sum we had agreed upon. I walked round for a bit looking for any note he might have left, but I couldn't find anything.

I will have reached the end soon. Everything feels strangely empty. I am still at Calle Joaquín Costa with a pen in my hand and the tops of the plane trees above me, but there aren't any sounds from the terrace below and no sounds either from the flat at my back. The terrace below is deserted, and Blosom and Mum are sitting behind closed doors watching Latin American soap operas on television. Sometimes I think of Auscias. None of us talk about Alba Cambó any more. It is as if we have already forgotten her, as if she never existed.

Alba Cambó died in a brightly lit antiseptic room at the Sant Rafael Hospital in Barcelona, one of those rooms whose only purpose is to allow people to die in peace without any distractions. There were no windows in the room, and the walls must have been soundproofed because the silence within felt padded and muffled. A lot of people had died in that room before Alba Cambó, and people would continue to die there that very afternoon while her body was still cooling under a sheet that had been stretched over her by two nurses and folded down just below her chin. The ironed and folded sheet lent her corpse an air of propriety almost, an impression that was completely at odds with the black hair she never brushed and that stretched across the pillow like a broom head despite the stillness of her body. There was a lack of solemnity to the situation. A mobile phone in someone's jacket pocket rang at the moment of death, and two nurses could be heard chatting about a colleague in the corridor outside. A patch of sunlight wandering through the room or a breeze entering suddenly through an open window, or a murmur coming from the street, would have provided that sense of the infinite, of something coming to a complete stop at moments like these. Looking back, there was nothing lofty about the situation, nothing to make it memorable. It was more as if the death that occurred that afternoon and in that room was routine and industrial, the inevitable and unspectacular forwarding of Alba Cambó's body from one dimension to another.

Once she was dead, she was transferred to the funeral home in a black van; it had no windows either. During the wake we all stood on the other side of the glass and observed her where she lay, surrounded by flowers, her skin glowing and a smile on her lips. That smile was achieved by pulling an invisible thread from the corners of her mouth to her ears, according to Madame Moreau. Even though it was Madame Moreau who shared this slightly macabre bit of information, she was the only one of us to cry. She blew her nose in a cloth handkerchief, and I must have been in a state of shock as well, because it wasn't her grief I was witness to – a grief that lent her a dignity the rest of us lacked – what I saw instead was her handkerchief filling with warm mucus and then being crumpled up and stuffed into her skirt pocket. Valentino Coraggioso, who should, formally at least, have been the one to mourn Alba Cambó the most, dished up his usual clichés, 'Now all the breaths have been taken, all the accounts settled,' and 'No one is master of the last moment of their lives.' That last one sort of jarred considering Cambó had said she could imagine dying any way at all (and it is courageous to say you can imagine dying any way at all), apart from in a hospital in an airless room without any windows. I tried to forgive him. I thought about that day in the car when he had cried and I had been forced to put up with his tears. Maybe I had been too cold toward him at that point; maybe I should have listened to him the way I listened to Auscias.

The day after the wake Cambó's body was transported to the cemetery in Sitges. With its old monumental graves and cypresses that provide shade for marble angels and strutting pigeons, the cemetery in Sitges is one of the most beautiful in Catalonia. It is completely quiet inside, even though the sea is pounding away right on the other side of the thick wall that surrounds the cemetery. The only thing you can hear is a bit of wind moving in the treetops and through the cellophane wrapped around the plastic flowers that stand in tall vases by the graves. This is a faint and rather chilly rustling sound, almost a whisper, like delicate voices, dry as paper. There are cigarette butts and the odd empty bottle on some of the graves, which makes it look as though people meet there at night and use the large graves as benches to sit on. Though it wasn't one of the grander graves that was waiting for Alba Cambó. Those graves were family graves and, as Madame Moreau observed in that know-all way of hers, if you haven't got a family then you cannot be buried in a family grave. Madame Moreau was the one who had taken care of the burial arrangements while Alba was still alive. She had looked into where Alba's parents and any siblings she might have were buried and discovered that Cambó had no siblings and, as for her parents, they were not lying in the same grave but at opposite ends of the enormous cemetery in Caudal de la Ribera, a village in the hinterland whose motto according to the inquiries Moreau made was: *pueblo chico, infierno grande.* She couldn't be buried there. Moreau managed to find a place for her by the sea instead without any scent of the hinterland, just of the coast, space and salt water.

The grave itself was of the simplest kind. A gap in a wall that contained coffins separated by a few decimetres in a kind of apartment block for the dead. Madame Moreau kept on sharing macabre bits of information and told us that there was a drainage system behind the wall, a Venice of death fluids that Cambó would soon be flowing into.

The words chiselled into the front of the grave were: *Alba Cambó Altamira, 1968-2010.*

The idea that Valentino Coraggioso really would stay on to deal with Cambó's effects was not one any of us believed. The last few months the two of them had lived in a kind of hell, with Valentino, who was an actor, after all, and accustomed to spending his days under a parasol on a cliff top in Liguria, foundering under a host of practical demands. Madame Moreau judged him harshly and stopped responding when he spoke to her even while Alba was still alive, which must have been painful for Cambó, bedridden, ashen-faced and locked inside an entirely hopeless struggle with pain. During the last days of Alba's life, Moreau slept on a mattress on the floor beside Alba's bed while Valentino slept on the sofa in the sitting room. Moreau also dealt with all the practical arrangements during those last few weeks and, if she delegated anything, it was to us in the flat above, never to Valentino, who ended up sitting listlessly on the terrace, drinking Italian beer and dressed in a pair of silky shorts with stripes that read *Milan* on one side.

The very first night after the wake Valentino moved into a hotel. Mum, Moreau and Blosom cleaned the flat and put everything they found of Valentino's in a cardboard box they left out on the street. One morning they said the cur had been to fetch his things. He must have crept over that night with his tail between his legs, because the box was gone by morning. Blosom rang to find out if he had really been the one to take the box. He replied that it had been him. Blosom hung up without saying anything because she couldn't think of anything to say to a man like him, a man who had lived in Cambó's home, eaten her food and slept in her bed, shared her life and now was backing away without exhibiting even a shred of grief or any desire to honour her memory.

That last bit wasn't quite true. The same night Valentino came to fetch the box, I went down to see him on the street. He threw a stone at the windowpane in the sitting room where I sleep. I saw him standing there and once I had shoved on a dressing gown I went down. He was wearing the same clothes he'd had on for the funeral and his hair was greasy and stuck to his scalp.

'I'm going to go home to Liguria now,' he said. 'I have to start living again.'

'I understand,' I said.

'First it was Alba's illness that was killing me and now it feels like the women around her are kicking my corpse. You can't win against someone like Moreau, I knew that the first time I met her, and Blosom could wipe any man out with that toughness of hers and a bottle of ammonia.'

He looked up at our terrace.

'Only Alba deserves an obituary I can't give her. And I need your help for that. I want you to write something about her.'

He took out his wallet and skimmed through the banknotes as though he was considering how much this particular service could be worth. He pressed some notes into my hand. I stared at him.

'I didn't know her,' I said. 'I can't write about her.'

'I didn't know her either,' he replied. 'Even though we lived together for almost two years, I really don't have any idea who she was.'

We stood there on the street and it looked so empty. Alba's terrace was abandoned, and the bougainvillea hanging over the wall had dried out a bit. The cellophane is rustling at the cemetery in Sitges, was what I thought in that moment. Valentino shook my hand, adjusted the stained white collar of his shirt, picked up his box and started walking down the street. His back was straight and for a moment just before he turned the corner, I thought I could hear him whistling.

Dear readers,

We rely on subscriptions from people like you to tell these other stories – the types of stories most publishers consider too risky to take on.

Our subscribers don't just make the books physically happen. They also help us approach booksellers, because we can demonstrate that our books already have readers and fans. And they give us the security to publish in line with our values, which are collaborative, imaginative and 'shamelessly literary'.

All of our subscribers:

- receive a first-edition copy of each of the books they subscribe to
- are thanked by name at the end of these books
- are warmly invited to contribute to our plans and choice of future books

BECOME A SUBSCRIBER, OR GIVE A SUBSCRIPTION TO A FRIEND

Visit andotherstories.org/subscribe to become part of an alternative approach to publishing.

Subscriptions are:

£20 for two books per year

£35 for four books per year

£50 for six books per year

OTHER WAYS TO GET INVOLVED

If you'd like to know about upcoming events and reading groups (our foreign-language reading groups help us choose books to publish, for example) you can:

- join the mailing list at: andotherstories.org/join-us
- follow us on Twitter: @andothertweets
- join us on Facebook: facebook.com/AndOtherStoriesBooks
- follow our blog: Ampersand

This book was made possible thanks to the support of:

AG Hughes · Aaron McEnery · Abigail Miller · Ada Gokay · Adam Butler · Adam Lenson · Adriana Maldonado · Aileen-Elizabeth Taylor · Aino Efraimsson · Ajay Sharma · Alan Ramsey · Alasdair Thomson · Alastair Gillespie · Alastair Maude · Alec Begley · Alex Gregory · Alex Martin · Alex Ramsey · Alex Robertson · Alex Sutcliffe · Alexander Balk · Alexandra Buchler · Alexandra Georgescu · Alice Toulmin · Alison Bowyer · Alison Hughes · Alison Layland · Ali Smith · Allison Graham · Allyson Dowling · Alyse Ceirante · Amanda · Amanda Dalton · Amanda DeMarco · Amelia Dowe · Amy Allebone-Salt · Amy Rushton · Anderson Tepper · Andrew Cowan · Andrew Kerr-Jarrett · Andrew Lees · Andrew Marston · Andrew McDougall · Andrew Rego · Andrew van der Vlies · Andrew Whitelegg · Andy Madeley · Angela Creed · Angus MacDonald · Angus Walker · Ann Van Dyck · Anna Dear · Anna Holmwood · Anna Milsom · Anna Solovyev · Anna Vinegrad · Anna-Karin Palm · Anne Carus · Anne Lawler · Anne Meadows · Anne Marie Jackson · Anonymous · Anonymous · Anonymous · Anthony Quinn · Antonia Lloyd-Jones · Antonio de Swift · Antony Pearce · Aoife Boyd · Archie Davies · Asako Serizawa · Asher Norris · Audrey Garcia · Audrey Holmes · Barbara Adair · Barbara Anderson · Barbara Mellor · Barbara Robinson · Barry Hall · Barry John Fletcher · Bartolomiej Tyszka · Belinda Farrell · Ben Paynter · Ben Schofield · Ben Smith · Ben Thornton · Benjamin Judge · Bernard Devaney · Bianca Jackson · Bianca Winter · Bill Myers · Blanka Stoltz · Bob Hill · Bob Richmond-Watson · Briallen Hopper · Brian

Rogers · Brigita Ptackova · C Mieville · Cam Scott · Candy Says Juju Sophie · Carl Emery · Carla Coppola · Carol Mavor · Caroline Rucker · Catherine Mansfield · Catherine Taylor · Catrin Ashton · Cecilia Rossi & Iain Robinson · Cecily Maude · Charles Lambert · Charles Rowley · Charlotte Holtam · Charlotte Middleton · Charlotte Whittle · Charlotte Murrie & Stephen Charles · Chris Day · Chris Fawson · Chris Gribble · Chris Holmes · Chris Lintott · Chris Stevenson · Chris Vardy · Chris Watson · Chris Wood · Chris Elcock · Christine Carlisle · Christine Luker · Christopher Allen · Ciara Ní Riain · Claire Brooksby · Claire Fuller · Claire Seymour · Claire Williams · Clare Quinlan · Clarissa Botsford · Clemence Sebag · Clifford Posner · Clive Bellingham · Clodie Vasli · Colette Dunne · Colin Burrow · Colin Matthews · Courtney Lilly · Craig Barney · Dan Pope · Dana Behrman · Daniel Arnold · Daniel Carpenter · Daniel Coxon · Daniel Gillespie · Daniel Hahn · Daniel Hugill · Daniel Lipscombe · Daniela Steierberg · Dave Lander · David Archer · David Gould · David Hebblethwaite · David Hedges · David Higgins · David Johnson-Davies · David Shriver · David Smith · Dawn Hart · Dawn Mazarakis · Debbie Pinfold · Deborah Jacob · Denis Stillewagt & Anca Fronescu · Dermot McAleese · Dianna Campbell · Dimitris Melicertes · Dominique Brocard · Duncan Marks · Duncan Ranslem · E Jarnes · Ed Tallent · Elaine Kennedy · Elaine Rassaby · Eleanor Maier · Eleanor Walsh · Elisabeth Jaquette · Eliza O'Toole · Elizabeth Heighway · Ellen Jones · Emily Diamand · Emily Jeremiah · Emily Taylor ·

Emily Yaewon Lee & Gregory Limpens · Emma Bielecki · Emma Perry · Emma Pope · Emma Yearwood · Emma Louise Grove · Eric E Rubeo · Eva Hdoherty · Ewan Tant · Finbarr Farragher · Finnuala Butler · Fiona Graham · Floriane Peycelon · Fran Sanderson · Francesca Caracciolo · Francis Taylor · Friederike Knabe · G Thrower · Gabrielle Crockatt · Gawain Espley · Gemma Tipton · Genevra Richardson · Genia Ogrenchuk · George Wilkinson · George Sandison & Daniela Laterza · Gill Boag-Munroe · Gillian Spencer · Gillian Stern · Graham & Steph Parslow · Graham R Foster · Gregory Conti · Guy Haslam · Hans Lazda · Harriet Mossop · Helen Poulsen · Helen Brady · Helene Walters-Steinberg · Henriette Heise · Henrike Laehnemann · Ian Barnett · Ian Kirkwood · Ian McMillan · Ian Smith · Íde Corley · Ignês Sodré · Inna Carson · Irene Mansfield · Isabella Garment · Isabella Weibrecht · J Collins · JA Calleja · Jack Brown · Jacqueline Taylor · Jacqueline Lademann · Jakob Hammarskjöld · James Beck · James Clark · James Cubbon · James Lee · James Portlock · James Scudamore · James Tierney · James Warner · James Wilper · Jamie Walsh · Jane Crookes · Jane Whiteley · Jane Woollard · Janette Ryan · Jarred McGinnis · JC Sutcliffe · Jeff Collins · Jennifer Hearn · Jennifer Higgins · Jennifer Hurstfield · Jennifer O'Brien · Jenny Diski · Jenny Newton · Jerry Simcock · Jess Howard-Armitage · Jess Parsons · Jessica Kingsley · Jethro Soutar · Jillian Jones · Jo Harding · Joanna Flower · Joanna Luloff · Joanna Neville · Joel Love · Johan Forsell · John Allison · John

Conway · John Down · John English · John Fisher · John Gent · John Hodgson · John Kelly · John Nicholson · John Royley · John Steigerwald · Jon Riches · Jonathan Ruppin · Jonathan Watkiss · Joseph Cooney · Joseph Schreiber · Joshua Davis · Josie Soutar · Julian Duplain · Julian Lomas · Juliane Jarke · Julie Gibson · Julie Van Pelt · Juliet Swann · Kaarina Hollo · Kaite O'Reilly · Kate Cooper · Kate Pullinger · Katharine Freeman · Katharine Robbins · Katherine El-Salahi · Katherine Wootton Joyce · Kathryn Bogdanowitsch-Johnston · Kathryn Lewis · Katie Brown · Katie Prescott · Katie Smith · Keith Dunnett · Kelly Russell · Kevin Brockmeier · Kevin Pino · Kiera Vaclavik · Kirsteen Smith · KL Ee · Krystalli Glyniadakis · Lana Selby · Lander Hawes · Laura Batatota · Laura Clarke · Lauren Ellemore · Laurence Laluyaux · Leanne Bass · Leonie Schwab · Leri Price · Lesley Lawn · Lesley Watters · Leslie Rose · Linda Dalziel · Lindsay Brammer · Lindsay Healy · Lindsey Ford · Liz Ketch · Loretta Platts · Louise Bongiovanni · Louise Rogers · Luc Verstraete · Lucia Rotheray · Lucie Donahue · Lynda Graham · Lynda Ross · Lynn Martin · M Manfre · Mac York · Maeve Lambe · Maggie Peel · Maisie & Nick Carter · Mandy Boles · Marcus Joy · Marella Oppenheim · Maria Cotera · Marie Donnelly · Marilyn Zucker · Marina Castledine · Marina Galanti · Marina Lomunno · Mark Ainsbury · Mark Lumley · Marlene Adkins · Martha Gifford · Martha Nicholson · Martin Brampton · Martin Conneely · Martin Hollywood · Martin Cromie · Mary Nash · Mary Wang · Mathias Enard · Matt & Owen Davies · Matthew Francis · Matthew Geden · Matthew O'Dwyer · Matthew Smith · Matthew Thomas · Maureen McDermott · Maxime Dargaud-Fons · Meaghan Delahunt · Melissa Beck · Melissa Quignon-Finch · Melvin Davis · Michael Harrison · Michael Holtmann · Michael Johnston · Michelle Roberts · Michelle Dyrness · Miranda Petruska · Monika Olsen · Najiba · Nan Haberman · Natalie Smith · Nathan Rostron · Neil Pretty · Nicholas Laughlin · Nick Chapman · Nick Sidwell · Nick James · Nick Nelson & Rachel Eley · Nicola Hart · Nicola Hughes · Nina Alexandersen · Nina Power · Octavia Kingsley · Olga Alexandru · Olga Zilberbourg · Olivier Pynn · Pablo Rossello · Pat Crowe · Pat Morgan · Patricia Appleyard · Patricia McCarthy · Patrick Owen · Paul Bailey · Paul Brand · Paul Gamble · Paul Jones · Paul Millar · Paul Munday · Paul C Daw · Paul M Cray · Paula Edwards · Penelope Hewett Brown · Peter Armstrong · Peter McCambridge · Peter Murray · Peter Rowland · Peter Vos · Philbert Xavier · Philip Warren · Phillip Canning · Phyllis Reeve · Piet Van Bockstal · PJ Abbott · Poppy Collinson · PRAH Recordings · Rachael Williams · Rachel Carter · Rachel Lasserson · Rachel Matheson · Rachel Van Riel · Rachel Watkins · Read MAW Books · Rebecca Atkinson · Rebecca Braun · Rebecca Carter · Rebecca Gillam · Rebecca Kershaw · Rebecca Moss · Rebecca Rosenthal · Réjane Collard-Walker · Rhiannon Armstrong · Rhodri Jones · Richard Ellis · Richard Gwyn · Richard Major · Richard Martin · Richard Ross · Richard Smith · Richard Steward · Rob Jefferson-Brown · Rob Plews · Robert Gillett · Robin Patterson · Robin Taylor · Robyn Neil · Ronan Cormacain · Ros Schwartz · Rose Cole · Ross Macpherson · Roz Simpson · Ruth Van Driessche · Ruth F Hunt · S Italiano · SE Guine · SJ Naude · Sabine Griffiths · Sally Baker · Sam Cunningham · Sam Gordon · Sam Ruddock · Samantha Sabbarton-Wright · Samantha Schnee · Samuel Alexander Mansfield · Sandra Hall · Sarah Benson · Sarah Butler · Sarah Kilvington · Sarah Pybus · Sarah Salmon · Sarah Salway · Scott Beidler · Sean Malone · Sean McGivern · Seini O'Connor · Sez Kiss · Sheila Beirne · Shelley Krueger · Sheridan Marshall · Shirley Harwood · Sigrun Hodne · Simon John Harvey · Simone O'Donovan · Sioned Puw Rowlands · Sonia Overall · Sophia Wickham · Stephanie Carr · Stephen Bass · Stephen Karakassidis · Stephen Pearsall · Stephen H Oakey · Steven Reid · Steven Williams · Steven & Gitte Evans · Sue Childs · Sue & Ed Aldred · Sue Eaglen & Colin Crewdson · Susan Ferguson · Susan Lea · Susan Tomaselli · Susanna Jones · Susi Lind · Susie Roberson · Suzanne Ross · Sylvie Zannier-Betts · Tammy Harman · Tammy Watchorn · Tania Hershman · Tara Cheesman · Thami Fahmy · The Mighty Douche Softball Team · The Rookery in the Bookery · Thea Bradbury · Thees Spreckelsen · Thomas Bell · Thomas Fritz · Thomas Mitchell · Thomas JD Gray · Tim Jackson · Tim Theroux · Timothy Harris · Tina Rotherham-Winqvist · Tom Bowden · Tom Darby · Tom Franklin · Tom Mandall · Tony Bastow · Tony & Joy Molyneaux · Tracy Bauld · Tracy Lee-Newman · Trevor Lewis · Trevor Wald · Tristan Burke · Troy Zabel · Val Challen · Vanessa Nolan · Vicky Grut · Victoria Adams · Visaly Muthusamy · Vivien Doornekamp-Glass · Wendy Langridge · Wenna Price · William G Dennehy · Yukiko Hiranuma · Zac Palmer · Zoe Taylor · Zoë Brasier

Current & Upcoming Books

Lina Wolff has lived and worked in Italy and Spain. During her years in Valencia and Madrid, she began to write her short story collection *Många människor dör som du* ('Many People Die Like You'; Albert Bonniers Förlag, 2009). *Bret Easton Ellis and the Other Dogs*, her first novel, was awarded the prestigious *Vi* Magazine Literature Prize and shortlisted for the 2013 Swedish Radio Award for Best Novel of the Year. Her second novel, *De polyglotta älskarna* (The Polyglot Lovers), is forthcoming from Albert Bonniers Förlag in 2016.

Frank Perry has translated the work of many of Sweden's leading writers. His work has won the Swedish Academy Prize for the introduction of Swedish literature abroad and the Prize of the Writers Guild of Sweden for drama translation.